RADIATION

CAMILLA OCHLAN
CAROL E. LEEVER

OF CATS AND DRAGONS BOOK 2

Copyright

Radiation

This book is a work of fiction. Names, characters, places, and incidents are the products of the authors' imaginations or are used fictitiously. Any resemblance to actual events, locales or persons, living or dead, is coincidental.

Dedication

For our siblings: Kim, Ted, Robert, Christina, and Csilla.

CONTENTS

Timeline of books

Counted from the year of the last Covenant, 14,000 years ago.

❖

14,021 *Autumn:* Night's Gift (Book 1)
14,021 *Winter:* Winter Tithe (Novella)

❖

14,022 *Spring:* Radiation (Book 2)
14,022 *Summer:* Summer's Fall (Book 3)
14,022 *Summer:* Hollow Season (Book 4)
14,022 *Summer:* Autumn King (Book 5)
14,022 *Summer:* Solstice Thyme (short story)

❖

You can get Night's Gift (Book 1 e-book) for free when you sign up for the Of Cats And Dragons Newsletter.

Radiation (Book 2 e-book) is also available for free when you sign up for the Of Cats And Dragons Newsletter.

We offer Winter Tithe as a seasonal gift for our newsletter subscribers.

Solstice Thyme will soon be available on our website at OfCatsAndDragons.com

Chapter 1: Quest

O men Daenoth stared hard at his pony-sized cat. Tormy had grown rapidly in the last six months — going from a fluffy, thirty-pound kitten to a robust adolescent that Omen was no longer capable of lifting. *He looks like a Shindarian tiger — without the black stripes. Must weight at least four hundred pounds.*

Utterly silent for once, the large cat balanced on his furry toes and stretched his long, orange body in an effort to reach a thick leather-bound book high on a shelf in the section of the sprawling library designated as *off limits*.

The Divine Library of The Soul's Flame, nestled in the realm of its namesake, had become Omen's latest refuge. He loved the quiet calm, the mythology-inspired art of the concave ceilings, the storytelling mosaics of walls and floors, and the smoke and vanilla scents mingled among the endless collections of books and scrolls.

While Omen's ability to focus had improved with Tormy's arrival, he still had needed to contend with the constant distractions at home in Melia — friends inviting him out, his sister asking to play with Tormy, his father piling on new fields of study, his mother surprising him with random magic quizzes, and Tormy "feeling peckish" and sweetly demanding second breakfast, pre-lunch snack, after-lunch nibbles, afternoon pudding, before-dinner appetizer, tummy-settling post-dinner digestive, or late-night test breakfast. The library had become his place of concentrated, uninterrupted study — until now.

Tormy swiped at the thick book again, catching its edge and scooting it a quarter inch off the shelf. Omen held his

1

breath, watching and waiting for the inevitable.

They were alone in the Divine Library of The Soul's Flame. Unable to take his eyes off Tormy's antics, Omen absently chewed on the tip of his quill, even as he pushed the scroll he'd been reading aside.

Tormy's claw caught the golden-lettered spine of the thick tome. The book tilted forward, hung suspended in the air for an infinitesimal moment, and then plunged to the floor with a loud *thump*. Omen thought he heard a brittle crack in the mosaic tiles. *I think Tormy just fractured the antler of the constellation of the Fallow Deer. Hope Etar doesn't notice.*

"Read this one, Omy!" Tormy squealed. The cat's sweet baby voice had deepened as he had grown, but his joyful enthusiasm still imbued his every word.

The cat pushed the enormous leather-bound tome across the gold-and-cream mosaic, passing more of the myriad of constellations and artistically-rendered calculations that made up this section of the floor. Diffused light from gleaming crystal ceiling orbs illuminated the long fluffy orange and white fur around the cat's ears and ruff.

Omen set aside his quill as he rose. He rolled his stiff shoulders back, blinked to clear his vision, and quickly crossed to Tormy's side, hoping to spare the ancient volume grievous mistreatment by the floor.

Tormy proudly planted a silken paw the size of a dinner plate on the book's textured cover.

He's so pleased with himself. The big kitten had been trying to *help* him study all day. Omen crouched down to look at the book, waving Tormy's paw away. He recognized the language the book was written in: Sul'eldrine, the Language of the Gods.

2

"The Book of Cats, by the Architect," he read the title —
upside down as it was facing Tormy — out loud.

"I is thinking this is the bestest book ever!" Tormy's amber eyes widened with excitement. His whiskers flared.

Curious in spite of himself, Omen opened the cover and
glanced at the first few lines written inside. "It does appear
to be a book about cats," he told Tormy. "But it's not what
I'm supposed to be doing, remember? I'm learning my
spells."

"I is knowing!" Tormy seemed undeterred as he pushed
his nose into the pages and then turned several of the sheets
of parchment with one paw, claws carefully sheathed. "You
is doing *this* spell!" He planted the same paw on the page
for emphasis.

Omen turned the book. He recognized the lines and
strokes of the pattern — a magical spell, just like the ones
he'd been studying. There was a drawing of a mouse above
the pattern — no doubt the reason for the cat's interest.
Clever cat — he recognizes it as a spell!

The books stacked on the desk behind him were filled
with magical patterns his mother had determined "beginner
level." The bulk were spells she believed Omen should
have learned long ago. "Remedial," he grunted under his
breath. To his burning embarrassment, his mother had
called his lessons *remedial.*

"You're not really supposed to cast spells from books,
Tormy," Omen explained to the cat — this was a lesson his
mother had drummed into him early on. "I have to memorize the patterns first, internalize them. When you cast a
spell out of a book or from a scroll you can't really control
the energy properly."

Tormy's excitement did not dim. His pink ears perked

forward, his long fluffy plume of a tail flicking uncontrollably. "I is not knowing what that is meaning," he purred. "You is casting my spell for me?" The cat's hopeful tone made Omen pause.

"It means that if I don't memorize the spell first I can't . . ." He trailed off, faced with Tormy's eager anticipation, and glanced down at the spell once more.

While he didn't exactly know what the spell was — it was labeled *MICE* just under the drawing of the mouse that had caught Tormy's attention — he could tell that it was a minor cantrip. The spell was uncomplicated — only two sets of circular lines describing the pattern. *Cantrips are harmless.* He reasoned that the spells his mother wanted him to study were of the same variety. *It is technically the type of spell I'm supposed to be learning.*

"Well, all right," he agreed. "Can't hurt to try once."

Tormy leaped in the air and spun around several times, before landing with his paws splayed, head down, hindquarters in the air as if ready to pounce. Amber eyes sparkling, he looked from the book to Omen and back again.

Chuckling to himself, Omen took a deep breath and sat on the floor in front of the book. He closed his eyes, concentrating on the sensation of magical energy all around him. *Magic feels amplified here, stronger. This is a divine realm — I bet all my spells will be affected!* A sense of glee flooded through him. *Maybe learning these spells will be easier than I thought!*

Normally he would pull the magic inside himself, and then push it into a pattern he'd formed in his mind. For this experiment, he simply gathered the diaphanous power around him like a warm blanket. He held it for a moment, listening to the tonal shift in the buzzing as strands of energy expanded and knitted together. Then he simply thrust the magic outward toward the book as if slapping it down on the page — it felt messy and disorganized. The energy slipped from his grasp and chaotically flowed down onto the ink and parchment, swirling into the diagram as if seeking shape and form.

The ink glowed brightly as the magic streamed into it. A moment later, the light coalesced into a small blue ball in the center of the page. Omen watched with wonder as the ball of light took the shape of a little glowing mouse. The glow-mouse instantly scampered free of the book and raced away. Tormy pounced after it, leaping with abandon.

The mouse flitted and dodged, swerving to avoid the enormous paws of the oversized kitten. But despite being a magical construct, the mouse was no match for the cat's speed and agility. A mere moment later, Tormy slammed his paw down upon the magical rodent with a loud *mer-rrowww*. The glowing mouse exploded into a shower of glittering sparkles.

Excited, Tormy swiveled around, eyes on the book again. Another mouse formed in the center of the pattern and ran off. Tormy charged after it.

Omen watched the chase, laughing. "Magical mice. I'm going to have to add this one to my list of must-learn spells."

A third mouse formed on the pattern and raced away. Tormy shrieked, torn between chasing after one mouse or the other. He leaped and pounced in one direction, then turned and hopped the other way. A fourth mouse skittered from the book, and Tormy flipped back around in mid-turn, trying to catch it too. His claws scraped against the marble as he skidded and slid. He bowled over several chairs in his single-minded pursuit.

Omen cringed at the sound of furniture crashing. "Don't knock into the bookshelves!" he called to the cat.

Luckily the bookshelves in question were all made of solid stone and would likely hold up to Tormy's flailing as he gamboled after the glowing mice through the maze of the great library.

A fifth mouse escaped.

Omen frowned down at the book, suddenly feeling a little ill. "That shouldn't be happening." The spell was a mere cantrip; as far as he knew, it should only have been able to produce a couple of illusionary mice. *The magic should have run out already.* Without Omen actively pushing magic into it, there should have been nothing to sustain the spell.

A sixth mouse escaped from the book.

"Rat's teeth! The spell is not stopping!" Omen called out to the cat.

"Hurrah! More mouses!" Tormy leaped, sending another shower of mouse sparkles into the air.

"It has to stop!" Omen knew the cat couldn't comprehend the gravity of the situation. *I am in such trouble!*

"You is the bestest wizard, Omy!" the cat praised loudly as he caught two of the glittering mice beneath one front paw, and another beneath a back paw at the same time.

Several more mice escaped from the book.

"Think," Omen muttered to himself as more mice swelled from the book. "I'm not pushing magic into it, so it's drawing the magic from somewhere else. All I have to do is block the flow."

Block the flow! Use a shield! The only sort of shield he

knew how to create was psionic, not magical. But he'd become quite adept at shielding psionically over the last few months. Ever since Tormy had appeared in his life, the mental shield he had to maintain to control his powers no longer debilitated him with mind-numbing pain. Something about the cat's presence calmed him, eased the chaotic jumble of thoughts that had tormented him through his childhood. *Feline focus,* his father had called it.

Omen touched the personal shield surrounding him. A slow, steady hum — a purr really — flowed through him and kept the shield in place. He used the hum as a base to craft a new song as an overlay. The song — a mnemonic device he used to trigger his psionics — started immediately. He felt a surge of energy rush through him as he formed a faint glowing shield around the book on the ground. *That should block the magic from flowing into the book. That should stop the spell.*

He could feel the outside pressure of magic swirling through the library and coalescing on the page. The pressure met his shield like water on stone — crashing against the barrier, held back by the sheer force of his mind. He steadied the shield against the onslaught of energy lashing wildly all around him.

I'm in a divine realm! He cursed himself for ignoring the location before attempting the new spell. *Mother always warns me not to take easy shortcuts!*

Tormy padded over to him a few moments later, crouching down in front of both Omen and the book, his amber gaze on the glowing dome of light covering the pattern. "No more mouses?" the cat asked plaintively. His voice cracked with disappointment.

"I don't think so," Omen replied, relief ebbing over him.

"I think I've stopped the flow of energy." *I hope.* "Sorry, little guy."

Omen took a deep breath and slowly relaxed his tense muscles, letting go of the energy of the shield, letting the song in his head wind down and stop, effectively erasing the pattern in his mind. The glowing shield vanished.

He felt it the instant he released the shield. Like water crashing against stone, the energy had not dissipated but merely backed up, building and building behind the barrier holding it. It all rushed forward now, like a raging river, flooding into the book and setting the pattern into a blinding flare. The mice formed instantly, and escaped — not one at a time, but dozens upon dozens rushing from the page and scattering in all directions. Omen felt them racing up his body and over his head, leaping past him to disappear into the stacks.

Tormy trilled and gave chase — dozens more escaped. *Hundreds!* Panic washed through Omen as he realized that in a matter of moments the library would be hip deep in glowing mice. He started whacking the glowing constructs as they came out of the book, striking them over and over again, making them explode into glittering flashes of light. "Tormy, get them!"

Omen could hear Tormy letting out gleeful snarls and trills while the happy cat raced around bookshelves and circled pillars, stalking his prey. Omen scrambled after him, swatting at the mice still crawling over his clothing. He shook his head — mice flew from his hair — every step he took sent explosions of light into the air. He stomped and spun, and tried to destroy as many sparkling rodents as he could.

Maybe I can crush them psionically? he thought, frantic

for a solution. *Or I can use my cloak — beat them out like a flame — fire! I can set the library on fire!* "Tormy, catch them!"

"I is catching them, Omy!" Tormy insisted. The cat whirled in a frenzied dance, his powerful tail knocking over what little furniture remained standing.

The mice raced up the walls, swarming over the book-shelves.

Omen couldn't even see *The Book of Cats* anymore. It had disappeared beneath the flood of mice erupting from the surface of the pages.

Omen turned and twisted, stomping and shrieking until — on one flailing swat — he crashed into Tormy, and they both went down in a heap on the floor. In moments they were buried under a cascade of glowing mice. The shimmering fiends simply trampled right over top of them, tiny claws scratching, and bolted toward the far reaches of the library. Omen pushed at the cat sprawled across him. "Tormy, we have to stop them!" he shouted.

The wave of mice grew, streaming over them until Omen feared he and Tormy would be smothered. *Drowned in a sea of rodents!* He reached for a song in his mind. *I have to. . .*

But from one moment to the next, it all just stopped.

One second they were choked beneath a glowing avalanche of mouse bodies, and the next they were not. The mice were gone; the library was silent — the blinding glow faded back to the simple light from the crystals illuminating the room from overhead.

Omen and Tormy sat up.

Standing a few steps away was Omen's half brother and current host — Etar, The Soul's Flame. Etar held *The Book of Cats* in both hands, the cover firmly closed.

The mice were gone.

Omen blinked. "Um, we were. . ." His thundering pulse slowed.

"You were supposed to be studying," Etar reminded him.

"Well," Omen searched for a response. "Technically, I was studying." When Omen had asked his mother's permission to visit his half brother that day, he had promised he'd spend part of the time studying in Etar's library, learning the spells she insisted he learn. "Mother asked me to study the cantrips — this was a cantrip."

Etar — firstborn of the Elder God Cerioth, The Dark Heart — looked skeptical.

Can gods tell when you're lying? Omen wondered. He wasn't entirely certain what powers Etar did or didn't have. He'd never seen Etar do anything particularly impressive in the time he'd known him — certainly nothing that would lead Omen to believe there was anything truly divine about him. *He's one of the younger gods. Godling? Godlet? Maybe they can't do anything powerful.*

Omen's close relationship to divinity stemmed all the way back to before his birth. His pregnant mother had been savagely attacked by a powerful elemental force. *Never did find out why the thing was trying to kill her.*

Omen's father, desperate to heal his beloved and save their unborn child, had enlisted the aid of a faerie healer and the Elder God Cerioth. While saving both mother and child, the strange and unpredictable magic had tangled the bloodlines of the healer, the elemental force attacking them, and the Elder God Cerioth, bestowing upon Omen the benefits and disadvantages of five bloodlines.

His connection to the Elder God Cerioth had meant little

to Omen until he had wandered into an Elder Temple on his tenth birthday and had discovered a doorway into the divine realm of Etar, The Soul's Flame.

Like Omen, Etar was one of the many children of Cerioth. But unlike Omen, Etar was a god himself — one of the younger gods of the world, capable of channeling the power of the Elder Gods. As a ten-year-old, Omen had not understood the implications of meeting a god — to him having a brother had been far more important. And in the five years Omen had known Etar, his brother had always appeared as nothing more than a regular man. Etar was generous and kind, and he'd always had time for the over-active child Omen had been.

"I hardly think your mother asked you to learn a spell to create magical mice," Etar remarked.

"Tormy wanted me to learn the spell," Omen admitted.

"I is asking!" Tormy agreed wholeheartedly. "And Omy is brilliantnessness at the magics!"

"Who's in charge?" Etar asked pointedly. "You or the cat?"

"The cat." Omen grinned at his brother and pointed a finger at the book Etar still held in his hands. "It says so in that book of yours — right there on the first page."

Etar's gaze narrowed as he opened the front cover and scanned the first page. *"Before we begin, you need to understand that the cat is always in charge,"* he read the first line of the book out loud.

Etar sighed in exasperation and shut the book, heading toward a nearby bookshelf to return the tome. "Didn't it occur to you to just close the book when the spell got out of hand?" he asked.

"Close the book?" Omen cringed. *Of course that's all I*

had to do!

"Is we not chasing mouses any more?" Tormy asked as he watched Etar put the book away. "I is liking the mouses. We is studying our books and we is chasin' mouses!"

Omen rose to dust himself off. Tormy was not going to be distracted by simply putting the book away.

"You two are a menace," Etar mused with a shake of his head, though Omen could see his eyes glittering with humor.

"You could find us something fun to do instead?" Omen suggested, seeing an opening in his brother's demeanor — a chance to possibly get out of several long hours of copying down magical spells that would likely not be half as interesting as the magical mice spell he'd just cast. "I know, send us on a quest!"

"We is going on a quest!" Tormy squeaked breathlessly. The cat's tail lashed back and forth.

Etar snorted in derision as he carefully righted some of the fallen furniture in the room.

"And not some dumb quest where I run around fetching something pointless — a real quest. An epic quest!" Omen continued, ignoring the fact that Etar had dismissed him.

"I'm not sending you on an epic quest," Etar stated flatly. He picked up a fallen chair.

"We is going on an epicnessness quest, and we is being fiercenessness!" Tormy was growing more excited by the moment, and a wary look entered Etar's glittering blue eyes. Once Tormy got an idea into his head, it was difficult to deter him from it.

"Omen, I'm not going to send you on a heroic quest that you'll abandon halfway through just to go to the Night Games with Templar," Etar said frankly.

Omen sputtered with outrage. "What . . . what . . . abandon . . . Night Games. . ." *Actually, the Night Games sound really fun and I bet that would amuse Tormy.* But Templar had been commandeered by his father. *Stupid princely duties. He's probably off fighting giants and I'm stuck here doing nothing.* "I'm not going to abandon a heroic quest. I'm not that irresponsible!" He moved to help pick up the fallen furniture, hoping to prove his point regarding his sense of responsibility.

"Yes, you are." Etar's words were blunt but said gently. They merely stated a simple fact. Nonetheless, it was probably the rudest thing Etar had ever said to Omen. *Even if it is true.* Normally Etar was less judgmental.

"Omen, I'm not saying that's a bad thing," Etar added with a soft smile. "I mean you're young — barely twelve years old — you're allowed to be—"

"I'm fifteen!" Omen protested in shock. *So much for divine wisdom!*

Etar looked quite startled. "Fifteen?" he asked, sounding amazed. "Most fifteen-year-olds are hard at work learning a trade or preparing to enter the military. Are you sure you're fifteen?"

"I is fifteen too!" Tormy agreed with gusto. "I is three weeks old, and now I is fifteen — Omy, how many is fifteen? Is we going on our epicness quest now, or is we chasin' more mouses?"

"See — it's mice or quest," Omen reasoned with Etar. "Send us on an epic quest! You're a god — that's what you do, right?"

"Is that what you think I do?" Etar asked.

"An epic quest!" Omen repeated as he lifted up one of the couches Tormy had knocked over in his hunt for mice.

"I swear I'll complete it!"

Etar paused at that, staring intently at him. "You swear?"

"I swear!" Omen insisted blithely, sensing victory. "You have my word of honor! But it has to be an *epic* quest, something no one else has ever done! Something no one else *can* do."

"Hmm." Etar scratched his chin thoughtfully. "Well, there is one thing . . . no, I don't think you're really suited to epic quests. Epic quests take you down dark roads that tend to have lasting consequences. You set foot on a road like that and you may travel it your whole life."

Offended, Omen glared hard at him. "You think I'm not suited? I can travel a dark road as well as anyone — I'm not afraid! What's this great quest of yours? I'm perfectly suited!"

Etar's holding something back — I can see it in his eyes!

"Well, there is one epic quest I can think of," Etar said thoughtfully, his gaze suddenly intense and probing as if trying to see into Omen's heart.

"What is it? I already gave you my word of honor!" Omen pressed.

"We is promising," Tormy added helpfully. "Honest honest! We is promising to be epicnessness!"

Etar's eyes narrowed suddenly, his expression darkening. "Oh, I'd need more than just a single promise before I'd give you this quest," he said softly. "If you really want this quest, you'll have to make several promises."

Anticipating victory, Omen and Tormy both nodded their heads in agreement.

"If I give you this quest, you must promise that you'll go right now, without question, taking only what I give you. No delay, no hesitation, no questions. No consulting your

14

father or mother. You'll go now and you will not stop until you have completed the quest." Etar's voice matched the intensity of his gaze, and already Omen felt excitement rising inside him.

This is sounding more and more interesting by the minute. "All right!" Omen clapped his hands together. "Agreed! I promise!"

Etar turned toward the door. "Then both of you, come with me." He strode away at a swift pace.

"Where are we—" Omen started to call out to him.

"No questions!" Etar shouted back, making Omen bite his tongue.

I did agree — no questions.

"Come on, Tormy!" Omen said, eager to get started. The two of them chased after Etar.

Servants lined the halls beyond the library door. They held packs and waterskins which Etar grabbed as he passed by.

Omen's brows knitted as he followed. "What are—" he cut off the question himself this time, remembering his promise. *How did Etar's servants know to have all that stuff ready?* But before he could puzzle out the answer, the castle melted away, and he found himself standing in the middle of a dark forest next to an equally startled Tormy. Omen gasped at the sudden display of grandiose magic.

As if in a trance, he stared in awe at the brilliant, icy sky overhead. It was filled with constellations he'd never noticed before.

What just happened? What was that?

Etar tossed an intricate-looking saddle on Tormy's back and nimbly strapped it down, ignoring the cat's sputter of shock. *Is that contraption specially-made for Tormy?* The quick saddling, even more than the magical transportation to the woods, stunned Omen. *It takes me ages to put any sort of harness on Tormy. Etar did it in a second.*

Etar fastened the numerous bags and heavy waterskins to Tormy's saddle. "You know, eventually you'll be able to ride Tormy. Maybe in another year or so. I suppose a small child could ride him now."

"He's just a kitten!" Omen protested. "All that water is way too heavy for him."

"I is strong!" Tormy proclaimed and stood up straight beneath the weight of the saddlebags. Etar produced Omen's great two-handed sword, a gift from his father, from seemingly nowhere and strapped it alongside the saddle beneath one of the leg stirrups.

When did he steal my sword?

"See! I is carrying everything!" Tormy proclaimed proudly.

"The bags are magical," Etar assured Omen. "They don't weigh as much as you'd think."

Before Omen could ask, Etar turned away and held out his hands to the darkness as if reaching for something.

"It's here," he announced, motioning Omen to come forward.

The sharp scent of pine and cedar blew past as a cold wind swept through the forest. Overhead, the tree branches rustled. Dry pine needles crunched beneath Omen's every step.

Deeply suspicious, Omen caught hold of Tormy's shoulder strap. "Etar, what is this—"

"No questions," Etar told him once again. "You promised. Now listen to me very carefully. There is a rift here — a rip in time and space—"

"What!" Omen barked in disbelief. "That's not—"

"A rip in time and space," Etar continued as if Omen had not interrupted, "that leads to another world. You're going to go through it and you will not return until you find our brother."

"Brother?" Omen exclaimed, anxiety flooding through him. *What did I get us into?*

"Our brother has been lost for a very long time," Etar told him. "You must find him. And you must bring him back, bring him home. Do not stop, and whatever you do, do not turn back. If you turn back, our brother will be lost forever. Now, come quickly. We're running out of time. Step through!" He caught hold of Omen's arm and pulled him forward.

When did I lose control of this situation? "Wait a minute!" Omen protested. "How am I even supposed to recognize our brother?"

"You'll know him," Etar assured him. "He's the only one."

He gave Omen a hard shove, and a moment later Omen found himself standing in another place, in another world. Harsh daylight pierced his eyes. He blinked at the bright glare and tried to comprehend the arid landscape that stretched out before him.

Chapter 2: Radiation

"**M**ewrr?" Tormy said, thoroughly confused. The large orange cat stood beside Omen, saddle and supplies on his back.

No sign of Etar or the doorway back. Rat's teeth!

The land around them was empty. *Empty — there's really no other word to describe it.*

Omen and Tormy stood in the shadow of a tall craggy rock at the base of a long range of foothills. While it had been nighttime in the forest, it appeared to be daytime here — though the exact hour was difficult to gauge because the sky was filled with dense, reddish-grey clouds.

The world around them was barren, just dirt and rock as far as they could see. *No sign of life anywhere.* The hills behind them showed no speck of grass or trees. The air was dry, painfully so, choked with ash that immediately burned its way into Omen's nose and throat. He coughed violently, eyes watering. The ground was grey, flat and just as lifeless as the hills. Beyond the protection of the craggy rock, a strong wind blew and carried the dust high into the air.

"Where is we?" Tormy asked and blinked his large amber eyes against the grit of the bleak landscape.

"I don't know," Omen admitted. He coughed again. "But I think Etar had this planned. Lured me in and sprung his trap. We just got played." Omen hadn't expected such trickery from his older brother. *It just doesn't seem like something Etar would do. Which means there's something else going on.*

"We is studying our magics and chasin' mouses," Tormy

reminded him. "We is not playing."

"All right, *I* got played," Omen grumbled under his breath. "Now what do we do? We're stuck."

"We is not to stop, we is not to turn back. We is to find your brother and bring him back here, that's what Etar is saying," Tormy outlined guilelessly. "I didn't know you had a losted brother, Omy. Your Deldano brothers is all safe in Melia. Who is losteded?"

"That's what we're here to find out."

"This is being a terrible place, Omy," Tormy said. "My paws is all dirty — and where is the trees and grass and the birdies?"

Tormy's normally white paws were coated grey and black. Omen crouched down to scoop up a handful of the dirt from the ground. The dust seemed brittle and dry, a mixture of crumbling stone, sand and ash as if the very ground had burned in a blazing inferno. *Did a terrible fire sweep through this area and burn everything? Hope my brother didn't get caught in that fire. Whoever he might be.*

He sneezed as the soot worked its way into his sinuses. Tormy followed suit, his entire body shaking, saddle straps flapping in the air as he let out several loud snort-like sneezes.

"You okay?" Omen asked. He'd always possessed an extremely heightened sense of smell, courtesy of his Machelli bloodline, and the burnt, lifeless environment was playing havoc with him. He looked at Tormy in sympathy.

"My nose is all stuffinessness," Tormy explained. "So I is sneezing. I is thinking the wind is being very loudnessness too."

Omen cocked his head, listening. Though they were both protected in the lee of the craggy rock, the bray of the

19

wind over the arid landscape was relentless. *It's dead — destroyed. As far as I can see. What happened here?*

Driving thoughts of consuming flames and massive destruction from his mind, Omen stepped past the shadow of the rock to get a better look at the land. "Come on, Tormy." He tried to wipe the soot off his breeches, but only managed to grind the black dirt further into the material.

The empty hill led out to a flat valley that stretched endlessly. The wasteland to his left was unbroken dead earth as far as he could see through the dust-choked air. Far off in the distance to the right, however, shadows rose against the grey haze of the sky. The shapes suggested enormous castle walls or tall buildings of a once great city. Even from this distance, Omen could tell that the structures were in ruins, burnt-out empty shells. *People lived there once.* High overhead, the wind howled as it crested past the tops of the mountains behind them and blew more ash into the air.

Omen glanced around, confounded. *Where in this joy-forsaken empty place does Etar expect me to go? If there is someone here — there is no sign of him.*

"Where is we going, Omy?" Tormy asked, uncertain.

Tormy is counting on me. I can't let him down.

Omen glanced back at the foothills and the mountains. From where he stood, he could see no trace of life anywhere — not even snow on the mountains. *Though judging by the temperature, there should be. And it'll get even colder when the light fades.*

Save for the empty ruins of the city, there was nothing. No matter where he turned, there were no markers that anything lived here — only rocks and sand and the occasional boulder dotting the land.

"Let's head toward that city," Omen decided, glancing at

Tormy to see if he agreed. The large cat looked utterly perplexed, ears twitching wildly as he continuously shook the grit out of his fur. Omen nodded his head with determination. "We might be able to find something there. And maybe that's where my brother is."

Tormy just twitched his tail. "That is being a long walk. I is wishing I could fly."

"Fly?" Omen chuckled. *What an imagination.*

"I is almost big enough," Tormy proclaimed. "When I is bigger I is flying in the sky and you is riding."

"You can fly?"

"I is not a birdy, I is not having wings, but I is flying! My daddy, King Largepaw, is a great flying cat. I is being a great flying cat as well."

"But not yet." Omen smiled, guessing it was another one of Tormy's tall tales. *King Largepaw? There's a cat king? Now I've heard everything.* "All right, let's start walking."

The city seemed a long distance away. Omen guessed it would take them several hours to get there on foot. *And we'll be filthy once we get there — good thing I know the domestic spell for. . .* With a sudden jolt, he realized what else was missing from this land.

Magic! There's no magic!

The normal hum and buzz of power he typically felt surrounding his body was gone as if the usual vortices of energy were just as dead as the rest of the land. *Not a speck of magic. Never been in a land without magic before.*

He hummed softly to himself, using his music to conjure the third Tevthis Pattern — the one he knew best and had used often to clean Tormy's fur of dirt and grime. *Can I summon any magic at all?* The pattern formed only sluggishly in his mind, and he felt nothing beyond a simple

21

shift in the air around him.

Rat's teeth! He felt naked. Exposed. Vulnerable.

He glanced down at his hands — they were still filthy from the dirt he'd picked up. *This is going to be unpleasant . . . Wonder if I can use my psionics instead.*

Psionics, unlike magic, came from internal power, not the world around him. But using his psionics to mimic magic wasn't something he'd tried before, and he suspected it would swiftly tire him out. Like a hummingbird swooping from bloom to bloom, his thoughts flitted over the possibilities and pitfalls of magical experimentation.

Had enough trouble with those mice. Why risk it unless I have to?

"Let's check the supplies before we move on," he called to Tormy. The cat paused in mid-step, ears twitching as Omen checked the saddle.

"I is being strongestest," Tormy assured him. "I is carrying all the bags and I is not rolling on the ground and kicking my paws in the air even if I is wishing to!"

Grinning in spite of their circumstances, Omen took stock of Etar's supplies. *No magic, and limited psionics. What else have we got?* Along with food and water, he found a cloak with a hood in one of Tormy's bags. He pulled on the cloak and hood over his outer coat, grateful to block out some of the dust blowing past him. At least now he understood why Etar had attached so many large water-skins to the saddle — as far as he could see, this land was utterly parched.

"Come on, Tormy," he urged again, and he and the cat headed off at an easy pace toward the ruined city. Now more than ever he was certain that Etar had planned the whole thing. *Except it was my idea. I asked him for a quest . . . but his servants were waiting with the supplies. How does that work? And if he wanted me to do this, why didn't he give me more information? And if he's so mighty, why didn't he just go himself?*

The city was much farther away than he'd initially guessed, and after several hours, they still had not reached even the outer wall. *I massively misjudged the size.* Though the city had not seemed to draw much closer, it had grown larger and larger. *Maybe we should walk faster — but I don't know how far we need to go, and I don't want to tire Tormy out.*

"How are you doing, fuzz face?"

He appraised the kitten's stamina — despite the saddle and the numerous bags and waterskins, Tormy had not complained. His paws, utterly black now, made no sound as he strode steadily along. Muck and dry dirt coated his orange fur and whiskers. From time to time he shook himself, the metal buckles of the saddle clanking together.

"I is walking," the cat answered, tilting his head in Omen's direction. "Omy, I is thinking the ground is being funny."

While they were still far from the city boundaries, the ground beneath them had started to change. Omen halted to investigate. Tormy sat back on his haunches, and Omen took a moment to drink deeply from one of the waterskins, quenching his thirst and clearing the dust from his throat. A large wooden bowl hung from the back of Tormy's saddle. Omen filled it with water and set it down in front of the cat. Normally Tormy needed very little water during the day, but everything was so dry here that the cat lapped the liquid up quickly while Omen inspected the land around them.

The ground seemed unnaturally flat. Omen crouched

down to sweep away some of the debris at his feet. Beneath a heavy layer of dust and ash, he found a firm surface made of smooth, hardened tar. He guessed they were walking upon a great road that led straight into the city.

Odd shapes lined the roadway. From a distance he'd mistaken them for boulders, but up close he could see clearly that they were man-made objects — enclosed carriages perhaps. Most were fairly small, capable of seating four or five people, but a few were much larger. He approached one of the larger enclosed wagons and touched its side.

The strange outer shell had been crafted from metal, but exposure — perhaps decades of exposure — had left it rusted and crumbling. What wheels remained were small metal hubs that seemed incapable of supporting the main structure. It occurred to Omen that there must have been something else surrounding the hubs — something that had long since decayed or burned away.

Omen cautiously stepped into the interior of the large carriage and stared down the long row of what might have once been benches. Bits and pieces of cloth and leather still flapped in the wind. He guessed that these seats had been padded at one time. But now they were nothing more than rusted, twisted hunks of metal that merely suggested their former shape.

Mounds of sand rose inside of the carriage at regular intervals. He sifted his fingers through the ashy granules and noticed tiny, sharp pieces mingled with the dirt. *Bones. Bleached bone shards.* He backed away quickly, flicking the dust off his fingertips with a deep shudder. *What happened to these people?*

Tormy, who had finished his water, was now peering into the interior of the carriage.

I can't tell Tormy what this is.

The sky was growing dark, night finally setting in, and the temperature started to drop sharply. They'd have to stop sooner than he'd planned. There would be no light at all once the sky-glow had vanished. No starlight or moonlight could pierce the thick cloud cover.

"What is this, Omy?" Tormy asked curiously, gazing at the inside of the large wagon.

"It's a transport of some sort," Omen explained. "Mechanized, I think. I think these were all machines."

"What happened to all the peoples?" Tormy wondered.

Of course he already knows. He's a cat. He can smell it.

The cat swished his tail back and forth. Omen guessed the oppressive lack of life was working on Tormy's sense of well-being.

No plants, no animals, not even any weeds or insects as far as I can tell. But someone obviously built these machines, and, based on the size of the city, it must have once been filled with hundreds of thousands, maybe millions, of people.

"I think there was a war, Tormy," Omen said softly, piecing together what he'd guessed from the evidence around him. "I think there was some sort of weapon used here that destroyed everything, that burned everything. My dad told me about weapons like that. Terrible weapons that can do this sort of damage."

It had been in one of the many science lessons his father had given him. *Physics, I think. I thought he made it up. Didn't pay much attention — magic always seems so much more practical. But this . . . I had better stay awake for his lectures from now on.*

"A bomb of some sort, I think," he told Tormy. "One that

25

spread fire and poison everywhere, burning and killing everything." He recalled something about such weapons poisoning the land.

"The land is poisonededness?" Tormy guessed immediately. His eyes were big and round. His fur stood on end as if it had been brushed the wrong way.

"Not anymore," Omen assured the cat. "I think it happened a long time ago. Maybe hundreds of years ago. I think all the poison has faded away by now."

"But there is nothing here, Omy," Tormy pointed out. "Where is the losted brother? There is nothing to eat, nothing to drink, not even any mouses."

True. Omen shuddered at the thought. He climbed all the way out of the large metal wagon and looked back along the flat road ahead toward the ruins. *If there's anyone left in this world, he'd still be in the city. But Tormy's right — what would someone in this world eat or drink?*

Etar had said that the person he was looking for was their brother — implying that he was a child of Cerioth, and would thus be immortal. *Could an immortal survive without food or water? Survive for hundreds of years? And what about this war — was my brother here when the initial cataclysm happened? Was he part of the war? Could an immortal survive the destruction of a world, or would he have turned to ash along with everyone else in this cursed place?* Omen swallowed hard.

He'd heard horror stories of the curse that went along with immortality. Templar had quite delighted in telling spine-chilling tales. His friend had suggested that it was possible to burn an immortal alive, reduce him to ash, and then leave him to re-form over years or centuries, held impossibly alive in a state of unimaginable pain in a body that could never die. *Doesn't seem likely.* And truthfully Omen didn't think Templar really believed the tales. *Those are just stories.*

Omen's thoughts returned to his father's lessons about the terrible weapons. He suspected if they had been used here, this world would have burned for decades. *Surely nothing, not even an immortal could survive what must have happened here.*

The wind picked up, the howling increasing, and Omen shook himself from his reverie, moving swiftly to retrieve Tormy's wooden bowl. The cat had consumed all the water, and Omen was grateful that Etar had supplied them with numerous waterskins. He had no idea how long this rescue would take. *If this goes on too long, we'll run out of water.*

He looked at his furry companion and felt a surge of guilt.

I brought Tormy here. I brought him here without finding out the first thing about this place. This world has no magic. If we run out of water, I can't conjure any. Not to mention I don't recall learning a pattern to create water — I know one to heat water. And even if I had a book with patterns, I don't have the weeks I'd need to learn the right one. I am so unprepared.

The light was swiftly fading, and the cold set in. "We won't reach the city before dark, Tormy. We'll have to camp for the night." Omen wondered what he'd do for fire. There was nothing to burn — no wood anywhere — just rock and dust and twisted pieces of metal. He imagined he might be able to scrape together a few meager scraps of cloth from the various wagons along the road, but nothing that would burn for more than a few minutes.

A flash of light momentarily illuminated the ominous

clouds overhead. A booming crack of thunder followed, heralding in a change as the temperature plummeted with the fading light. A moment later rain began to fall, startling Omen more than just about anything he'd seen so far. There had been no sign of water anywhere, and now suddenly they were in a heavy rainstorm.

Perhaps water won't be an issue after all.

He held out his hand to inspect the rain falling on his skin. A strange prickling sensation startled him. It swiftly turned from prickling to burning, and the skin of his palm grew red. Tormy cried out in pain, and Omen turned swiftly, motioning the cat back toward the large wagon.

"Get inside! Quickly!" he shouted at the cat. Tormy was already moving, squeezing through the human-sized opening of the wagon and pushing his furry body into the interior. Omen had to help him shove forward as the bags attached to his saddle caught on the edges of the door. But once he was clear, Omen followed, getting himself out of the poisonous rain.

His skin was still burning, and he could see now that Tormy was also suffering. The cat had flung himself down on the floor of the wagon and was about to start licking the pads of his paws which were showing signs of blistering and bleeding. Omen dove forward, catching hold of the cat's head before he could lick anything. "No, Tormy, don't lick!" he commanded, knowing that if any of that burning water got onto the cat's tongue, they'd be in real trouble. "It's poison!"

"My paws hurt!" Tormy wailed, and Omen's heart clenched, his own pain forgotten as he frantically tried to figure out what to do.

He replayed every lesson his father had ever given him

in those endless science classes. One conversation in particular stuck in his head.

"You know, one day you'll want this information and you won't have it," 7 had chided him.

And with his usual defiant attitude, Omen had scoffed, "Right, as if I'm ever going to need to know about acids or alkalies. Why don't you just show me something fun — like how to blow things up?"

That lesson, faint though it was, came back to haunt him, and he scrambled for the waterskins on Tormy's saddle. *Clean water will dilute it — wash it off. Best way to stop the burning.*

"This will help, Tormy," he assured the whimpering cat as he pulled the stopper from the waterskin and began rinsing the pads of Tormy's paws, washing away the built-up grime. Then he held Tormy's head firmly against his chest while pouring the water over both of the cat's ears and rinsing away the rain.

When he was done rinsing Tormy clean, he set aside the waterskin and pulled out a second container he'd found in the pack. It held an unguent that smelled strongly of sweetroot, a powerful healing herb. The cat stopped whimpering as Omen soothed the ointment over the paw pads and the tender skin of his ears. The rain had blistered even the thick callouses of the cat's feet. But the bleeding stopped as Omen spread the cream over the pads, and the blisters slowly faded away.

When he'd finished with Tormy's paws and ears, he checked the rest of the cat, removing the saddle so that the kitten could rest comfortably. The animal's thick fur had protected most of his skin, though Omen dabbed more of the ointment on the cat's nose for good measure.

29

When he was finished tending to Tormy, and the cat sat with his paws folded beneath him, his whiskers drooping miserably, Omen inspected himself. Save for his hands, he'd had little direct exposure to the rain. Etar's cloak and hood had protected his head and face.

Despite his body's own natural healing abilities, his hands were heavily blistered and bleeding, and Omen took the time to carefully wash his skin before applying a thin coat of the ointment to them. The pain faded quickly, and he knew that in a few hours the blisters would be gone. His clothing, like Tormy's fur, was somewhat the worse for wear, damaged in places. But while the rainfall was acidic enough to blister the skin, it wasn't truly strong enough to burn through the thick leathers he was wearing.

"Why is the rain burning, Omy?" Tormy asked after a while. He was staring at the long rows of open windows along the side of the wagon they were sheltering in. There was no glass remaining in any of the windows, but the wind was blowing from the back of the wagon and for the most part, the rain was kept out by the thin metal roof above them. Omen imagined the rain would eventually eat right through the metal and one day the wagons would be gone from the barren land, no trace left behind.

"It's the poison, Tormy," Omen explained. "The wind carried all the dust and poison into the sky and when the temperature drops, the rain starts and all that poison gets pulled back down in the water."

We can't stay here. It's too dangerous for Tormy. He couldn't possibly consider continuing to subject Tormy to this horrible world. Once the rain let up, they'd have to find their way back to that rocky crag and return to their own world.

30

"Poor losteded brother." Tormy sighed heavily, resting his chin on his folded paws. "Poor losteded brother with the burning rain. We is going to save him. Right, Omy?"

Omen stared at his cat in silence. Etar had made him promise that he would not turn back. Had told him that if he did turn back then their brother would be lost forever. *But if Etar knew we had a brother trapped here, why didn't he just save him . . . unless . . . he can't. But that doesn't make any sense — Etar is a god. What would stop him? And unlike us, he wouldn't be bothered by dead worlds and acidic rain.*

Tormy was staring at him with such an honest and hopeful expression on his face that Omen was momentarily at a loss for what to say. How could he possibly suggest they abandon anyone here in the face of that childlike hope staring at him?

"We'll try, Tormy," Omen agreed reluctantly, and the cat fluffed his fur as if accepting that trying would mean succeeding.

Omen didn't hold out much hope of finding anyone left alive here — and if by some miracle someone had survived, that person would be far from sane.

Digging through Etar's packs, Omen found several large woven flax canvases. He covered the windows around them in case the wind changed directions and began blowing the poisoned rain inside the wagon. There was little he could do about lighting a fire to drive away the cold. Luckily his cloak was warm, and Tormy's thick fur coat would protect both of them through the night.

He shared some cheese and dried meat with the cat, both of them eating in silence and accepting the fact that they would not be filling their bellies anytime soon. Typically such lack of food would set the cat to wailing in protest, but tonight Tormy just settled down and allowed Omen to lean into his side to share his warmth.

The howling wind sounded like the voices of the dead, and it was a long time before either of them managed to drift off to sleep.

Chapter 3: The Thing that Crawls

Eventually dawn arrived. The sky grew lighter gradually, the air warmed, and the rain stopped falling.

Knowing he'd need to do more to protect Tormy's skin from further damage, Omen cut strips from one of the canvases to fashion cat boots. The cat waited patiently while Omen tied the cloth around each paw. When Omen was done, Tormy took a couple of tentative steps. It was obviously strange for the cat to walk with strips of cloth wrapped around his feet, and he made several twitchy high stepping motions. Omen laughed out loud. After a few more steps, the cat adjusted.

When they stepped out of the large wagon, the ground was still damp from the rainstorm. Tormy carefully inspected his new boots, lifting one paw and then the next as if to assure himself that his tender pads would be safe.

While the rain had fallen steadily, it had made little impact on the land. Most of the precipitation had already soaked completely into the ground, and with the howling wind still blowing relentlessly around them, the earth would be bone dry in less than an hour.

Omen repacked their belongings, saddling a remarkably complacent Tormy, and the two of them continued their journey toward the ruined city.

It took several hours to reach the edge of the city, and Omen marveled at the total destruction of this once great metropolis. Some of the buildings in the city center had to have been thousands of feet tall, made of stone and metal. All was in ruins now, the metal girders melted and twisted from terrible heat, leaving only the skeletal remains of broken frameworks and crumbling stone reaching toward the dust-filled sky. More rusted carriages sat along the roadway, but up ahead at the outer edge of the city Omen spotted standing figures.

"Is those peoples, Omy?" Tormy asked. The shapes seemed humanoid. But all of them were frozen, standing perfectly still in the relentless wind.

"I think they're statues, Tormy." He remembered reading stories of volcanic eruptions that would coat cities and people in molten lava, preserving their forms in stone for all eternity. He hoped that was not the case here. *Bad enough that the dust and ash we're breathing is filled with burnt and crushed bones.*

As Omen and Tormy drew closer, they could both see that the shapes were indeed statues placed at regular intervals along the city's boundaries — statues of people captured eternally in the motion of talking or walking or standing in place.

At first Omen thought someone had dragged all of these strange creations onto the road, positioning them in various spots by the city entrance, but as he got close enough to inspect them individually, he saw that the statues had been carved where they stood. The base of each was unfinished stone, salvaged from the decaying buildings. These forms had been hewn from the very remains of the city they now inhabited, all made of granite or marble or concrete.

Bewildered, he approached. Some sculptures were life-sized, some gigantic, carved into the enormous blocks of stone that had once made up the monstrous buildings of this

city. Other massive blocks of stone had been carved in relief — hundreds of faces emerging from surfaces, staring
out at the empty world around them. And interspersed
among effigies were smaller representations, carved from
smaller rocks: some children, some tiny people, some animals of various sizes and shapes, all populating a city without life.

"Who is carving all these, Omy?" Tormy asked in awe
as he inspected a large statue of a horse and rider who appeared to be entering the city at a gallop. "It must be hundreds of peoples."

"Or one person working for a very long time," Omen
said, uneasy. Moving further into the city, he studied the
sculptures for similarities. While there were no structures
still intact around them, no signs of anyone inhabiting the
area, the statues were everywhere.

"Etar is a master sculptor," Omen told Tormy.

"I is 'member 'membering," the cat agreed. "Is Etar carving these?"

"I don't think so," Omen replied uncertainly. It didn't
make any sense to him. *Why would Etar carve some random statues and then leave our brother trapped here?*

One group of statues seemed crudely done in comparison to most of the collection. Omen touched the hard
jagged surface of the arm of a young woman. These art-
works seemed older than the rest, and showed signs that the
rain had eaten away at the stone for years. *Decades. Longer
maybe.* He followed the evolution, each shape carved pro-
gressively with more and more skill, growing more lifelike
with each passing attempt, until the work eventually
reached a master level that left no doubt in Omen's mind
that whoever had carved these shapes shared Etar's genius.

Etar, The Soul's Flame, inspired artists the world over, and his own exquisite creations were considered sacred objects.

Whoever did this has to be our brother.

The mysterious sculptor's skill was unmistakable, and though the technique and style were far different from anything he'd ever seen Etar create, there was no denying the artistry or craftsmanship. Etar tended to sculpt beautiful and fantastical things. While the skill level on display here was breathtaking, the subjects of these statues were commonplace. These were normal people, some ugly, some pretty, some with expressions of conceit and pettiness, some faces dull and drudging, others kind and serene. And mixed among the common statues were disturbing ones, men and women carved with arched backs, and skeletal hands outstretched to the heavens. Their faces were twisted in agony, flesh melted away and bone exposed. So detailed and terrible were these works that there was no doubt in Omen's mind that the sculptor had witnessed the cataclysm that had annihilated this world.

That's awful. So awful. How . . . He couldn't put his thoughts in order. A wrenching pain gnawed at his insides. *Such misery.*

"Look over here, Omy," Tormy called. The cat peered into the ruined cavity of one of the numerous destroyed buildings. The ground floor was partially intact, three of the walls and the roof still sound enough to form a protected room beneath. Many of the statues were clustered around this area, one or two carved in the position of looking down through a broken window casement at whatever was housed inside.

He looked through the large opening Tormy had discovered. This room showed signs of habitation. The ground against the far wall was cleared of debris. And there was a small pile of bits and pieces of cloth forming a makeshift sleeping pallet that looked more like a large rat's nest than anything else. Throughout the room, other items showed evidence of careful collection — small cans made of rusted tin, an assortment of tiny pieces of metal that still held their original shapes — gears and bolts, and tiny useless pieces of machines that had long ago failed. What must have been a metal sign leaned against one of the walls.

Omen stepped into the interior and brushed his hand over the sign. He noticed the faded marks of paint still stuck to the surface, the words once written there so worn away he could not read them. He suspected it was a city's welcome sign, crafted by people long dead and gone. Whatever name they had given this once great city was lost now to history.

He turned back toward the opening where Tormy was still waiting and caught his breath when he saw the far wall. Unlike the rest of the interior, it was carved in full relief. This edifice depicted a family. The mother was tall and re-gal looking — beautiful in a way the other statues outside had not been, her face proud and fierce and yet somehow gentle. The father's face was common but kind, showing a warmth and a depth of soul in the expression that spoke of a great compassion. And standing next to them was a young boy who bore an expression of joy and mischief, eyes alight with youthful innocence that belied everything Omen had seen here. Next to the boy was a hollow, rough area of stone that suggested that at one time there might have been another form standing next to him.

Omen stepped forward and ran his fingers over the chis-el marks of the last shape beside the family — this last figure had been chipped away and obliterated — the crudity of the marks suggesting rage.

"Is that him, Omy?" Tormy asked, peering around the opening to get a better look at the carving. "Is that your losteded brother?" He was looking at the shape of the happy boy standing beside the man and woman. But Omen did not think that was the case, and he shook his head.

"No, Tormy," he said softly. He touched the hollowed, empty area. "I think this was him."

A small tin can sat nearby on a stone shelf. Omen picked it up and heard the rattle of metal inside. Reaching in, he pulled out several long, thin pieces of steel. Unlike the rest of the metal he'd seen, these strips were bright and shiny as if someone had carefully cleaned away all the rust and had sharpened the edges. At first, he thought they were meant to be knives, but after holding them in his fist a while longer he guessed that they had been used as chisels.

Setting the crude chisels aside, he stepped outside again and stared at the hundreds of statues in the street. He thought of Etar's home far away from this pitiful disaster. The castle of The Soul's Flame housed a great art studio where Etar joyfully carved his masterpieces. That chamber was filled with finely crafted tools.

How could Etar leave someone here? How could he just sit around reading and playing and pursuing his hobbies when—

The idea that someone had carved all these figures using nothing more than a few rusted pieces of metal defied Omen's imagination. *This brother must have incredible mental stamina and discipline.*

"Can you smell anything, Tormy?" Omen asked, wondering how he was going to find his lost brother in this

38

place. He sniffed the air, but the acrid dust swirling around him made it nearly impossible to scent anything. He choked back a cough. "Someone is obviously living here — can you smell him?"

Tormy shook his head. "My nose is being all stuffiness-ness," he admitted. The constant exposure to the noxious air had left Tormy's nostrils heavily caked with residue. Omen suspected his own face was just as grimy. His fingers itched to throw a cleaning spell.

"Let's keep looking around," he suggested. He didn't know what time of day it was, and he wanted to make certain they had a place to shelter should the rain start falling again. *This is obviously the carver's home. He can't have gone far — not if it rains every night. He'd have to return by sunset.*

Omen picked his way carefully around the numerous statues, taking care to avoid stepping on or knocking over any of the smaller forms surrounding him. So intently did he study the sculptures that he did not notice the pile of rags lying upon the ground.

The pile of rags leaped at him suddenly and landed on his back. It snarled and hissed like a wild animal, fists flailing at Omen's head.

Omen hollered and grabbed for the flailing rags. He flung the thing from him.

Tormy let out a high-pitched *merow.*

The rag bundle flew through the air and crashed with a muffled crunch against a stone wall at the edge of the street.

Tormy bolted to Omen's side, and they both stared at the bundled-up creature, which now lay motionless.

As his initial shock wore off, Omen noted first that he

39

had not been injured — though the thing had attacked him like a feral animal, there had been no strength in the blows. The second thing he realized was that his attacker had barely weighed anything at all — seeming more a small pile of old rags and dried sticks than an animal or person. It sprawled lifelessly in the dust.

"Hello?" Omen said, carefully taking a step toward the bundle, his hand moving to the dagger at his belt. His sword was still strapped to Tormy's saddle, but he didn't think this fragile thing was enough of a threat to warrant a two-handed great sword.

"Is it killeded, Omy?" Tormy asked softly when the heap of rags did not respond.

Omen's stomach sank, fearing that he had just injured something truly helpless. He took another careful step forward, the heels of his boots crushing pebbles beneath his feet. At the sound, the pile of rags moved suddenly, drawing in upon itself and folding into a tight ball. The movement at least gave Omen a better glimpse of what was under the rags — not an animal or a pile of sticks, but rather a person. Its arms and hands moved to cover its head, legs and feet wrapped with dirty strips of cloth.

Judging from the size of the form, Omen guessed it had to be a young boy — but the poor thing was so filthy Omen couldn't even tell the color of his skin. The boy's arms and hands were little more than thin bones covered with filth-scabbed skin. Every bone was clearly defined, the skin lacking flesh.

"Did I hurt you?" Omen asked gently, fearful that he'd damaged the boy beyond repair. "I'm sorry. You startled me." Omen took several more steps forward, and the boy raised his skeletal arms over his head and sat up, back still turned to Omen as he pressed his bony, blackened hands against the stone wall he'd crashed into.

"Real flesh, real body, hard as stone, how can this be?" a painfully hoarse voice choked out from the small form. Omen shuddered at the sound of the strange words. *That's Kahdess — the Language of the Dead!*

While Omen had been required to learn the rudimentary vocabulary of Kahdess as part of his schooling, it hadn't actually been something he'd ever heard spoken out loud. Unlike Sul'eldrine, the Language of the Gods everyone revered, Kahdess was so abhorred that none of his tutors had wanted to pronounce the words for him. No one living save mystics or necromancers who consorted with spirits spoke Kahdess. It was a language that belonged solely to the dead. Omen only knew the basics because his mother insisted he understand how to ward off necromantic curses.

"Was that the dead tongue, Omy?" Tormy asked, startling Omen again. *How would Tormy have ever heard such a thing? Tormy wouldn't have studied ancient languages — maybe the Cat Lands have their own legends about the dead.*

"I think so," Omen admitted.

Since his tutors were thorough and afraid of his mother, Omen knew the basic vocabulary and structure even if he was uncertain how to pronounce many of the words. He'd only studied the language in its written form. "I greet you," he said hesitantly in Kahdess — the closest equivalent to *hello* he could remember.

The small form stiffened and turned, head and face still completely obscured by the rags. "It speaks?" the figure whispered. "It has words, a voice, a tongue. The others do not have tongues — they have voices but they do not have

41

tongues. What is this meaning?"

Uncertain what was happening, Omen crouched down carefully in front of the small form. "Do you. . . " he corrected his vocabulary, "are you hurt? I didn't mean to throw you so far. You scared me."

The small form spun toward him at that, face turned upward, and Omen found himself biting back a gasp. The boy's face was like a skull, thin skin barely covering the bones beneath. His skin was black with soot and grime; his lips cracked and bleeding. He wore strips of cloth around his head, covering parts of his face and most of his scalp, but Omen could see strands of hair tangled among those lengths of cloth, though the color of the meager strands was indistinguishable. His skull seemed a matted clump of filthy hair and old rags caked together with years of blood and ash and old seeping fluids from too many wounds to count. But in the center of that shrunken, skeletal face, a pair of large heart-rending eyes the color of a brilliant, violet sky at sunset gazed back at him.

"This thing is broken and bleeding," the boy said simply, holding his hands up as if to show the bleeding scrapes coating what little flesh covered his palms. "This thing is scary."

Strange innocence resided in the boy's eyes, making the statement almost laughable.

"No, I only meant you startled me." Omen smiled gently. "I didn't expect you to jump on me." He knew his sentence structure was flawed, but he hoped the boy understood his meaning.

"I was not expected?" the boy asked and then turned suddenly to hiss at something off to his left. "Yes, I heard what it said! You don't need to repeat it!"

Omen and Tormy both turned in the direction the boy was looking. Save for the statues, there was nothing there.

"It says I am not expected — but *it* is the new thing, the unexpected thing. I did not expect it. I did not prepare. There have been no other voices with tongues and bodies," the boy exclaimed, still looking at something Omen could not see.

"Who is he talking to, Omy?" Tormy asked curiously, his ears twitching as if to catch hold of any stray sound.

At the cat's words, the boy leaned over and peered around Omen to stare at Tormy. The boy's large, violet eyes, so prominent in his sunken face, gleamed with deep confusion.

Tormy flared his whiskers and gave a hesitant, toothy smile.

"Its words are lost," the boy exclaimed. "I hear its voice, but its words are lost."

Guessing that the boy meant he had not understood what Tormy said — he'd been speaking in Merchant's Common — Omen tried to explain. "He doesn't speak your language — Kahdess." He shifted closer. "Do you have a name?"

The boy pursed his lips at the question, and Omen found himself wincing as the movement split open one of the numerous cuts on the child's mouth.

"A name," the boy repeated. He turned again, glaring up at something Omen couldn't see. "Yes, I remember names! You don't have to shout at me. I remember a world filled with names!" He suddenly thrust his arms upward, his hands in the air, bony fingers stretched out to the heavens as he looked up at the dust-choked sky.

Startled by the sudden action, Omen stepped back.

"I remember," the boy said, "before when the voices of

the dead did not scream across the surface of the world, and the tears of fire did not fall from the heavens. I remember names of things that lived and breathed and did not crumble away to ash." He dropped his arms suddenly, as if all the life had drained from him, his shoulders drooping, his head bowing. "Kyr," he said simply. "I was called Kyr."

Though Tormy might not have understood the words the boy was saying, he latched onto the name as if understanding it. "Keeeeeeerrrrrr," the cat purred, drawing out the name as if testing it on his tongue.

"Kyr," Omen repeated. "That's a good name." He wondered if it was really the boy's name or simply the only thing he could remember. He didn't suppose it mattered.

"I will ask!" the boy said again to someone Omen could not see, and he and Tormy watched helplessly as Kyr waved his arms about as if shooing away a crowd. "They wish to know what its name is," he said, looking up expectantly at Omen. Save for the statues there was no one else there.

"Who are they?" Omen asked, wondering if he could get the boy to explain who exactly he thought he was talking to.

Kyr turned to glare at someone who wasn't standing beside him. "I told you already, you have voices, but you do not have tongues, you do not have bodies, it cannot see you." He growled in exasperation at something else that Omen could not hear and frowned at something just past his shoulder. "You heard me — I have already asked. If it does not tell me, I cannot guess at its name."

Not entirely certain why the boy was calling both him and Tormy *it,* Omen pressed his hand to his chest. "Sorry, my name is Omen and this is Tormy."

44

"Hallowwww," Tormy greeted, guessing Omen's words were meant as an introduction.

Kyr tugged at one of the blackened bandages wrapped across his nose and leaned over again. Dumbfounded, he looked at Tormy in silence for a long moment. "Omen, Tormy." He repeated finally, then turned to glare at something beyond them. "No, I don't know why it has two names. I didn't ask it that!"

Really confused now, Omen scratched his head. "There's two of us," he explained. "There's me, and there's Tormy."

That caught Kyr's attention, and he stared fiercely up at Omen, striking his bony fist against his rag-covered chest. "No! There is not two, there is not three. There is only the one. There is only the thing that crawls, the thing that bleeds, the thing that burns and screams. In this land with the fire and the ash and the bone there is only one!"

Etar's words came flooding back. *Etar said that our brother was the only one.* Deeply troubled, Omen understood the gravity of what it meant — what a truly horrific thing Etar had said. Here, in this empty dead world, Kyr was utterly alone, quite literally the only one left.

"We're not from here," Omen explained gently to the boy, not certain the child was capable of understanding what he was saying. "We're from someplace else."

Kyr's brow wrinkled in confusion. "There is an else-where?" he asked, his voice a quiet squeak.

"Yes," Omen assured him. "Lots of places — filled with people."

The boy looked around, sadly staring at all the statues and the ruined remains of the city. "There are no people here," he stated. "There is only the dead and the dust."

The boy started to cough, choking on that very dust he'd

45

just mentioned. Omen watched as the thin child raised one bony hand to his mouth, pulling back his bleeding lips to reveal blackened teeth which he sank into the palm of his hand.

A moment later black and red rivulets of blood seeped from Kyr's mouth, and horror overtook Omen as he realized what he was seeing. The boy was sucking blood from his own hand to quench his thirst.

Chapter 4: Green

"**K**yr!" Omen grabbed the boy's wrist, pulling his hand away from his mouth. "Don't do that!"

Looking petrified, the boy froze, offering no resistance as Omen drew his hand toward him. Omen pulled a hand-kerchief from one of the inner pockets of his coat and carefully wrapped the bleeding wound, tying the ends of the handkerchief together. The tiny wrist felt utterly thin and delicate in his grip as if it would break from the slightest pressure. *It's like holding a hummingbird.*

When Omen was done, he released Kyr's wrist, and the boy drew his hand back to stare at it. Uncertain, he offered up his other hand. Omen glanced at Tormy to see if the cat understood what the boy wanted.

"I think he's trying to share, Omy," Tormy said carefully, his voice subdued.

Omen gulped and blinked several times. "That's . . . kind of sweet." He cleared his throat. "And extremely gross." He retrieved one of the waterskins from Tormy's saddlebags.

"We don't have to drink blood, Kyr." He held out the heavy waterskin. "Drink this."

The boy grasped the waterskin, its weight dragging his arms toward the ground. Struggling with the leather strap, the boy poked at the sack with a bony finger. Finally he bent his face toward it and tried to sink his blackened teeth into the thick leather.

"No," Omen exclaimed, taking the heavy container back. He pulled out the stopper and turned the skin over, letting a thin trickle pour onto the ground. Fascinated, the boy immediately stuck his fingers into the stream of water, then pulled them back and stuffed them in his mouth. At the first taste of fresh water, his eyes widened. He quickly reached out and grabbed Omen's wrist to tilt the waterskin downward and pour the liquid directly into his open mouth. He drank desperately, frantically gasping and choking as he tried to swallow mouthful after mouthful.

Alarmed, Omen watched for a few moments before he finally angled the waterskin upward, the boy's grip on his wrist too weak to stop him. "You're going to make yourself sick . . . Slow down."

Kyr cried out in protest as the stream of water was pulled away, his eyes frantic and panic-stricken.

"It's all right," Omen assured him. "Just drink slowly. I'm not taking it away from you. Just drink a little at a time."

Omen tilted the waterskin again, measuring out the liquid more carefully, but letting the boy drink his fill in gulps.

Kyr drank for a long time and more than once Omen and Tormy exchanged concerned looks. But eventually the boy sat back, exhausted, and pressed his hands against his stomach, a look of such profound incredulity on his face that Omen didn't have the heart to tease him.

"You going to be sick?" he asked.

Kyr shook his head, still holding his stomach and rocking back and forth as if trying to keep the water down. A great deal of the water had spilled down the boy's chin and neck. It dripped onto the dirt where he was still kneeling in the ash. The water had washed away some of the black from his teeth and the centuries of caked-on muck from his skin, revealing pale flesh underneath. His chin showed no signs of a beard, suggesting that he was either extremely young, or came from a people who did not grow facial hair.

It would have taken him years to carve all these statues — maybe even hundreds of years. He has to be older than I am. But looking at him, I'd guess he's barely nine or ten.

Kyr's bone structure was sharply angular, but given the boy's filthy and emaciated appearance, Omen couldn't guess if he was human, elvin or faerie. *Maybe he's something I've never even heard of. Those eyes of his are certainly unusual. He is Cerioth's son.*

"Did you make all these statues?" Omen asked while they waited for the boy's stomach to settle.

Kyr ducked his head hesitantly, the dry wind lifting away a dirty bandage from around one of his blistered and filthy ears. "I gave the voices bodies, but they do not walk, they do not talk, they do not breathe."

"They're amazing," Omen told him. "Very beautiful."

The boy's eyes lit up. "Do you want to see my treasure? I can share it with you." He scrambled to his feet, his water-bloated belly forgotten as he reached out with one bony hand and caught hold of Omen's cloak to pull him along. As he passed, he also caught a handful of Tormy's dirty orange fur and pulled at him too. Bemused, both Omen and Tormy followed. Kyr pulled them past a row of statues and down one of the crumbling streets.

The light was beginning to fade from the sky, and Omen hoped the treasure the boy wanted to show them was close. *Can't get caught unprotected if the rain returns.* "Is it far?" he asked Kyr, glancing back at the shelter where the boy had been living. It was big enough for the three of them and would keep the rain off for the night.

"Not far," the boy explained and then released them to

climb over a large rock in the middle of the street. He pointed down at the ground on the other side. "There it is! I found green!"

"Green?" Omen wondered if he'd mistranslated the boy's words. He moved around the rock to see what the boy was pointing at. Tormy followed closely behind.

There on the ground, growing out of a crack between the stone and the street in a dark patch of dirt was a tiny, green weed no larger than Omen's thumbnail. It was so innocuous, and at the same time so out of place, Omen wasn't certain what to say. Tormy was peering over the edge of the rock and studying the weed intently, ears perked forward as if he found it utterly fascinating.

"I is thinking it's a clover," Tormy announced, seeming quite pleased by the sight.

"It's a weed," Omen agreed and then watched as Kyr lay down on the ground beside it, placing his head in the dirt, face turned toward the weed, eyes fixed upon it.

"It's beautiful," the boy breathed as if it were the most extraordinary thing he'd ever seen in his life.

A loud crack of thunder overhead signaled a change in the atmosphere. While they had been talking, the temperature had dropped, night settling in as the light quickly faded from the sky. The first drop of rain struck, and Omen waved his hand toward Tormy. "Quickly Tormy, back to the shelter!" he shouted. The cat did not need to be told twice; he sped across the statue-filled street toward Kyr's small shelter. Omen moved swiftly after him.

He glanced briefly over his shoulder to aid Kyr only to realize that the boy was not following him. He raced back and was startled by what he saw. Kyr crouched protectively over the small weed, his hands braced in the dirt on either side of the clover, using his own body to protect the little plant from the burning rain. He seemed oblivious to the blisters already forming on his exposed skin.

Omen lurched forward, grabbed Kyr around the waist, lifted him out of the dirt, and carried him back toward the shelter.

Kyr shrieked and wailed, arms outstretched toward the plant, limbs flailing as he tried to free himself. But there was no strength in his broken little body, and Omen didn't slow down as he carried him back to the shelter and ducked inside.

He carried Kyr to the far side of the room and set him down on the filthy pile of rags, bracing himself, ready to grab the boy if he tried to run back to the plant. But any fight seemed to have left Kyr, and he curled himself into a small ball, arms once again wrapped around his head while he sobbed softly.

Omen's eyes teared up, and he had to blink several times before speaking. "Have you been protecting that weed with your body?" Omen asked, loath to think of the damage and pain the child had suffered while shielding the tiny clover.

Kyr did not answer.

At a loss, Omen turned toward Tormy. "You all right?" he asked, his gaze roving over the cat, assessing if he'd taken any more damage from the rain.

"I is wellnessness," Tormy assured him. "My boots is saving me!" He waved one of his paws at Omen, his canvas boot still firmly in place.

Omen's hands were blistered again, but he could see that Kyr was in much worse shape. The rags the boy wore around his body were thin and left patches of his skin fully exposed. There were blisters on his arms and hands, face

51

and neck. His matted skull was covered with oozing sores. Grabbing another full waterskin from Tormy's saddle, as well as the healing unguent, he set about trying to repair the damage the rain had done.

Kyr stopped crying when the water first poured across his skin, his eyes opening to watch in bewilderment as Omen cleaned his wounds with the water to neutralize the remaining acid. The boy's body was so filthy there was really no chance of cleaning the wounds properly — the cloth Omen dabbed against the blisters quickly turned black with soot and ash. He eventually gave up and smeared a generous dose of the sweet-smelling ointment on all visible blisters.

Kyr was utterly silent and compliant throughout the entire process, merely watching Omen with big eyes.

He doesn't seem to even feel this. After so long, his pain tolerance must be extremely high.

When he was done, Omen tended to his own wounds, promising himself that the moment he got home he would get his father to teach him everything he knew about psionic healing. He'd seen his father heal deep sword wounds in a matter of seconds. *Never thought how amazing that really is.* Despite his own ability to heal with the speed of an immortal, Omen was beginning to see how important the skill was when responsible for others. Kyr might be immortal — time might heal the wounds of his body — but Omen certainly didn't like seeing either him or Tormy suffer while they waited for nature to cure them.

"I is hungry," Tormy admitted after a while, and Omen smiled at him. Moving forward, he unfastened the heavy saddle and saddlebags still strapped to the cat.

Tormy hasn't complained at all about carrying such a

heavy load.

"Let's see what we can do about getting some dinner," he told the cat. He glanced over at Kyr who was watching in silence. Omen searched his memory for the proper words in Kahdess. "Food," he explained. "It's time to eat."

Kyr shook his head. "No food. There is nothing. I looked." He scooped up a handful of rocks and dust from the ground and held it out to Omen. "There is only this. You can't eat the dust. I tried."

Omen stilled as Kyr's words sank in. *He must be starving — if there's no water, there is certainly no food left in this world. How could I be so thoughtless?*

There were apples in one of the saddlebags, and Omen swiftly sliced one of them up before handing a sliver of the fruit to Kyr, not wanting the boy to gorge himself as he had with the water.

Kyr's eyes widened as he took hold of the fruit slice and hesitantly raised it to his mouth. At the first taste, his violet eyes watered, tears dripping down his face. He gobbled the apple down and then began sobbing and shaking uncontrollably. He collapsed on the ground and lowered his head to the dirt.

Without hesitating, Omen sat down beside him and lifted him up, carefully handing him slice after slice until all of the apple was gone. The boy stopped sobbing eventually, but the uncontrollable shakes never ended. Omen feared he would rattle his poor bones apart from the sheer force of the tremors.

Omen removed some bread, cheese and more of the dried meat from the satchel. He gave the meat to Tormy and shared the bread and cheese with Kyr. While it was obvious Kyr was starving and desperate for the food, his stomach simply could not handle much. The boy eventually curled up on the pile of rags and fell asleep.

Omen and Tormy finished in silence, neither certain what to say. When they were done, Tormy climbed behind Kyr and settled himself on the pile of rags to sleep in a large furry ball. The tired cat purred softly to himself, and the deep rumbling sound soothed Omen's nerves.

Omen packed up the supplies he'd pulled out before settling beside Kyr and Tormy. He sneezed briefly, his nose tickling, but his sinuses were still too stuffed up to smell anything. *Probably a good thing,* he considered, guessing neither he nor Tormy smelled particularly good. Certainly Kyr had to reek from filth and decay.

He leaned back against Tormy's warm belly, listening for the rumbling purr and Kyr's shallow breathing. Omen gazed across the darkened room to where the relief carving of the family ornamented the bleak wall. Though it was too dark to see, he could still make out the forms from memory. He wondered if Kyr even remembered the names of the people he'd carved.

Were those people his adopted parents? Was that boy his friend, or perhaps his brother? Whoever they were, they were long gone, long dead, and Omen wasn't certain it would be wise to ask Kyr to remember.

Omen woke when the sky began brightening beyond the confines of their shelter, and he discovered that during the night Kyr had wormed his way under Tormy's right paw and was lying half hidden beneath the sleeping cat's furry body. The boy had also wrapped one bony fist around Omen's left wrist and was holding on tightly as if terrified of letting go. Omen smiled faintly at that and tried to gently free himself. His movements woke Kyr instantly.

For a moment Kyr stared at them in confusion, then he turned to gaze at the light coming in from the open doorway. His eyes widened suddenly. He leaped to his feet with startling speed and raced toward the door.

"Hey!" Omen shouted. He jumped up and ran after the boy. Kyr leaped over stones and raced around statues with practiced ease. In seconds Omen realized the boy was not fleeing, but racing toward the little weed he'd shown him the day before.

Kyr disappeared behind the large boulder that had sheltered the weed, and a moment later a wail of despair echoed through the air. As Omen rounded the stone, he saw the boy with his face once again pressed into the dirt, beating the ground with bony fists — all that was left of the small weed was a faint greenish smear of dissolved plant material mixed in with the slowly drying muck on the ground.

"It's all right, Kyr," Omen assured him.

"It's all gone!" Kyr wailed. "All the green and growing — all gone! I try to remember the green but it's all gone."

"It's all right," Omen said again. "There are plenty of plants back in my home."

"We is having to show him some trees," Tormy suggested as he approached, his cloth boots still firmly fixed to his paws. "And flowers and vegetables. He is liking vegetablenessness."

Kyr stared at the two of them, trying to process Omen's words. "Omen is going home? Tormy is going home?" he asked uncertainly. "There is just the one left here alone, the thing that crawls, the thing that bleeds, just Kyr, and no green?"

Omen crouched down in front of the broken child, his heart clenching. "No, Kyr," he said gently. "Omen and

Tormy and Kyr are going home. You're coming with us. All three of us are going home."

The boy started shaking again, his entire body trembling violently, but when Omen held out his hand, he did not hesitate to take it. Omen helped him to his feet and led him back to the shelter to pack up their things.

Tormy did not complain as he fastened the saddle once more. "I don't want to stay another night, Tormy," Omen told the cat, and Tormy flicked his tail violently in agreement.

"I is not either," the cat stated firmly. "This is being a bad place. I is not liking it."

"We'll have to move quickly. Do you think you can carry Kyr? I don't think he can run that entire distance." Omen removed his heavy two-handed sword from Tormy's saddle and fastened it across his own back instead. He also pulled a couple of the saddlebags free, strapping them over his own shoulders to remove some of the weight from the cat's load.

"I is carrying him." Tormy pricked up his ears confidently and crouched on the ground, belly low to make the saddle easier to access.

The boy doesn't weigh much. Hope we can keep up the pace the entire time. Omen lifted Kyr's skeletal form and settled him on Tormy's back. "Can you hold on tight, Kyr?"

Kyr sank his bony fingers into Tormy's ruff in response, holding on with all of his might.

"Try to relax, Kyr." Omen patted the cat on the flank. "Let's do it."

They took off at a brisk trot, Omen running alongside the cat, down the road, out of the city, back toward the craggy rock, and back to the rift in time and space that led home.

Chapter 5: Home

Desperate to leave before another night fell on that terrible, barren world, Omen urged Tormy to travel swiftly. The large cat had never run full speed with someone on his back, the extreme flexing of the young cat's spine not suited to the weight of the saddle; he could, however, manage a very fast trot. Their trip into the city had been at a moderate pace, but now Tormy raced along their previous path, heading unerringly toward the distant rocky crag.

Gripping the cat's fur tightly with one skeletal hand while clinging to the saddle horn with the other, Kyr stayed completely silent throughout the journey.

Omen jogged alongside, keeping pace with the cat's long strides and ready to catch the boy should he fall or, worse yet, bolt.

Kyr must be terrified, leaving the only shelter he's known for who knows how long. Tormy and I are basically strangers to him.

But Omen remembered how he'd woken to find Kyr gripping his wrist. While Tormy and he were strangers to the boy, they were also the only other living beings in this entire world. *Kyr's been utterly alone for years, maybe centuries. Of course he won't let us out of his sight.*

Kyr had been responding to his words, but Omen was uncertain how much the boy truly comprehended. *I doubt my Kahdess is that good — I'm probably mixing up the verbs and the nouns. And Kyr can't understand Tormy at all.*

The cat might have recognized the sound of the Language of the Dead, but he did not speak it. In the months Tormy had lived with Omen he'd made great headway in learning both the common tongue and Omen's native Melian, proving himself far more clever than Omen had initially suspected. But there had been no need to teach Tormy anything as exotic as Kahdess.

The lack of a shared language, however, did not seem to bother Tormy in the slightest. The cat chatted loudly the whole way, telling Kyr story after story about things he found fascinating — trees, grass, birds, mice, lunch. Kyr listened dutifully even if he couldn't comprehend the cat's words.

Despite their swift pace, it still took many hours to reach the craggy rock. Omen knew Tormy had to be exhausted. The cat's voice had become more and more breathy as they traveled. *This is a hard pace even for me, and Tormy is carrying extra weight. And he keeps rattling on to comfort Kyr. Sweet little guy.* He would have removed the saddle from Tormy, but without it he feared Kyr would fall.

As the sky began darkening, Omen grew nervous that night would find the three of them without shelter. He'd run through several scenarios in his mind. He still had the heavy tarps that Etar had provided. If night came, he could rig a makeshift tent for the three of them. *Seems like the best option.* He supposed it would be possible to hold a shield over them using his psionics.

But I'm not sure how long I could keep a psionic shield up. I've gotten much better but I've never held one that long. He'd only ever used the stronger shielding patterns in battle to block momentary blows to his body. Maintaining a long-term shield through an entire night was not something he'd ever practiced.

I use the third Medzin Pattern in battle — but this would be domestic use against elemental forces. He tried to reason out the proper pattern. *That means I would use one of the Asric Patterns to shield from the elements — but I only know the first and it's only meant to last for a few minutes.* He'd never bothered learning any of the more advanced Asric Patterns as they'd seemed too tame — too boring.

I really have to start listening to my father when he's trying to teach me things!

The light was fading, and the wind had turned cold when they finally reached the craggy rock. "It's getting late, Tormy," Omen called worriedly to the cat who was scrambling purposefully up the hillside. "Maybe we should set up a tent."

"We is almost there, Omy," Tormy called down to him, seeming unconcerned with the approaching nightfall. "I is hearing the forest!"

"The forest?" Omen called. "You mean you can hear the rift?" Omen had no idea how to find the rift in time and space himself — he hadn't even seen the one Etar had shoved them both through. His nose stuffed up, he tried to scent the air. *Nothing but dust and dirt.*

"I is smartinessness!" the cat assured him.

The large cat climbed over several rocks and then leaped toward one cracked rocky surface. When the cat vanished from sight, Omen rushed after him. Instantly, he landed back in the middle of the forest with a loud *oomph*. Relief washed over him like a wave of warm water. *Back where we started. Did Tormy know we could have gone back at any time? I just assumed the portal closed behind us.*

Night had been approaching back in Kyr's world, but in

the forest it was just past dawn, the blue sky brightly lit with golden sunlight, the cluster of pine, cedar and birch trees still fresh with morning dew. The sound of songbirds was enchanting after the endless moan of the empty wind, but it was the overwhelming pulse of magic that flooded through Omen's body that gave him immeasurable joy. *Hadn't realized how much I missed that!* He breathed deeply, letting the magical aura of his world flow into him.

Omen heard Kyr gasp.

The boy had raised his skeletal hands above his head as if trying to reach the blue sky. Omen paused to take in the sight. *Seeing the sky and the forest after centuries of nothing . . . He must be ready to burst.*

It was late in the winter season, spring nearly upon them, and though there were still signs of the cold — patches of snow on the ground, frost in the air — life was flowering all around them. Winter had always seemed lifeless to Omen, void of the vitality of the other seasons. But after the bleakness of a dead land, he could see now how false that impression was.

The evergreen trees blazed vibrantly against the clear sky, and there were numerous flourishing plants of every shade of green around them. The long verdant stalks and lilac flowers of blooming crocuses grew right at their feet.

Smiling at the wonder on the boy's face, Omen lifted Kyr from Tormy's saddle, guessing he'd want to investigate further. Kyr's legs gave out beneath him as Omen set him down on the ground. The child sank into the dirt of the forest floor and dug his fingers into the fallen pine needles before laying his head down against the ground amid the colorful blooms.

"He is liking the flowers," Tormy told Omen. "I is saying flowers is smelling nice."

Which was true — Tormy had spent a great deal of their journey talking about plants and their various smells, but Omen was quite certain Kyr had not understood any of it.

"Omen." Etar's voice startled all three of them. Kyr shrieked in fright and dove at Tormy, scrambling between the cat's two front paws and wrapping his thin arms around Tormy's right front leg, hiding himself in the dense belly fur. Perplexed, Tormy leaned his head down and peered upside down at the boy.

Both surprised and relieved that Etar was still there, Omen turned to see his older brother standing next to a tall pine tree. Etar's gaze was fixed on Kyr, a mixture of grief and pity in his expression as he studied the boy.

"I have a lot of questions—" Omen began only to be cut off by a sharp look from Etar.

"Not now," Etar insisted, urgency in his tone. "No time. It's not safe. You must take him home — to your home. Quickly. Introduce him to 7."

"What . . . Why—" Omen began, only to be cut off again.

"I'll explain later. There is no time." Etar waved his hand past the three of them. Instantly the forest began fading.

A moment later Omen found himself standing on the glowing Cypher Rune transfer portal in his father's office in Melia. Tormy stood beside him, Kyr still hidden behind the cat's front legs.

He could see his father seated at his desk beyond the portal's alcove. 7's golden hair shone in the bright morning sunlight filtering in through the large window behind him, and his heterochromatic eyes — one blue, one dark — widened at the sight of the three of them.

Etar's magic must have bypassed the portal's warning bells.

"Hi, Dad," Omen said simply.

"Omen?" 7 exclaimed and rose to his feet. "The warnings didn't sound!"

He would hate that. Doesn't want people randomly teleporting into his office.

7 moved around his desk. "Wow, you've come home dirty before . . . but this . . ." He shook his head.

Omen glanced at Tormy. The cat's orange and white fur was almost completely grey with a heavy coating of ash, his nose and eyes crusty with black grime. The pieces of cloth wrapped around his paws were beyond filthy. Omen guessed he didn't look much better.

"That's it!" a rich, husky voice protested. The slender form of his mother, Avarice, stood in the doorway of the office, silver eyes flashing. Dressed in a gown of dark blue, her long black hair braided loosely and pinned up by gem encrusted clips, she had her hands on her hips, her face set in a frown of distaste. "I'm putting cleaning spells on all the doorways and portals into this house. What on earth do you two think—"

The sound of terrified whimpering coming from behind Tormy's paws stopped Avarice's words as both she and 7 realized at the same moment that Omen and Tormy had not arrived alone.

"I is thinking that Kyr is being very frightenednessness," Tormy stated, peering between his own front paws where Kyr was hiding. Omen quickly knelt down and held out his hand to the boy.

"Kyr," he said softly. "It's all right. You're safe. This is my home."

He heard his mother hiss in shock at his words, and knew it was the language he had spoken that had startled her.

"Was that Kahdess?" she demanded sharply.

Omen threw her an apologetic look. "It's the only language he speaks."

Avarice made a warding gesture with her right hand, shaking her head firmly. "You'll bring the wrath of the dead down on this house — and we've got enough enemies as it is!"

He didn't really think speaking Kahdess would bring the wrath of the dead down on them. *Then again, my mother knows more about curses and magic than most people.*

"Don't have a choice — it really is all he knows."

7 approached the cat and crouched down to study the small form hiding in Tormy's fur. "Are you going to introduce us, Omen?" Though his voice was deceptively mild, Omen could see that his father was actually quite alarmed by the boy's appearance — what little he could see of it.

"This is Kyr," Omen explained. "My brother." *How many people get to say things like that to their parents? I'm forever introducing them to brothers they are not related to.* With Omen's complicated bloodline, all of them had become used to the oddity of new relatives appearing at random intervals.

"Cerioth?" 7 asked, since it was equally possible he'd have an unknown brother from his faerie bloodline, the Deldanos.

Omen quickly recapped where he'd found Kyr, and why the child was in such frightful condition. Both 7 and Avarice listened silently, and Omen could see the growing horror in their eyes when he explained the years the boy had spent without food, water or company. He doubted his mother understood what he said about the technology of Kyr's world, but his father certainly did, and Avarice understood the concept of being burned by both fire and acid.

"Well . . ." Avarice said when Omen was done, looking out of sorts. She cast her gaze around the room as if searching for something to do, at a loss in light of the story. "Why don't I clean the three of you—" She raised her hands to cast a powerful cleaning cantrip, a swirl of energy gathering around her.

7 stopped her, placing a hand on one of her raised arms. "I'm not sure that is a good idea," he explained. "Some of those rags look like they are stuck to his skin — particularly his scalp. You'll likely scour off what little flesh he still has with a spell. The rags will have to be soaked off."

Omen grimaced at the thought. *This won't be pleasant . . . But it has to be done. The sooner we can heal Kyr, the better.*

"Well then," Avarice amended. "All three of you into the baths, and I'll see about getting that boy something to eat."

"Hurrah! Lunch!" Tormy exclaimed happily, his filthy whiskers flaring as his ears perked forward.

"Bath first," Avarice insisted, but Tormy shook his head stubbornly. He lashed his tail back and forth.

"I is not going into the water," the cat insisted, only to receive a dark glower from Avarice, which he endured for about half a second before wilting. His ears drooped pathetically. "I is going into the water," he sighed.

Satisfied, Avarice left the room.

"Come on, Kyr," Omen encouraged, hand held out. It took some doing, but Kyr finally took hold of his hand. Omen lifted him up, figuring it would be easier to carry the boy. Kyr weighed very little, and the constant trembling of his small form was worrisome. *Not sure if he can walk right now.*

While Daenoth Manor had private bathing suites off most of the main bedrooms, the lower level was made up of a huge subterranean bathing chamber with open baths large enough to hold even a rambunctious Tormy.

7 followed, calling to several servants and sending them ahead to fill the pools with hot water. All the manor's servants were practiced at bathing the large cat.

The water was already pouring in from numerous spouts when they entered the baths. The sound of rushing water and the rising steam caused Kyr to tremble all the harder.

Gleaming lamps illuminated the stone room and brightened the surface of the four large sunken pools of water. Steam, perfumed with exotic oils, billowed about them.

Tormy balked at entering the largest pool, but a quick psionic shove from Omen's father had the cat sitting grumpily in the water an instant later.

Three young servants approached to begin the arduous task of washing all of Tormy's filthy fur. While the servants glanced curiously at Kyr, none of them said anything, taking care to avert their eyes when the boy looked up.

Omen sat Kyr down on a bench near one of the pools. It had obviously been a long time since the boy had seen so much water, and he stared in disbelief at the flowing liquid and the clouds of steam forming above them. The water pouring in through the ornamented spouts was heated by rare sun stones, and the baths were stocked with soaps and oils.

Remembering the starkness of Kyr's world, Omen saw through new eyes the wealth and casual magic that ran their home. *I am so lucky.* He looked at his father. *My parents provide all of this . . . for me. For us.*

7 collected one of the larger jars of oil from a shelf and added more to the water of the nearest pool. As the steam began to clear Omen's dust-choked senses, he thought he smelled jasmine. *He's worried about Kyr's skin. It's so fragile.*

While the rags draped around Kyr's body were easily removed, Omen discovered that beneath them were more bandage-like wrappings — strips of foul-smelling cloth tied around the child's skeletal form that were stuck fast by years of dirt and seeping wounds. Like Tormy, Kyr had been wearing layers of cloth around his feet that acted as boots, but the crusty rag-boots too were stuck to his skin. Omen could easily remove only the top layer of bandaging.

The rest will have to be soaked off.

When Omen lifted him up, the boy bellowed frantically, his pitch climbing higher and higher as he tried to scramble away from the water. Omen put him down again gently, ignoring Kyr's out-of-control flailing even as the boy's bony hand slapped the side of his head.

"Get in first," 7 suggested.

Omen stripped down and climbed into the pool, urging Kyr to follow. Kyr calmed at the sight of Omen standing uninjured in the water. The boy hesitantly touched the surface, and did not protest as 7 lifted him carefully and lowered him into the pool.

The child's eyes widened as he sank down into the water against the edge of the bath. He raised his hands to stare at the droplets dripping from his fingers before sticking them into his mouth to taste the liquid. The soap and oil made him pull a face, and Omen quickly reached out to remove the fingers from his mouth, shaking his head.

The boy slapped the top of the water and then grinned joyfully, slapping it again and again as if in complete disbelief. Despite Kyr's blackened teeth and skeletal appearance, Omen had to smile at the obvious happiness sparkling in those violet eyes and the unexpectedly childish mannerisms. The boy looked as pleased as he had when he'd shown Omen the small weed back in his desolate world.

7 removed his own boots and seated himself at the edge of the pool to help carefully peel the rags away from Kyr's body. While Omen didn't know how much Kyr actually understood, the boy did not fight or protest. Even when one of the rags he unwound from Kyr's left arm took off a strip of skin, leaving a bloody, oozing wound, the child just stared at his bare, bleeding arm and said nothing. He gave no indication he felt any pain.

Alarmed, Omen glanced at his father who just took Kyr's arm into his hands and focused his gaze. Omen felt the faint hum of power in the air as his father directed his psionics toward the boy's wound. Slowly, the damaged flesh began to regrow and smooth, knitting itself back together.

That at least got a reaction out of Kyr. The boy clutched his head, mouth agape, and stared up at 7 in alarm.

Kyr can feel that. Which means he must have the potential for psionics. Someone without any abilities wouldn't be able to feel anything.

Omen pulled Kyr's hand away from his head before he could injure himself by clawing at his brain.

"We're going to have to teach him how to shield his mind," his father said, pausing momentarily to wait for the boy to calm down.

"It's all right, Kyr," Omen assured him quickly in Kahdess. "It's just magic. My father is a . . ." He searched for the proper word, glancing up at his father in confusion. "There is no word for healer in Kahdess," he stated in Melian.

"The dead don't need healing," 7 replied, still waiting while Omen tried to explain further.

"He's going to fix . . . stop the bleeding," Omen continued. Kyr's large, soulful eyes watched him with a sense of trust that Omen found both reassuring and humbling. "Make it stop hurting. He's . . ." Again he struggled for a good word.

"Father?" Kyr asked simply in Kahdess, the first word he'd spoken in a long while.

Omen smiled. "Yes, he's my father." And that, it seemed, was enough for Kyr, and he relaxed and looked expectantly back at 7. Omen couldn't help but think of the image of the family carved into the stones of Kyr's small shelter and wondered if he could still remember something from the time before his world had gone to ruin.

The wave of power surrounding 7 grew again as he continued healing the boy's arm. Omen trusted his father to heal whatever he could.

"His pain threshold is extraordinary," 7 commented mildly, speaking in Melian and modulating his tone softly so that the boy calmed further. "But I'm going to numb his nerve endings — no sense in making him suffer needlessly."

I should get him to show me how to do that, Omen thought as he continued removing the rags — taking care to soak them first so that they sloughed off instead of having to be pulled free.

The water around them quickly turned black with dirt, old blood and grime. But the servants efficiently set the drains and the spouts so that the water drained out and re-filled constantly. When Omen began to pour water over the boy's head, he could see that Kyr's tangled hair was a pale golden blond under all the dirt. But the constant damage to his scalp by the acidic rain had left his skull raw and ooz-ing, and he and 7 ended up having to cut away the matted mess of hair and rags.

"No saving the hair I'm afraid," 7 told Omen.

Kyr was still playing with the water, running his fingers over the surface and making waves that moved across the pool and back again. He looked blithely unconcerned with the state of his hair.

"I don't think he really has any sense of vanity," Omen replied. "He refers to himself as 'the thing that crawls.'"

7's brow furrowed as he continued cutting. "The poor boy," he muttered as he peeled off long tangled strands of hair and knotted rags and tossed them aside for the servants to clean up.

When Kyr was at last free of all the filthy rags, his skin healed and cleaned, the true state of Kyr's emaciated form became obvious. Omen's first assessment of a pile of dried sticks was more accurate than he wanted to admit. The boy was nothing more than fragile skin stretched over bones — no flesh at all remaining. He looked like a living skeleton.

Kyr's teeth were the last things 7 cleaned, coaxing the boy to open his mouth. 7 threw a powerful cleaning cantrip on the blackened teeth that had the child gasping in shock. Kyr stuck his fingers into his mouth and rubbed his gums. Eventually, however, he grinned up at both Omen and 7 — showing off a pearly white smile in that fragile bald skull that had both 7 and Omen smiling back at him.

Cerioth's genes bred true. No gum disease or rot. After all that time.

The most surprising thing Omen noticed about the boy's appearance was the faint point to both of his delicate ears. Once they had removed the tangled mess of bandages from his head, and 7 had healed the oozing flesh, they had been surprised to see the pointed tips.

Elvin, Omen thought. *What in the Elder's Names was an elvin child doing in that horrible world?*

Chapter 6: Family

A varice entered the bathing chamber a few moments later, carrying a pile of clothes with her. Tormy shrieked with outrage at her entrance.

"Avarice! I is naked!" the cat cried.

Avarice set down the pile of clothing. "You're a cat," she said, unfazed. "You're always naked."

Tormy met her words with a rumble of discontentment. "Sometimes I is wearing a hat."

"I brought some things that should fit him," she told Omen, who was climbing out of the pool. 7 tossed him a towel before getting a second one to dry Kyr.

Avarice had brought clothes for Omen as well. Amid the pile, he noticed several cast-off tunics and trousers from when he was younger. His mother had chosen pieces made from soft material, brushed cottons and silks, that would not harm Kyr's delicate skin. And because it was winter-time in Melia, Avarice had also brought one of his sister's fur-lined coats for the boy.

She left the clothes for 7 and Omen to sort out while she motioned the still grumbling Tormy out of the water. Using several drying spells to dry his fur, she also insisted on cleaning the cat's teeth and ears with more focused magic. The lack of wet fur went a long way to cheering up the cat, and he purred loudly a moment later, backing away from the pools and chattering about lunch.

Kyr accepted the new clothes without protest, stroking his fingers over the silk of the tunic when they pulled it over his head. There were even soft slippers for the boy's feet, the soles thickly cushioned.

When Omen had finished dressing himself, he took note of the last item his mother had brought. Apparently she had anticipated more than he'd expected. Omen picked up a knitted stocking cap from the bench. He carefully pulled it over Kyr's bare skull. The boy patted it several times before grinning contentedly.

Avarice returned to inspect Kyr. He did not protest when she cupped his chin in her hand and turned him toward her, studying his features intently. She turned his head briefly to the side, making note of the delicate point to his freshly healed ears. Omen wondered who the child's mother might have been.

"Elvin," Avarice stated. "And probably from the Venedrine line if his fine bone structure is any indication."

Her words startled Omen as he remembered the Venedrine he'd met months ago in Hex. *Haughty, self-involved, and poisonous. That's not Kyr.*

7 looked quite impressed by her assessment. "That's what I thought as well."

"Aren't the Venedrine under some awful curse?" Omen asked, recalling the tale Templar had told him.

"Only the royal caste," 7 said. "Legend has it that they angered the wrong god, and he wiped them out of existence. Very few Venedrine tribes survive today — and none of the royal caste remain."

A trickle of alarm ran down Omen's spine. Etar's urgency and insistence he take Kyr home became clearer to him. *Etar said I was not safe. "You must take him home — to your home. Quickly. Introduce him to 7."*

"Do you know any of the Venedrine — or have any connection to them?" he asked his father.

7 shook his head. "Not that I know of. That curse happened thousands of years ago. It would have to be very
powerful to still be in effect today."

"Time to feed this poor boy," Avarice announced.

"Woohoo!" Tormy cheered and happily hopped toward
Kyr while babbling about sandwiches with sweet berries
and whipped cheese.

The boy grew frightened again when he realized they
were leaving the bathing chamber. He clutched Tormy's fur
tightly with one hand and Omen's wrist with the other. But
nevertheless, he valiantly walked out on his own two feet,
managing one step after the next without stumbling.

Avarice ushered them to one of the smaller dining rooms
where servants hurried to place the last of the dishes and
flatware. Omen noted the crisp, white lace tablecloth. *Not
even the clouds were that white in Kyr's world.*

His ten-year-old sister Lilyth was already seated in one
of the padded brocade armchairs. She kicked her feet impatiently as she'd obviously been told to wait for the rest of
the family to arrive and was annoyed by the delay. She
twisted the silver and hematite cuff Omen had given her for
her birthday. *Glad to see she's wearing it.*

His eyes on the people moving about the room, Kyr
tripped on the woven rug.

"Careful," 7 said in Kahdess.

"Thank you," Avarice pronounced to the servants in
carefully chosen Melian. "That will be all." Her tone im-
plied that while she was dismissing the young men and
maids from the room, she expected them to see to other
tasks immediately. Well-trained and genuinely respectful,
the Melian servants scurried from the room, leaving
Avarice to set out the remainder of the meal.

"Who is that?" Lilyth demanded, silver eyes widening with curiosity when she spotted Kyr half-hidden behind Tormy's fur and still clutching tightly to Omen's wrist.

"This is Kyr," Omen informed her with a pointed stare. *Be nice,* he tried to will her. "My brother."

Lily rolled her eyes and tugged at the end of her long dark braid, feigning indifference. "Beren's or Cerioth's?"

"Cerioth." Omen cleared his throat, hoping Lily would spare a kind word.

"Well, what's wrong with him?" she demanded. "He looks ill. How can one of Cerioth's sons be ill? You're never ill!" She sounded put out.

Used to Lily's careless brattiness, Omen quickly conjured the picture of Kyr's world firmly in his mind and pushed it toward his sister. He felt the faint buzz of her psionic shield resisting momentarily before recognizing his touch and allowing the image past it. Long hours of practicing psionic communication with their father had left them both able to send each other images easily.

While Lilyth was still quite young, she was quick and clever and seemed to understand what Omen's image suggested. But she also had an edge to her that made Omen somewhat wary of her reaction. *She can be such a spoiled baby. Hope she'll be nice to him.*

Lilyth looked taken aback by the image. A glower twisted her features as she kicked her chair again. She looked toward Tormy and then back to the boy. Then she huffed and turned her head away briefly, biting her lower lip as if restraining herself from speaking. That more than anything set Omen's fears to rest — if she were going to react, it would have been now.

She doesn't mince words. But she's never spiteful or

backbiting.

"I wasn't certain what the poor boy would be capable of eating." Avarice frowned. "There's oatmeal and soup for him. Something light will be best."

Avarice set a bowl of warm oatmeal with a pad of butter down in front of Kyr after they had managed to coax him into one of the chairs between Omen and Tormy. At the sight of the bowl, the boy immediately shoved his fingers into the oatmeal and began stuffing it into his mouth, earning a snicker from Lilyth and a heavy sigh from Avarice. But no one said a word as they joined him, helping themselves to pastas and thin, breaded cutlets. Along with an assortment of lighter foods were more substantial dishes that Omen and Tormy tended to crave after strenuous activities.

Omen closed his eyes and sniffed. *White sauce with mushrooms. I bet they used the hard cheese from Scaalia,* he guessed. "What meat is in the red sauce?" he asked his mother. They usually bonded over cooking.

"Braised beef and pork," she said. "Your favorite."

There were also large amounts of grilled, almond-crusted salmon, which Tormy waxed poetic over. The cat happily devoured the fish and most of the winter squash served with melted butter, chatting all the while to Kyr who ate several mouthfuls of oatmeal and slurped some of the soup. At Tormy's coaxing, the boy grabbed small pieces of squash and fish from the cat's plate and shoved them into his mouth. He chewed with vigor, grinning as Tormy continued jabbering.

Avarice opened her mouth to scold the boy when she saw him eating off the cat's plate, but she seemed to change her mind at the last minute and graciously looked away.

It's not like cat germs are going to kill him, Omen

thought, amused. He didn't want to stop Kyr either. The look of delight on the boy's face was heartbreaking.

Despite his enthusiasm, Kyr could not eat very much, and he finished long before the rest of the family had. He waited patiently, seeming content to listen to Tormy chatter and the others talk. Eventually Kyr put his head down on the tabletop and fell asleep, though one hand snaked out and grasped Omen's wrist first, holding tight as he drifted off.

"Ooh, naptime!" Tormy exclaimed when he saw Kyr sleeping. "I is teaching him that word — I is teaching him all the important words — food, dinner, naptime. I is teaching him Melian really goodnessness!"

"I'm sure that's going to work out well," 7 commented with a smirk. He glanced at Omen who realized at once that teaching Kyr to speak something other than Kahdess was going to have to be a priority. Avarice wouldn't tolerate Kahdess around the house.

"You can put him in the blue room next to yours," Avarice told Omen.

He carefully picked the boy up, trying not to wake him. Tormy trotted after them, and Lilyth followed them upstairs, seeming quite curious about the new addition to the family.

"Doesn't he talk?" Lilyth asked as she watched Omen lay Kyr down in the large four-poster bed.

"He speaks Kahdess," Omen replied.

Lilyth's eyes widened. "Bet Mother loved that."

"Rather." He turned to study his sister. She stood near the foot of the bed, eyeing Kyr mistrustfully. Omen again took note of the unnatural thinness of the boy's frame. The stocking cap had shifted, revealing one delicate, pointed ear and the bald skull. "He's very fragile. You know that, right?" Omen asked. His little sister had next to no experience being around anyone or anything so vulnerable.

Her silver eyes flashed. "I haven't broken you or the rest of your friends yet, have I?"

"He's not like my friends. He can't fight back," he said as gently as he could.

She just turned on her heel and headed toward the door. "Then I'll teach him," she called over her shoulder before disappearing down the hallway.

"Tormy," Omen called to the cat who was running around the room investigating various items. But Tormy anticipated exactly what Omen was going to say. He gingerly hopped up onto the bed and curled around the sleeping boy.

"I is napping too," the cat agreed, already purring heavily as he settled down. Omen smiled and ruffled the cat's fur. He pulled the curtains over the floor-to-ceiling bay windows before leaving the room. His mother and father were standing in the hallway, talking quietly.

"It's his choice," Avarice said evenly as Omen approached, her gaze on 7. "Just make certain he knows what he's choosing." With that she turned sharply and walked away, disappearing down the stairs.

"What choice?" Omen asked as he approached his father. While he knew 7 typically took charge of their political affairs, it was Avarice who made major decisions concerning the family.

7 looked grave, his eyes studying Omen with probing intensity. "What are you going to do with him?" he asked, and there was a certain weight to his words that left Omen unsettled.

"Do with him?" Omen asked, confused. "What do you

mean?"

"Are you going to keep him here, or send him somewhere else?" 7 clarified.

"Somewhere else?" Omen nearly shouted. The idea of
sending Kyr away had never occurred to him.

"Omen," 7 said patiently. "If you want to keep him, your
mother and I will accept him into this family as one of our
own. We'll even give him the Daenoth name. But you have
to understand that he's extremely damaged. He may be a
demigod, and his body will eventually heal from what's
happened. But immortality does not protect the mind — in
fact it is a curse that subjects the mind to things no mortal
can ever imagine. A mortal would die long before enduring
the things that boy has suffered. Avarice and I can give him
a home, security, wealth, an education — but it is you he's
going to follow. He sees you as his savior — his dependen-
cy on you and Tormy is already written in stone. If you decide to keep him, it will be a heavy burden you will not
soon be free of. Choose carefully."

But Omen just shook his head, trying to imagine a reali-
ty where he'd abandon Kyr, or the aftermath of trying to explain such a decision to Tormy. In his mind there was no
choice to be made. "He's my brother," he stated simply.
"He's family."

"So be it." 7 turned and walked away.

Around him, Omen could already feel the dozens of
spells and wards his father and mother had placed over the
house, changing and altering to accommodate the new addition.

Kyr was home to stay.

❖

Omen sat in his mother's overgrown solarium, the morning winter sun shining through the frosted glass. The table before him was laden down with steaming tea, braided pastries, and red fruit compote. Next to him by the tall winter roses, Tormy and Kyr were seated on a thick rug placed on the mosaic floor. They chatted away while rare songbirds frolicked around them. Or rather Tormy chatted — Kyr simply listened and stared in fascination at the colorful birds and the lush exotic flowers blooming out of season within the solarium. From time to time, the boy would run his fingers along the nearest flower petals as if not believing they existed. Kyr gave no indication that he understood what Tormy was saying, not that it deterred the cat. Yet the boy appeared quite happy to simply stare and listen to the endless chatter.

Occasionally Tormy would urge Kyr to repeat a specific word — usually food related. After the cat coaxed and coached with long, drawn-out syllabic repetitions accompanied by theatrical grimaces and encouraging smiles, Kyr would oblige, quietly and simply. Beyond that he said nothing more.

I wonder if he's figured out that Mother doesn't like Kahdess. Or maybe he just doesn't know what to say?

Occasionally the word Tormy would urge Kyr to repeat was so heavy with the cat's odd accent and verbal oddities — extended syllables, drawn-out vowels, broken consonants, made-up conjugations — that Omen would immediately correct Kyr's pronunciation, worried that the boy would pick up bad habits. In those instances Kyr would look back and forth between Tormy and Omen, as if trying to decipher something, but would then dutifully repeat Omen's pronunciation with the proper Melian accent, indicating that at least he understood the difference and could hear the discrepancy in the sounds.

Tormy took matters into his own paws at one point, correcting Omen by saying, "No, Omy, the word is 'exactedednessly!' It means even MORE than 'exactly.' Say 'exactedednessly,' Kyr!"

Kyr dutifully repeated *exactedednessly* back to Tormy, but upon hearing the sigh Omen uttered, he said it again correctly, looking curiously back at Omen. The boy gave him a toothy grin.

Just because he doesn't understand the language doesn't mean he's dumb. He understands Tormy better than I thought.

"How's he doing?" his mother asked. Both his mother and father had arrived quietly and each took a seat at the table. Kyr shifted slightly, moving subtly closer to Tormy.

"Good," Omen told them. "We ate earlier, and he managed more this time. And he seems quite clever."

"I checked on him last night," Avarice told Omen. "He wasn't in his room."

Omen smiled at that. "I woke up in the middle of the night to hear him and Tormy in the bathroom. Apparently Tormy taught him how to use the facilities."

"Stars and scales!" Avarice exclaimed, rolling her eyes at the thought.

"No, he did fine." Omen grinned at her. "As I said he's very clever, and Tormy's pretty good at nonsensical communication — he did a good job explaining. In any event, afterward, they both climbed into my bed and fell asleep. I don't think he wants to let either me or Tormy out of his sight."

"Has he said anything?" 7 asked.

Omen shook his head. "He was talkative enough back

81

where we found him. But hasn't really said anything here. I think he may be too overwhelmed to even know what to say." He thought of something then, guessing it would probably be a good idea to forewarn his parents. "I should probably mention — a lot of the times he did talk, he was speaking to imaginary people. Carried on whole conversations with them."

Neither Avarice nor 7 looked particularly surprised, but Avarice's gaze turned immediately sharp. "Are you sure they were imaginary?"

Omen poured tea for his parents, silently replaying the events in his mind. "Well, I couldn't see anyone." He was not sure what she was getting at, but he had a bad feeling in the pit of his stomach. "Neither could Tormy." *Mother has an instinct for dark magic.*

"He speaks Kahdess," Avarice said, her voice low and husky. "Are you sure he wasn't speaking to the dead? A world like the one you described would have a lot of dead. The dead aren't always quiet."

"I hadn't thought of that." Omen swallowed hard. "He said they were voices without tongues, without bodies. He said he'd tried to give them bodies, but they wouldn't move."

Avarice drummed her fingers against the armrest of her chair. "Give them bodies? Like a necromancer?"

"No, like a sculptor," Omen explained. "He created hundreds of statues — maybe thousands. He'd carved them all out of the stones on the street. I saw them before I saw Kyr. The artistry. There was no doubt in my mind that the sculptor was related to Etar. Kyr's work is amazing."

"Thousands of statues?" Avarice questioned. "How long could he have been there?"

Omen drew a blank. "I have no way of knowing. I'm pretty certain he was there when the original calamity happened. He must have burned with the rest of that world. But that must have been at least a century or two ago. The radiation—" He stopped himself, knowing that his mother had no use for his father's scientific explanations.

"A long time," 7 amended for him.

"So aside from all the trauma suffered from the disaster itself, he's been alone for *centuries,* with nothing but the voices of the dead to speak to?" Avarice's silver gaze flicked away uncomfortably as she watched the flight of a songbird overhead. "You do understand that his mind is not likely normal?"

"I know," Omen agreed, wondering if this was his mother's attempt to talk him out of keeping Kyr. As far as he was concerned, it was too late for that. "But what passes for normal in our group of friends? Besides, you see how Tormy reacts to him. If there was anything bad inside Kyr, Tormy would know."

"You're putting a lot of faith in that cat of yours," Avarice commented doubtfully.

"Absolute faith," Omen insisted without hesitation. "And with good reason."

He waited for further criticism from his mother, thinking she was ready to pass judgment. He was startled by the next words from her mouth.

"Well," she looked over at the boy, "he's going to need more clothes if he's staying. He can't wear your hand-me-downs indefinitely. I think he'd look good in blue — maybe something with a Lydonian flair." As if suddenly distracted by an idea, she jumped up and hurried away, disappearing down the hall.

Startled, Omen glanced at his father who had an amused grin on his face.

"She's decided to start a new business venture. She wants to turn her sewing into something more," 7 replied. "It's been on her mind since the fall."

"What?" Omen asked, dumbfounded.

7 just smirked. "I think it bothers her that every single person she knows gets to show off their art. She's decided to turn a profit off her creative endeavors."

While Omen knew his mother was an extremely skilled fighter, not to mention adept at various forms of magic and potion-making, he'd never thought of her doing more than putting together a few outfits for Lily. "Really?"

7 looked unconcerned. "She usually accomplishes any-thing she puts her mind to, so I'm curious to see the results. He's trying to eat the flowers, by the way."

Startled by the non sequitur, Omen glanced back at Tormy and Kyr. Kyr was indeed putting rose petals into his mouth, despite Tormy's insistence that he stop.

"Kyr!" Omen leaped up, heading toward the boy. "If you're hungry, we'll go eat lunch." While rose petals were edible, they weren't particularly nutritious, and Kyr needed all the help he could get.

"Hurrah! Lunch!" Tormy crowed with delight. "It's not even lunchtime — so this is brunch, so we is getting break-fast, brunch, and lunch today which is the bestest."

Kyr, still holding the rose petals, watched the cat in con-fusion. Omen guessed he recognized the word *lunch* by now.

"Are you hungry?" Omen asked in Kahdess, and the boy nodded his head up and down. "Come on then. I'll show you where the kitchen is. If you ever get hungry you can get whatever you want. You don't have to eat the flowers."

Kyr took the hand Omen held out to him, though he didn't release the rose petals, choosing instead to stuff them in his pocket. But he seemed happy enough to follow Omen and Tormy toward the kitchen and the promised food.

Chapter 7: Curse

Etar waited in the shadows, masking his presence and watching for the creature he knew would come. He stood a silent sentinel through the long hours, until his patience paid off.

A dark entity appeared from deep in the forest. It was little more than a shadow upon the ground, possessing neither form nor substance, but it swallowed all light as it passed. Even the winter sunlight amid the trees dimmed.

It paused at the entrance to the other world. Though Etar had closed the rift, the creature seemed to know exactly where the opening had been, and it moved around the area, scenting.

Etar waited and watched, hoping that over the centuries, the thing had grown weaker, its power faded as it lost its physical form and shape. It had not needed a body in a very long time, its task all but completed. Etar was hopeful that the creature was little more than an echo now — powerless, able to do nothing more than haunt the world until it faded from existence.

But a moment later, he felt the land around him shake. The shadow rose up, momentarily darkening, its misty form growing dense as it swirled and twisted in violent streams of blackness, like a tornado made up of ropy arms and grasping hands. Etar felt the rift ripping open once again. The shadow creature stepped through the opening and vanished from the forest.

Etar shuddered at the confirmation that the thing had lost none of its powers — anything that could so easily rip open a portal through time and space, sealed by a god no less, was nothing to be trifled with.

He continued to wait, wondering how much time the thing would take. When it wished, the curse could move swiftly. Perhaps no more than an hour had passed when it reappeared from the barren world and swept through the forest, moving like a dark breeze and leaving the portal behind it gaping open. It was gone a moment later, and Etar knew he would have to warn Omen.

He was about retreat when he saw more movement below in the woods and realized he had not been the only one observing the entity. There at the entrance to the rift, hidden beneath the leafy branch of a winter-blooming camellia bush was a small orange cat, little more than a kitten, tiny and fragile looking. By appearance, his markings were nearly identical to Omen's cat, Tormy. But this cat was not one of the larger variety; it was instead small enough to fit in the palm of his hand. For several moments the little kitten sniffed around the entrance to the rift, then he fluffed his tail and leaped through. That, even more than the shadow creature's appearance, took Etar's breath away.

Alarmed, he scrambled toward the rift, following after the orange kitten. The appearance of this cat so soon after the shadow could not be coincidence, and he was determined to discover its meaning. But first he had to retrieve the kitten from the empty land.

He found the cat almost immediately; the little creature sat perched upon a craggy rock and stared out at the arid, ash-covered landscape. His orange fur was already turning grey from the dust in the air. He was staring determinedly forward as if trying to decide the best path to take. Etar knew the kitten would not likely last out the night in a place like this.

"You is looking too?" the little kitten asked, turning his head to look up at Etar. He had the same amber-colored eyes as Tormy, but there was a shrewdness in them that was different from the larger cat's demeanor. The kitten spoke in the holy language of Sul'eldrine like all the cats did, marking him definitively as the same race as Tormy. Tormy had learned to speak both Melian and Merchant's Common in the months he'd been with Omen, but Sul'eldrine was his native tongue.

"Looking?" Etar asked, wondering what this cat could be seeking. Surely the cat had not been sent by his father.

"For the boy," the kitten explained. "The losted boy. I is looking, and I is finding this place. This is being a badness-ness place."

"What do you want with the boy?" Etar asked, suspicious.

The little cat flicked his ears and stared at Etar as if bewildered about why he would ask such a question. "He is a boy; I is a kitten. We is going to play games. And probably eat lunch on account of the fact that I am a mite peckish. That means my tummy is all growlingnessness and I is hungry, and I is looking for a long time."

"But why are you looking?" Etar pressed.

Again the kitten fixed him with a perplexed glare. "You is not listening. The boy is losteded. I is looking on account of the fact that he is losteded — when he is foundeded, I is stopping."

Etar sighed; sometimes these cats took things far too literally. And though they came off as simple-minded, he knew they could hold their secrets if they wished.

"What is being that other thing?" the kitten asked suddenly. "The shadow with the bad feeling?"

Etar looked back toward the opened rift. "Something else that is looking for the lost boy," he told the cat. "That thing was a curse."

The kitten flicked his tail back and forth. "I is cursing sometimes — Drat! Darn! Blegh! It is not turning into a shadow thing."

Despite everything, Etar had to smile — it was rare to hear one of these creatures using a bad word — especially since Sul'eldrine did not have a vernacular. It was also a remarkably astute observation from the little cat. "This was a curse spoken by a god, little one," he told the kitten. "A very old and very powerful god. And a very angry one. A god's curse takes on a life of its own."

"The boy is curseded?"

"Not just the boy." Etar found the memory painful — so much death had resulted because of the curse.

The kitten fluffed his fur suddenly, puffing himself to twice his size. Even still, he looked so tiny perched on the craggy rock. "Blegh on the curse! I is cursing the curse! I is a fierce fighting cat and I is saving the losted boy!"

Amused, Etar smiled. "He's not actually lost anymore."

The little cat's eyes widened at that. "Most wonderfulnessness! I is really good at cursing! I is just saying my curse, and now he is foundeded! I is not even having to scratch anything!" He gave the air a good swipe with one of his little paws, needle-like claws extended as if to demonstrate his abilities.

"Shall I take you to him?" Etar asked.

"Yes, please," the kitten agreed, nodding his head up and down fiercely. He stretched his front paws upward to Etar, asking to be picked up. Etar opened his coat and deposited the kitten in one of the inner pockets, charmed when the little cat instantly curled up and went to sleep. The little creature, despite his ferociousness, seemed exhausted.

Etar returned through the rift, and once again sealed it shut, he hoped for the last time. He paused momentarily to study the forest around him, searching for any more watching eyes. But the woods were silent, though shadows lingered. He shuddered and moved on, thinking that he would avoid this part of the forest for years to come.

❖

After brunch, Omen returned to the solarium. While Omen sat at a small wrought iron table, Kyr and Tormy had spread out on the stone pavers at his feet. Tormy snored in the sunlight. Kyr happily stared at the world around him.

I suppose to Kyr, everything is new and fascinating. The boy had been equally enchanted by the flowering plants, the blue sky visible through the glass ceiling of the solarium, and the flittering collection of tiny songbirds that lived within the protective confines of the garden. Forced inactivity was unusual for Omen, but to his surprise he didn't really mind. Seeing the world through Kyr's eyes made him realize just how blessed he truly was.

A shift in the air caught Omen's attention. Suddenly a presence manifested beside him. Omen started, getting half out of his chair before he grasped that his eldest brother was slowly materializing into view next to him. Etar rarely demonstrated such power — the ability to come and go with a thought. To Omen, Etar had always appeared as nothing more than a simple man. In the past days he'd displayed more magic than he had in all the time Omen had known him.

Beautiful, like all the children of Cerioth, Etar for one

brief moment seemed to shine brighter than the sunlight. A shiver ran up Omen's spine at the overt reminder of who Etar really was. *The Soul's Flame.* While Omen, circuitously, was the son of an Elder God — Omen was not a god himself. He was beginning to wonder just how well he truly knew Etar. *Until now, he's never shown his power to me — why now? What's changed?*

A moment later the light faded, and Etar's handsome features took on a more human appearance, his eyes blue as the sky. Casually sitting in what had been an empty chair at the table, Etar smiled and turned his gaze toward the cat and boy — now both fast asleep. He paused to study them for a moment, then held up a small piece of wood, barely longer than his smallest finger. In his other hand, he held a carving knife.

Purposely ignoring the stick and the knife, Omen glowered at his brother. "Explain!"

"I imagine you have questions." Etar's tone was low and measured. Surprisingly he answered in Sul'eldrine instead of reverting to Melian.

"Kyr is our brother, right?" Omen demanded. Etar's calm demeanor made his anger flare suddenly. *He might at least show some sign of remorse!*

"Yes." Etar again answered in Sul'eldrine. A dozen birds fluttered to a landing on the table. The birds burst into song.

Omen forced himself to remain calm. His insides boiled, but he waited and watched. While the songbirds in the solarium were used to the presence of people, the little birds weren't tame. They rarely landed close to anyone. *Is it the Sul'eldrine? Are they drawn to the sound?*

Omen wondered if Etar was concerned about Kyr overhearing his words — the boy was asleep, so it was unlikely. *And even if he does overhear us, he speaks Kahdess, not Sul'eldrine or Melian. He wouldn't understand what we're saying.*

Omen switched to the divine tongue himself. "You knew where he was, what he was suffering?"

Etar nodded. He raised the small knife he was holding and began carving tiny slivers of wood from the stick in his hand.

"And you did nothing! Why? How could you just leave him there for all those years?" Omen tried to keep his voice down, but did not bother to mask his outrage.

Etar paused in his carving and looked upward toward the glass ceiling of the solarium. "It's a long story, Omen. And I did do something — I sent you to retrieve him."

"A little late!" Omen protested. "He must have been there for centuries."

"One hundred and eighty-seven years to be exact," Etar replied, his expression a mixture of remorse and sorrow. He turned his gaze back to the wood and knife, cutting away another small shaving.

Omen watched the slow, calculated movement of Etar's knife. *A hundred and . . . wait a minute, the dates for all this aren't matching up!* "As near as I can figure Kyr was a child when he ended up in that land . . ."

"He was an infant," Etar confirmed.

"A hundred and eighty-seven years ago, Cerioth was still imprisoned — trapped in the form of a lute," Omen argued. "How can Kyr possibly be his son? And how can he be almost two hundred years old? He looks like a little boy."

Omen knew the story of Cerioth's imprisonment by the Elder Gods. Fourteen thousand years ago Cerioth, The

Dark Heart, had broken the first Covenant, releasing the denizens of the Night Realm into the mortal lands, resulting in unspeakable slaughter. The other Elder Gods had punished Cerioth by imprisoning him, though they'd given their brother the chance to choose his prison. Cerioth had chosen a musical instrument, which had allowed his voice to still be heard throughout the world when the strings were strummed.

Etar turned the piece of wood over and carved another shaving from the edge, whittling down its shape. "His imprisonment didn't stop you from being born."

"That's different." Omen slapped his hand down on the table, causing several of the songbirds to flutter away while scolding him with musical tweets. Surprisingly, they did not fly far and settled down again on the tabletop. "Mine were . . . unusual circumstances. And as far as I've ever heard, until my father came along, no one could even touch that lute, let alone play it." 7's discovery of the magical lute was a story Omen also knew well. "And I only exist because my father freed Cerioth so that he could save my mother — and me."

"You're right of course." Etar paused to inspect his carving. He'd whittled away the end of the wooden stick to a tapered point, long and rounded like a fine needle. "While Kyr is still a child — he's elvin after all — he is a hundred and eighty-seven years old. But he was conceived over fourteen thousand years ago, a few hundred years before Cerioth was imprisoned."

History wasn't Omen's strong point, but he knew that after Cerioth had broken the first Covenant, several hundred years of chaos passed before the second Covenant had been formed. The Elder Gods had closed the great Gates into the other lands. They had imprisoned the Night Dwellers and safeguarded the mortal races of the world. It was only then that Cerioth had been imprisoned. "You mean he was born before the second Covenant?"

"Before the first Covenant was broken," Etar corrected. "Before Cerioth ripped open the Gates and unleashed the Night Dwellers on the world."

"But why did he break the Covenant in the first place?" Omen asked, wondering what any of this had to do with Kyr. No story he had ever heard had adequately explained why Cerioth had broken the first Covenant.

"Do you want to hear about the Covenant or about Kyr?" Etar asked. "Kyr's story takes place before all of that."

Omen grumbled — he wanted to hear both, but decided that Kyr's story was the more pressing. *Etar isn't very forthcoming. But he seems willing to talk about Kyr.*

One of the little birds nearest Etar tweeted happily. Omen flicked a finger at it, wondering why it wasn't flying away. It just fluffed its feathers and hopped to the side, avoiding his hand. Two more alighted on the table. "Tell me about Kyr," Omen conceded.

Etar inclined his head and turned his attention back to his carving. "Long ago, Cerioth met Kyr's mother, Cira deKyrel, a Venedrine princess."

"So my parents were right — he is Venedrine."

Etar looked impressed. "Considering the condition he's in, I'm surprised they were able to tell. The Venedrine are considered the most beautiful of all the elvin races, and the most powerful, the most magical. They are also the most vain, self-indulgent and hedonistic. Even today with their numbers so diminished, that has not changed."

While Omen knew very little about any of the elvin races, he had heard stories about the Venedrine elves. And he'd met a few in Hex not long ago. The Venedrine flaunted their power and were notorious for their decadent lifestyles.

"Even among the Venedrine, Cira was a rare beauty," Etar continued. "And extremely clever, talented at magic. Cerioth took an interest in her." He turned the wood again, and Omen could now see he was flattening out the remaining portion of the wood so that it resembled the end of an oar.

"He fell in love with her?" Omen asked.

Etar gave him a wistful smile. "Cerioth liked to walk the earth disguised as a mortal — forever seeking something he lost long ago. But even in such a disguise, there are many who would still recognize him for what he was. Cira was one such person, and he took an interest in her, but only a passing interest. He took passing interests in a lot of people. But she, unlike many others, was clever enough to know this — clever enough to know that her time as his favorite would be fleeting. She determined to get something of great value out of their liaison. While others were content to simply be allowed into his realm, she set about to uncover its secrets. She found a library with documents in it older than most of the mortal races, and she tried to uncover some ancient power to make her people rise in prominence."

"Did she find anything?" Omen didn't consider himself a scholar, but he knew a dozen people who would kill to get access to a library like that. He was reminded suddenly of Etar's library and wondered if there were such secrets there. *Who am I kidding? The Book of Cats almost did me in.*

"Cira found a whole lot of things," Etar explained. He blew briefly against the piece of wood, clearing off the shavings collecting on his fingers. "Unfortunately she also found the one thing that could set Cerioth into an unimaginable rage."

Omen knew Cerioth was called The Dark Heart for a reason — his name was spoken with both reverence and a great deal of fear. While the stories claimed he could be generous beyond all imagining, he was also capable of unspeakable vengeance. He wondered what Cira could have found that would send the god into a rage.

"She found reference to an ancient race — the Lithi. The first race," Etar explained.

"First of what?" Omen asked, the word *Lithi* unfamiliar to him. Several more birds landed on the table, hopping about, heedless of Omen's presence. He slowly raised his hand to poke at one, only to get his finger bitten by a tiny beak.

"The first of everything," Etar explained. "The first race of creatures the Elder Gods ever created. Before the Enshrined or the Dominions or the Revanants or the Powers."

Omen had no clue what Enshrined, Dominions, Revanants or Powers were, and he searched for some frame of reference that might be familiar. "Before the Night Dwellers or Dawn's Children?" he asked skeptically. *As far as I ever heard they are the eldest of all the races. If there were any older, everyone would know about them.*

"Not Night Dwellers or Dawn's Children, Omen," Etar corrected. He turned the sliver of wood again, twisting his knife slowly and carefully, and Omen realized he was carving tiny ribs in the flat part of the oar-shaped wood. "Enshrined and Dominions. They are nothing like the creatures you are thinking of. This was long ago — before the Night Dwellers or Dawn's Children existed."

Etar paused, as if searching for more to say. Several birds trilled at him, hopping closer to his side of the table. There were now over a dozen of the tiny creatures on the table between them. "Perhaps one day I will tell you the true history of the Elder Gods and the Old Ones who came from the abyss," Etar continued. "But that part is unimportant right now. The first creatures, or rather the first people, the Elder Gods created were the Lithi — and this was a very long time ago. Hundreds of millions of years in the past. And Cira found out about them and went in search of them when she left Cerioth's realm."

"What do you mean went in search?" Omen protested. "You just said they lived hundreds of millions of years ago." He noticed one of the little birds, small and brown, was moving oddly, his left wing hanging awkwardly at its side. Despite the injury, the little creature was singing.

"The elder races were immortal," Etar told him. "Are immortal," he corrected. He cut another shaving of wood free, slowly and methodically working away at the shape in his hand. "They may be gone from this world, but they are not dead. Most of them lost interest in this world and turned their minds to other things. But they're still out there. The Lithi were no different. They lost interest in life itself and one by one they fell asleep and vanished from the pages of time."

"You're telling me there is an entire race of people hidden somewhere in the world who have been sleeping for millions of years — what, like in a cave or something?" Omen scoffed at the story. While he wasn't the best student, he also knew his understanding of the world far exceeded the knowledge of most scholars. His father's understanding of the universe and their world was utterly unique.

97

"That's impossible," Omen proclaimed. "The world isn't even shaped the same way it was millions of years ago. The continents break apart and move, crash into each other, form mountains. Even if the physical location of one of these caves was put on a map somewhere it wouldn't mean anything — entire mountain ranges might not even exist anymore, let alone still be in the same place."

Etar chuckled, clearly amused by Omen's impromptu geology lecture. "So you actually *do* listen to 7's lessons from time to time," he teased. "The Lithi's fortresses were hidden by magic, Omen. The world could change around them but leave them untouched. It takes magic to find them, not a map."

"What kind of magic?" Omen asked, his curiosity starting to burn. *This sounds even more interesting than the Night Games. I wonder if Templar knows anything about this — ancient races hidden throughout the world?*

"Not something you should concern yourself with!" Etar gave him a dark, warning glare. He gestured with his knife, pointing emphatically. "Trust me on this, Omen. The Lithi are a race that should never be disturbed. There is nothing in this world save for the gods themselves that were ever a match for the Lithi. It is likely that they wouldn't even notice the races of this world, so insignificant are mortals to them." He took a halting breath. "The Venedrine paid a terrible price for Cira's curiosity."

"She awakened them?" Omen asked, anticipating the end of the story.

"No." Etar shook his head and returned to his carving. "The world you know wouldn't exist if she had. Not even the Covenants would have contained the Lithi. But she did find one of their fortresses, and with the aid of other members of her family she tried to drain magic from the sleeping immortals to enhance her clan's power."

Appalled, Omen cut his gaze to the tiny carving in Etar's hands — not an oar, he realized, but a tiny feather. "She drained the sleeping Lithi?" he asked, thinking that hurting a person trapped in an eternal slumber and unable to defend themselves might be enough to drive a god to rage.

Etar carefully sliced away more pieces of wood, detailing the ribbed lines of the little feather. "No, the Venedrine didn't have the power to hurt them. The sleeping Lithi didn't even notice what she had done — never even disturbed their sleep."

"I don't understand." Omen frowned.

"Cerioth found out what she had done," Etar explained. "And that was all it took. You have to understand that of all the races of the world there has never been a race that Cerioth loved more than the Lithi. When he discovered what Cira had done, his wrath was unimaginable. He cursed her and all her people — it was a curse so strong and so virulent it took on a life of its own and became a living entity whose sole reason for existing was to carry out Cerioth's vengeance. This curse, this creature, attacked the Venedrine and began killing them, all of them. The slaughter was terrible; the curse was unstoppable."

"It must have been stoppable," Omen reasoned. "The Venedrine still exist today." One of the little birds landed on Etar's shoulder, chirping joyously.

"That's because we intervened." Etar's gaze was still focused on his carving despite the little bird chirping in his ear.

"We?"

"The children of Cerioth, me and my other brothers and

sisters. We went to Cerioth and begged him to stop the curse."

Omen drummed his fingers lightly on the table, watching the birds nearest him. One or two scolded him briefly, but all of them clamored to get Etar's attention. *The children of Cerioth. They are not all as pleasant or kind as Etar.* "Why would all of the children of Cerioth care about one single tribe of elves?"

Etar held up the tiny feather he was carving, turning it around in the sunlight as if inspecting it for flaws. "This was about more than one tribe of elves. The curse was killing all the Venedrine and any creature with even a fraction of Venedrine blood in them. There isn't an elvin race today that doesn't have some Venedrine blood in their background."

Etar pinned him with a sharp gaze. "Cerioth was going to wipe out all the elves. Complete and total slaughter of one of the great races of the world."

Chapter 8: Tyrin

As Etar's words sank in, Omen swallowed hard, unable to find a reply. *I didn't realize that Cerioth was so ruthless. No wonder he's called The Dark Heart. All that power. And he used it to kill innocent people.* "Horrible," he finally stammered.

"You're beginning to understand." Etar worked the point of the knife against the very edge of the little wooden feather, shaving away some tiny imperfection. "We threw ourselves at Cerioth's feet and begged him to call off the curse. He was unyielding, insisted he would have his vengeance. We implored him to contain his wrath, to only punish those who had wronged him. In time our prayers for mercy moved him, and The Dark Heart agreed to limit the curse to the Venedrine royal caste. But he dictated a condition. We all had to swear an oath never to interfere in the curse's revenge. Powerless, we agreed. One by one, we all took a blood oath. Cerioth relented. The elves were saved."

The little wounded bird with the gimpy wing had paused in his hop across the table to pick at some tiny crumb left behind from breakfast. "This doesn't explain anything about Kyr." Omen tried to focus. *All these stories are making my head hurt.*

"None of us knew about Kyr." Etar took a long, slow breath. He seemed younger, vulnerable. "You see, by the time all this had happened, Cira was already long dead. The curse found her early, and killed her instantly. But upon killing her, it discovered her unborn child. Even though Kyr had not yet been born, and his mother was dead, he was

101

still a demigod and immortal. The very nature of the curse demanded that Kyr be killed, but even the curse could not kill a demigod. Instead it ripped Kyr from his dead mother's womb and abandoned him in a place where death would have been preferable. Back then none of us understood how truly powerful the curse was. I'm not even sure Cerioth knew. His rage was infinite."

Etar paused and studied his carving intently. Seeming pleased with the shape of the little wooden feather he had carved, he set his knife down on the table amid the flock of small birds. "The curse ripped open a rift through time and space," he continued his story, haltingly. "It hurtled Kyr thousands of years into the future to a dimension that was about to be destroyed by unimaginably powerful weapons. It left him there to burn."

"It took him into the future?" Omen asked, disbelief pinging through his mind. *Come on.* He knew it was possible to travel through dimensions and teleport across vast spaces, but he'd never heard of anyone actually time traveling. *How is that even possible? Dad says there is some sort of paradox that makes time travel impossible.* But his father had never actually said the word *impossible*, only *difficult*.

"Time travel isn't something you . . ." Omen began, only to trail off as the little wounded bird suddenly froze in mid-hop. Etar reached out and lifted the little creature into his hand. Around them the rest of the birds grew silent, peering at Etar with complete attention.

"Remember, we didn't know Kyr existed," Etar explained. "Not until our own timelines caught up with him, one hundred and eighty-seven years ago." Etar pulled gently at the little bird's wing, extending it outward and revealing the unnatural bend in the fragile bone and the missing primary feathers along the edge.

"But why didn't you go get him then?" Omen tried to focus on their conversation instead of the strange spectacle of the little bird and Etar. "Once you became aware of his existence, why didn't you rescue him?"

"Because of the oath we had sworn." Etar ran his finger over the bend in the bird's wing bone. With each pass of his finger, the bone grew straighter, smoothing out. "We were bound by the promise we had made. We couldn't even speak about any of this to anyone outside of our circle. Why do you think I am telling this story to you instead of any one of a thousand people I know who would have gladly gone into that world to rescue Kyr?"

"What?" Omen replayed Etar's words over in his mind. "You can tell me because I'm a child of Cerioth!"

"Exactly." Etar gave the little bird's back a gentle tap. "I knew the day you were born that you were Kyr's only hope."

"I knew it!" The tangled truth unfurled. "You tricked me into going."

"How did I trick you?" Etar asked reasonably. "You asked me to send you on an epic quest — I did." Still holding the bird's tiny wing, he picked up the little wooden feather from where he'd placed it on the table.

"You manipulated me into asking," Omen insisted. "You just said that I was his only hope. You had to send me on that quest because I was the only child of Cerioth who had not sworn the oath, because I hadn't been born yet."

Etar studied him closely — so closely, Omen felt his cheeks burn with a trace of heat. "I recall," Etar said lightly, "a library filled with glowing mice and a boy and cat insisting I choose between mice or sending them on a quest.

How did I trick you?"

Makes sense when he says it like that.

But Omen was certain, deep in his bones, that Etar had somehow set things in motion. And he was glad of it. *But did he have to trick me? I would have done it if he'd only just explained. Why did he have to trick me? Doesn't he think I'd do the right thing?*

Uncertain, Omen watched as Etar took the delicate wooden feather and slipped it between the tiny bird's remaining primary feathers. The moment he pressed it into place, the wood shimmered and changed in his hand, turning a brilliant blue, the same color as Etar's eyes. The wooden spines of the feather softened and grew downy in appearance. For a moment it looked as if the entire bird shivered and shook. Etar released the bird and it fluffed its body, flicking its wings before it took to the air once again, flying effortlessly as if the injury had never existed. The other birds at the table took flight after it, all of them chirping exuberantly as they lifted into the air.

Something stirred in Omen's heart, and he felt the corners of his eyes growing moist with pride for his brother and genuine respect for the kindness of Etar, The Soul's Flame. *He is a god.*

Omen watched the fluttering birds for a long moment before turning his attention back toward his elder brother. Etar was carefully cleaning his small carving knife, inspecting the blade before he slipped it into the sheath he'd removed from his coat pocket.

"Is Kyr still in danger?" A fissure of worry ran down Omen's spine. "When we came back through the portal, you told me he was still in danger, and that I should introduce him to my father. Why?"

"Because the curse is still out there." Etar pressed his lips together in distaste. "After you left the rift, the curse swooped in and tore through to the other side. It knows Kyr has been rescued. It is hunting for him."

Cold bands of anxiety wrapped around Omen's heart. "It's coming here?" He asked the question, knowing the answer.

Etar nodded. "It will have to get past the dragons, which won't be easy. But it is extremely powerful. 7 is the only one with any hope of fighting it, or of getting Cerioth to call it off."

While Omen was more than confident in his father's ability to fight anything that came their way, the second part of Etar's statement made no sense. "Why do you think my father could get Cerioth to call off this curse? Cerioth hates my father. If you can't convince Cerioth to stop, why do you think my father can?"

"Cerioth doesn't hate 7." Etar chuckled as if the very idea were preposterous. He placed the sheathed knife back in his pocket. "Why would you think that?"

"You do remember the whole imprisonment thing, right?" Omen asked. "My father owned the lute that Cerioth was imprisoned in for fourteen thousand years. He was in essence his jailer for the last stretch of his sentence."

"7 wasn't responsible for Cerioth's imprisonment," Etar reminded him. "If Cerioth hated 7, he would have killed him the moment he touched that lute, just like he did with the thousands of other people who tried to claim that lute over the centuries. And it was your father who freed Cerioth. For you."

Omen swallowed the words he'd meant to say.

Etar stood up then, looking ready to leave. "You should

tell your parents the story I just told you," he informed Omen. "I'm still bound by my oath. I cannot speak of it to anyone but you."

"Wait a minute!" Omen jumped to his feet. "I have about a million questions!"

"Oh, I have something for you." Etar ignored Omen's protest. "Or rather for Kyr." He reached into his inner pocket and pulled out a ball of orange fluff which he deposited into Omen's outstretched hand. A moment later Etar was gone, soundlessly, as if he'd never been there.

Stunned, Omen glanced down at the wiggling ball of fur. Two familiar amber eyes stared up at him from a tiny kitten face, white whiskers splayed, orange ears perked forward and tail twitching wildly. The kitten looked like a very tiny Tormy.

"By our king's whiskers!" the kitten exclaimed. "That is being a very excitingnessness story I is not supposeded to be listening to on account of the fact that I is pretending to be asleep! We is in the middle of an epicnessness adventure, isn't we! And I is really hungry! When's lunch?"

At the sound of the kitten's voice, Tormy awoke, ears turned forward as he lifted his fuzzy head to look around. "TYRIN!" the large cat yelled, waking Kyr.

"TORMY!" the little orange kitten yodeled and leaped from Omen's hands. He raced across the patio, miniature claws clicking furiously. The two cats danced around each other in frantic excitement, and Omen cringed, fearing that Tormy would step on the little cat and squish him.

Kyr, still seated on the solarium pavers, watched the entire display with a look of puzzlement on his thin face. The two cats were babbling at each other, their words coming so fast and so disjointedly that Omen couldn't really follow the gist of the conversation. He did note, however, that both cats were speaking Sul'eldrine.

That's why Etar was speaking in Sul'eldrine. He knew the kitten was eavesdropping. He can't speak directly about the curse because of his oath, but he knew the kitten would listen in. Omen was beginning to think his brother was a great deal sneakier than he'd previously considered.

Eventually Omen gave up on trying to follow the two cats' conversation and joined them on the pavers, seating himself next to his brother. "Apparently they are discussing how late Tyrin is, and that mice are really fun to chase," Omen whispered a translation to Kyr.

"Are you going to introduce us, Tormy?" Omen asked.

Tormy looked startled. "This is Tyrin!" he said, as if it were obvious.

"I is Tyrin!" the kitten trumpeted.

"We is twins!" Tormy continued.

"Twins?" Omen looked from the large cat to the small kitten. "As in twin brothers?" He could readily believe the two cats were related — they looked identical except for the size difference.

"Yep!" they both insisted. "We is born on the same birthday."

Wondering if the cats perhaps had a slightly different definition of the meaning of the word twins, Omen sought to clarify. "But not in the same year?"

The cats tilted their heads in unison.

Omen bit his lip to keep from laughing.

"We is born at the same time," Tormy insisted. "We is three weeks old!"

Which was exactly how old Tormy had told him he was when Omen had first met the cat six months ago. "Tormy, you've been living here for half a year. You can't still be three weeks old." Not that he thought the cat had been three weeks old when he'd found him — most kittens could barely crawl at that age, their eyes only newly opened.

"We is not knowing how to count any higher than three," Tyrin explained patiently.

"I is learning how to count to nine," Tormy announced.

Tyrin's eyes widened, the little kitten looking genuinely impressed. "Nine!" he exclaimed. "That's really high!"

"I know." Tormy nodded in agreement. "It is being really hardnessness!"

Might explain how Tormy manages to spend so much money when I'm not watching. Maybe I should teach them some basic arithmetic. "So, you two are brothers. And you're twins. Born on the same day, same year, same time, to the same mother?" He made an attempt to clarify further.

"Queen Flitterwhiskers!" both Tormy and Tyrin announced in unison.

First there was a King Largepaw, and now there is a Queen Flitterwhiskers! Tormy occasionally talked about the fabled Cat Lands he originated from, but Omen hadn't exactly believed that there were really other cats like Tormy in the world. *I thought he was the only one!*

"Your mother is queen of the Cat Lands?" Omen asked. Tormy had been wearing a crown when he'd found him, and had insisted that he was a prince. But Omen had had a lot on his mind at the time. *Night Dwellers. Necromancers. Giant undead worms. Psionic combat. Corzika.* He shuddered involuntarily.

"Our mommy is the queen and our daddy is the king," Tormy explained, unruffled.

"King Largepaw," Tyrin offered helpfully.

At least their stories match.

"On account of the fact that he is having really large paws," Tormy added.

Flitterwhiskers and Largepaw. Omen wondered if his life would always be this unpredictable. That he could go from a conversation with a god about the near extinction of an entire race of people and a dark curse which was hunting his helpless brother, to talking about cat queens and kings seemed unusual — even to him.

"All right." Omen decided to change the subject. "What brings Tyrin here, all the way from the Cat Lands?" Omen assumed it was a far distance. He didn't actually know where the place was — if it truly existed.

"He is living here now!" Tormy exclaimed happily, and little Tyrin took several tentative steps toward Kyr.

"I is here for the losted boy!" Tyrin explained.

The boy fixed his sunset-violet eyes on the little cat.

"I is Tyrin," the kitten told Kyr. The little cat folded his tail around his paws. "Teeeee-rin!" he repeated, waving his front paw in the air as he pronounced the name slowly as if picturing it printed in large letters upon a wall.

Omen had to smile, remembering how Tormy had repeated his name to him several times until he got the pronunciation down. Apparently Omen's initial attempts had not captured the roll in the *r* in Tormy's name to the cat's satisfaction.

"Teeeeeeeeeeeeerrrrrrrrriiiiiiiinnnnnn," the little cat repeated, stretching his name out as he waved his paw again. He looked expectantly at Kyr, who glanced over at Omen and Tormy.

"Tyrin!" Tormy said encouragingly as he bumped Kyr's arm with his nose. Omen knew Kyr didn't comprehend what was going on. When Kyr looked toward Omen again, he just nodded his head.

"Tyrin?" Kyr repeated.

Little Tyrin leaped up and spun around in several tight circles. "Hurrah! He is knowing my name!" Which didn't seem particularly remarkable to Omen since the cats had told Kyr the name repeatedly.

Tormy, however, looked quite impressed. "I is saying Kyr is very smartinessness!"

"I is Tyrin," the little cat said again. "And you is the losted boy, Kyr. And I is going to stay with you forever and ever."

Kyr tried to smile; confusion was written all over his face. Omen switched to Kahdess to translate. "His name is Tyrin. Apparently he's now your cat — or you're his boy. I'm not really sure how it works. He's going to live here with us. He's Tormy's brother. Like you're my brother."

"Brother?" Kyr's voice cracked with emotion.

It occurred to Omen then that he'd never really explained any of it to Kyr. "It's a long story," he told the boy. "But we're all family now — and Tyrin is going to stay with you."

Kyr took in a big breath and reached out to pick Tyrin up. Omen tensed. He knew Kyr's mind wasn't quite right, and he wasn't certain Kyr would understand how fragile such a small kitten was. But the boy held the little cat very gently in his hands as if afraid he would hurt him.

"Tyrin is the green," Kyr stated clearly. "I like green."

The little weed Kyr tried to shield. Omen's eyes pricked again with tears as he understood the meaning of the words. Kyr had protected the little plant with his own flesh and blood, sacrificing his well-being and enduring terrible pain for the sake of *the green*. Any concern Omen had had over Kyr accidentally harming the delicate kitten evaporated. And though the two cats didn't understand what Kyr had just said, both seemed to sense the profound nature of the boy's words. The felines settled down and started purring.

Kyr stretched out and rested his head against Tormy's furry body, his skeletal hands cupping Tyrin against his bony chest. Both boy and cats fell swiftly back asleep in the warm sunlight, leaving Omen sitting beside them, thoughts swirling in his head like colored beams of a kaleidoscope.

Overhead a small songbird flew past — a bright blue feather prominent in one of its tiny wings.

Chapter 9: Templar

After feeding Tormy, Tyrin, and Kyr braised lamb shanks, sautéed greens, and sugar squash along with a mild chicken soup that was easier for Kyr to stomach, Omen returned them all to the solarium to rest. Kyr's appetite had increased dramatically, and he'd tried small bites of everything after eating his soup.

Stuffed and yawning, Kyr followed after Omen like a hapless puppy.

He tires so quickly.

The overwhelming events of the past days and the rapid healing of his body had left the boy exhausted from the moment he woke up to the moment he fell asleep.

But rather than nap in a chair as Omen thought he would, Kyr stretched out on the ground, a piece of charcoal in his thin fingers and several large pieces of paper in front of him. *Servants must have brought those. Wonder who—* He looked at the cats.

Tormy and Tyrin perched beside Kyr, fuzzy heads bent over the paper as they chatted with the boy, instructing him what to draw — salmon it seemed. While Omen knew Kyr did not understand a word they were saying, the boy was nonetheless filling the page with sketches of swimming fish. The cats purred with pleasure.

For once, Tormy wasn't clamoring for attention or activities — content in Kyr and Tyrin's company. *Having another cat keeps him entertained, so I can catch up on my studies.*

Omen had taken a few books from the library on their

way back. The subject of the first one concerned water elemental magic. His sister had mentioned finding a water breathing spell, but she had not said where she had discovered the spell, nor given any hint what source of magic it belonged to. *She could have been lying.* Omen sat with the book in his lap, intrigued by the detailed description of the circulatory system of sea dragonettes.

"We is studying our lessons now!" Tormy proclaimed as soon as Omen had lost himself in the pages. Tormy rolled on his side and succumbed to a comatose nap.

Kyr continued drawing, but Tyrin proclaimed himself a brilliant scholar and followed Tormy's example. He hopped onto Tormy's head and disappeared in the fur of the larger cat's thick ruff. Soon, tiny snores — in harmony with Tormy's deep rumbles — echoed through the solarium.

Omen picked up a book with red leather binding. *Better get to it.* The volume was one of the many books his father had suggested when Omen had asked him about the various uses of his psionics. The content was theoretical and dry. *Of course.* While the magical patterns could be written down and learned from any book or scroll, the psionic patterns could only be learned from another psionicist. The patterns had to be transferred mind to mind. But numerous books expounded on the theoretical use of the psionic patterns, as well as their philosophical relevance and ethical application.

Omen had always tried to avoid such books. *And can you blame me?* The content was presented in dull, repetitive rhetoric laced with digressions and academic parlance. *This is dustier than a lich's lair.* However, since his little sister — supposedly — had already read all the theoretical works and had mastered much of the basics, Omen could

113

not give up. He found the text mind numbing, but dug into it, remembering his ill-preparedness in Hex and in Kyr's world. He was now responsible for Tormy, Kyr, and Tyrin. Word by word, sentence by sentence, he forced his attention on the material. *This is useful. This is useful. This is useful,* became his mantra. He even set the words to a little tune, humming absently while he turned page after page.

He was surprised to see the light had changed and hours had passed when a loud yelp in the hallway outside the solarium caught his attention. He turned toward the arched entrance to the glass-encased garden to see Templar. His friend was just as elegantly dressed and well-groomed as he always was, his dark hair curling artistically past his shoulders as if arranged by his valet just moments ago. But Templar did not look altogether well. His face flushed and jaw tight, the crown prince of Terizkand limped across the room. Silently, he stopped at an armchair next to Omen.

Kyr scrambled to hide behind Tormy. He dragged a rather startled Tyrin with him.

"What happened to your leg?" Omen asked, watching Templar rub his knee.

Templar unhooked the twin swords hanging from his belt and hung the weapon straps over the back of the chair before he dropped down into the seat. Dressed in a dark leather frock coat with silver studs and gem-adorned buttons, he looked as if he'd just come from a Terizkandian garden party despite the swords and the thin daggers peeking out from the cuffs of his polished boots. The Terizkandian prince had always been a flashy dresser, but this was extreme even for him.

"Your sister Lilyth kicked me." Templar's eyes, yellow as a cat's, flashed with irritation.

114

"What did you do?"

Templar looked offended. "All I did was say hello!" He pulled off one leather gauntlet and then the other, revealing the jeweled rings he wore on every finger. Several more gem studs lined his ears.

Omen nodded. "That would do it."

"What do you mean?" Templar asked, confused. He reached across the table and stole one of the biscuits on the plate next to Omen's pile of books.

"She doesn't like you," Omen replied. Truthfully, Omen rather suspected that his little sister did in fact *like* the flashy prince. While Templar possessed a posh elegance that annoyed his sister to no end, he also had a dangerous edge to him that most girls seemed to love. *But she's just a kid.*

"What's not to like?" Templar broke off part of the biscuit and popped it into his mouth. His gaze flicked briefly toward the two cats, and he suddenly sat up straight. "Hey, there's two of them!"

Tyrin had managed to squirm out of Kyr's grip and was sitting next to Tormy. The two cats blinked placidly at Templar with identical steadfast stares.

"Where'd the other one come from?"

"That's Tyrin," Omen explained. "Tormy's brother. Etar brought him by."

Templar's eyes widened with outrage. "So the gods are just handing them out to you now? That's not fair! Why didn't I get one?"

Startled, Omen looked up from his book. "You want a cat?"

Templar frowned. "Well, they are quite useful. Tormy fights and stuff."

115

"I don't think Tyrin is going to be much help in a fight any time soon," Omen pointed out.

Templar broke off another piece of biscuit and tossed it toward Tyrin. Tyrin caught it with one raised paw and pinned it to the ground triumphantly. "No, but I'd bet he'd be dead useful at finding out people's secrets. Cat like that could sneak in almost anywhere."

"And you wonder why Lilyth doesn't like you."

Templar's brow furrowed, and he leaned forward, his gaze on the pale-faced form of Kyr who was peeking cautiously around Tormy. "Who's the weird-looking kid?"

Omen slammed his book shut and kicked Templar hard in the shin, causing him to yelp again in pain.

"He's my brother, Kyr," Omen growled. "And he's not weird looking — he's just . . . He's been ill. He's getting better."

Templar held up a hand in apology while rubbing his doubly bruised shin with the other. "Sorry," he stated quickly. "Brother . . . Beren or Cerioth?"

"Cerioth," Omen muttered, still annoyed.

A look of confusion crossed Templar's face. "How does a demigod get sick? And where did you find him?"

"Actually, I rescued him." Omen gloated as he set aside his book. "It was an epic quest."

"Really?" Templar asked skeptically. Not one to let his moment slip by, Omen proceeded to launch into a detailed retelling of the story, embellishing where appropriate. Templar listened in silence, occasionally glancing over at the still cautious Kyr.

"So basically what you're saying is," Templar stated when Omen had finished, "you wandered into an empty wasteland, got rained on, and came home. And that's what

116

you call epic?"

Omen scowled at him. "It was more than rain and coming home!" he protested. "And besides, it's not over yet. We still have a god's curse hunting us!" Omen proceeded to relay the rest of the information Etar had given him.

Templar looked slightly more impressed with the second part of the tale.

"So why is he afraid of me?" he asked, motioning toward Kyr who continued hiding behind Tormy.

"He's sort of afraid of everything," Omen said. "You would be too."

Kyr peeked around Tormy again, staring mistrustfully at Templar before speaking a word in Kahdess that Omen did not know.

Omen frowned, puzzling the root of the word, trying to translate it as best he could into Merchant's Common. *Shadow . . . infernal . . . sunless . . . oh!* "That means—" he turned toward Templar to explain.

"I know what it means." Templar was staring hard at Kyr, an odd expression on his face. "Nightblood."

Is Templar offended? In all the time Omen had known Templar, he'd never made any attempt to hide the fact that he was part Nightblood. As far as Omen could tell, everyone in Terizkand knew that the royal family was part Night Dweller; bizarrely, it seemed almost a point of pride among the warlike Terizkandians. And since King Antares, Templar's father, had freed Terizkand from a race of man-eating giants who had ruled their beleaguered country for centuries, the people of the land would forgive their royal family anything — even possessing the cursed blood of a Night Dweller.

A lot of curses going around.

117

And if Omen was truthful, Templar's heritage was one of the reasons the two of them were able to be such good friends. Templar was one of the only people his age who could match him in strength. Immortal, quick healing, and unnaturally strong and fast, Templar could more than hold his own against Omen on the battlefield or game field.

Outside of Terizkand, however, Nightblooded were viewed mistrustfully, fearfully. Even among the eternally polite Melian population, Omen had seen people covertly making the warding sign against evil as Templar passed by. Unlike Templar's blue-eyed father and sister, Templar possessed flame-yellow eyes — the sure sign of the Nightblooded. While many Night Dwellers could take on any shape or form, if angered their eyes always flashed yellow with rage, unmasking them.

Templar claimed he had been born blue-eyed like his family, but his eyes had changed permanently to yellow when he was a child, and since then he refused to hide who he truly was. No matter the consequences.

"Where did you hear that term in Kahdess?" Templar asked Kyr.

Omen realized with some relief that far from being offended at the term Kyr had used, Templar was simply surprised at the language his brother had spoken it in. He also knew that Kyr would not have understood Templar's question. "He can't understand you — he doesn't speak Merchant's Common."

Templar looked even more intrigued. "What?"

Merchant's Common was spoken the world over — the universal language of trade. Though it was in fact the native tongue of the Kingdom of Narache, it was also the language of the Covenant of the Gods, and something every

118

child learned early in life.

"He speaks Kahdess — and nothing else," Omen explained.

"That's impossible," Templar protested. He turned his gaze back toward Kyr. "Who taught you Kahdess?" he asked, this time speaking in flawless Kahdess himself. His accent, Omen noticed, was far better than his own — he spoke it with the same ease as Kyr.

Kyr tightened his grip on Tormy's fur and leaned against the large cat. "The wind screams and the voices are never silent, always howling amid the dust and fire. I listen. I learn." The boy's voice was soft but clear.

Omen forced an encouraging smile on his face, despite the fact that Kyr's words made him want to shudder.

"What was that?" Templar demanded, his voice cracking with alarm.

"I just told you about where he came from," Omen hissed through his teeth.

"You mean you weren't making that up?"

"No, of course not!" Another wave of annoyance swamped through Omen. "And where did you learn to speak Kahdess? Your pronunciation is better than mine."

Templar leaned back in his chair, long legs stretched out in front of him. "I spend a lot of time in Revival," he replied, referring to one of the larger cities in the kingdom of Terizkand. "Between the swamp — you remember Cornelia. *That* swamp — the graveyard and the Cursed Garden, Revival is neck-deep in the undead: zombies, vampires, wraiths, liches, necromancers. Speaking Kahdess is a survival skill in Revival."

Impressed by the list of preternatural creatures, Omen pushed his stack of books aside. "Then why do we spend so

119

much of our time hanging out in Hex?" he demanded. *Revival sounds brilliant.*

"Because the Night Games are in Hex," Templar pointed out, which Omen had to concede was a good reason. "Speaking of which — there's a big party tonight in the Glass Walk. Everyone is going to the games afterward. That's why I'm here — I came over to get you. Free you from your toil and studies." He gave the pile of books a dismissive look.

"I can't leave Kyr," Omen said without missing a beat.

Templar tossed another piece of biscuit at Tyrin. The little cat pinned it under his other paw. "Get your parents to watch him."

A cold pain stabbed Omen's chest. *Leave Kyr?* He covered with a quip, "Get my parents to do something? Really? If you asked your father to do something you were supposed to be doing, what do you suppose he'd do?"

"Throw me off the tower wall," Templar replied without hesitation. "Or at least that's what he did the first time I tried."

"What happened the second time you tried?"

"There wasn't a second time." Templar offered a smirk. "I generally learn my lesson the first time. Can you get the cats to watch him?"

"Really . . . the cats?" His frustration mounted. "There's a god's dark curse hunting him. You expect the cats to protect him from that?"

"Then we'll bring him with us," Templar suggested brightly. "He speaks Kahdess — he'll get along famously with the Night Dwellers. And the Venedrine will think he's a mystic — he'll be an instant hit."

Omen rubbed the tight muscles in his neck. "I'd rather

the Venedrine stay away from him, considering his history. Kyr isn't nearly strong enough yet for that sort of complication. And he's afraid of people. I'm not taking him anywhere tonight, and I'm not leaving him alone."

"Isn't that going to be awfully boring?" Templar asked. "How long is this babysitting going to last?"

"Rat's teeth! As long as it takes!" Omen barely kept himself from yelling. "You weren't there. You didn't see how bad it was. I'm not leaving him alone."

Templar sighed theatrically and threw himself back into his chair in defeat. "You're supposed to be my irresponsible friend! How did this happen?"

Omen's mouth fell open. "Me?" He pointed an accusing finger at Templar. "You're the irresponsible one!"

"What are you talking about?" Templar sniffed indignantly. "I have a job. I do actual work. My father made me responsible for lots of things. I actually have to do paperwork and make reports and . . . stuff."

"And you do them?" Omen crossed his arms.

"Of course, I do them," Templar huffed. "He'd throw me off two towers if I didn't. He says you're a bad influence on me."

Omen thought about that for a moment. He'd always thought his parents were harsh taskmasters, but the truth was they didn't actually force him to do much of anything. "My parents say you're a bad influence on me."

"We can't both be bad influences on each other, Omen. Wouldn't that sort of negate the whole thing?"

"Well, you're definitely not a good influence," Omen reasoned.

"Neither are you!"

They both sat quietly working out the argument that

would indict the other and clear themselves of any wrong-doing, when Lilyth pattered in, looking even more out of sorts than the two of them. "Omen, Mother says we're eating early and that you're to come to dinner now," she announced. She folded her arms and tapped her foot. "And I suppose the Terizkandian will—"

She broke off suddenly, her gaze falling on Tyrin. Her silver eyes widened in complete shock. "Where did he come from!" she exclaimed. "Did you clone Tormy?"

Clone him? Omen looked at his sister, uneasy. *Don't tell me she also reads all the science books Dad gives us? I really have to start studying more.* "No, of course I didn't clone him. That's Tyrin, Tormy's brother. He's Kyr's."

Lilyth's expression twisted to one of outrage. "That's not fair! Why didn't I get one?"

The fact that her words perfectly echoed Templar's made Omen laugh, more so when he saw the look of embarrassment on Templar's face. "You want a cat too?" Omen teased his sister, knowing the answer.

Lilyth stomped her foot. "I was supposed to get one next! I'm next!"

"I don't think it works that way," Omen said, honestly trying to soothe her hurt feelings. "They're not pets. You can't buy them. They get to decide where they want to live."

"Well, I'm going to protest!" Lilyth insisted. "I've been waiting patiently all this time. Didn't even get one for my birthday! It's not fair!" As far as Omen knew, his sister had never waited patiently for anything — though she had made it clear that she wanted a cat of her own.

"Lily, I don't think . . ." Omen began, only to be silenced by his sister's glare.

"If you go out and get one for the brat prince before me, I'll never forgive you!"

"I didn't get Tyrin; Etar brought him. And I wasn't planning on getting anything for the brat prince," Omen avowed.

Templar looked mildly affronted at being called a brat prince — twice. "I do have an actual name, you know."

"Oh, shut up." Lilyth glared at him. "You're named after a building!"

"Actually, I'm named after an order of knights who guard a very important building," Templar corrected, his annoyance turning to amusement.

"It's still a stupid name," Lilyth insisted.

"And you're telling me that *Omen, Avarice,* and *7* aren't?" Templar argued. Omen had noticed that his friend and his sister seemed to enjoy arguing with one another.

"Those are hex names!" Lilyth exclaimed, stamping her foot again. "There's a good reason for them!"

"Yes, your weird Melian superstition about names." Templar laughed with a dismissive wave of his hand. A mischievous gleam entered his eyes, and Omen thought his friend liked baiting his ten-year-old sister far too much. Omen couldn't help wonder if this was how he treated his own sister back home.

"Speaking of which, why are you the only one in the family without a hex name?" Templar asked.

"It's not a Melian superstition," Lilyth snapped. "And Lilyth is a hex name. It means *assassin* in Scaalian."

Templar, who didn't speak Scaalian, frowned at that. "If Lilyth is your hex name, then what's your real name? Doesn't your Lydonian grandmother insist you all have proper names like Armand, Ava and S'van?"

Lilyth rolled her eyes, exasperated. "Lilyth is also my *proper* name because it doesn't mean anything in Merchant's Common. It's a double hex! Or are you too addlebrained to figure that one out for yourself!" She turned on her heel and stormed for the door. "I'm writing a letter of protest!"

"About Templar?" Omen laughed.

"NO!" Lilyth threw her hands up in the air. "I don't care about him! I'm writing a letter about the cats!" She left a deafening silence in her wake.

"Who is she going to send it to?" Templar asked after a few moments.

"Probably my dad," Omen reasoned.

"Is the superstition Scaalian then?"

"No, it's a Machelli family superstition," Omen explained, referring to his mother's bloodline. "All Machellis have hex names. The family believes that anyone with a weak name will come to a bad end. They've got these really strict rules about names — not only do you have to have a hex name, but it has to be something dark in nature to ward off bad luck. I've actually got two uncles named Massacre and Shroud. The entire Machelli clan is filled with oddly named people. Sometimes they even rename close acquaintances who they think might fall prey to ill fortune."

"Your father isn't a Machelli," Templar pointed out. "How did he end up named after a number?"

"How did you end up named after a building?" Omen shot back.

"An order of knights that guard a building," Templar corrected again. "My grandfather named me. He wanted me to serve in the Temple of The Redeemer."

"That didn't work out." Omen laughed at the thought of his friend serving in a temple. "My dad's real name is S'-

van. 7 is just a nickname from his childhood — not an actual hex name, but my mom liked it. She thought it was lucky."

"Your family is very strange," Templar told him, and Omen had to agree.

And strange is just the way I like it.

Chapter 10: Hex

Lilyth waited at the dinner table for her brother and the others to join them. She hadn't gotten very far with her letter, not certain her father would appreciate her argument that as the youngest in the family she needed the most watching over, which is why she should have a cat. *That's likely to get me a governess instead of a cat . . . so, no.*

She eyed her mother who was busy directing the footman at the sideboard where he was setting up the evening meal. "You should give him to me for safe keeping," she told her mother, trying to sound as reasonable as possible. "After all, Kyr can't take care of himself, let alone anyone else."

Her mother, in the process of inspecting two bottles of wine, turned with one dark eyebrow arched upward. "I beg your pardon?" she demanded, her tone making it clear that she was neither begging nor asking out of politeness. "You wish me to give Kyr to you?"

Lilyth grimaced. "Of course not! I meant Tyrin!"

"And who, pray tell, is Tyrin?" Avarice's voice had risen in tone, growing hard around the edges.

Outrage flooded through Lilyth. "He didn't even ask first? That's not fair! He gets away with everything!"

Before her mother could respond, an exuberant Tormy flounced into the room, nose in the air as he sniffed the aromas of the evening meal. "I is here!" he exclaimed happily. "We is eating dinner please!"

Behind him came Kyr, hands outstretched as he held

Tyrin before him as if serving him up on a platter. Omen and Templar trailed behind him, watching as the thin, skeletal boy showed the little kitten to Avarice. "Green!" he proclaimed, speaking the word proudly in Merchant's Common.

Her mother's anger faded instantly as she smiled down at the boy. She patted him benevolently on the stocking cap he wore over his bald head. "Very good, Kyr. You're learning to speak properly." She eyed the little orange kitten, and Lilyth held her breath.

Give him to me! Give him to me!

"And who is this?" Avarice asked, reaching out to pluck the kitten from the boy's hands. She placed him in her open palm, holding him up.

Tyrin, tail curled around his fuzzy little body, tilted his chin, ears perked forward. "I is Tyrin!" he explained. "I is telling everyone this, but you is not hearing, on account of the fact that you is in a different room when I is saying it."

"We is twins!" Tormy exclaimed. "On account of the fact that we is identicallynessness and you is not being able to tell us apart."

The sight of the food upon the table drew Kyr's attention, and Omen had to wrestle the boy into a chair as he tried to climb over the tabletop to reach the breadbasket. Avarice quickly placed a plate in front of Kyr while Omen buttered a hot scone for him. Templar sat down across from Lilyth, watching the proceedings with amusement.

"How wonderful!" Avarice proclaimed. "Now, you'll have time to do your studies, Omen. Two cats to keep each other company and occupy the boy. Excellent." She placed Tyrin on the seat cushion beside Kyr.

Lilyth's hopes were dashed. *She's fussing over them! She*

127

never fusses! And two cats will just get Omen in twice the trouble!

Tyrin clawed the edge of the fine tablecloth and pulled himself upward, planting his front paws on Kyr's plate. He sank his teeth into the other half of the buttered scone.

"Not on the table!" Avarice scolded the little cat. "And not off Kyr's plate. . ." Before she could finish, Kyr had sunk his fist into the crock of butter and removed a large handful of the thick yellow cream which he began licking from his fingers with joyful abandon.

"I is liking butter too!" Tyrin proclaimed, ignoring Avarice as he rose up on his hind legs and helped Kyr lick the butter from his hand. The laughter erupting from Prince Templar simply made Avarice huff in annoyance.

"First thing you're teaching them is manners!" She pointed a sharp finger at Omen who wisely nodded.

7 entered, and they all sat down to dinner.

Throughout the meal, Lilyth eyed Tyrin, strategizing ways to steal the tiny orange kitten. *I could hide him in the pocket of my skirt and say he ran away.* She'd barely speared the apple slivers and walnuts out of her winter salad when the footman removed her plate. She ignored the conversation about dark curses and Venedrine princesses in favor of plotting. *I could catch him with a net.*

By the time the pudding was served, she was fairly certain no amount of scheming was going to get her what she wanted. *Difficult to steal a cat who will just tattle on me. And he is a clever little thing — smarter even than Tormy, I think.* Tyrin had already won an argument with Avarice over the proper place for a cat at the table.

"I is civilizedednessness and I is not eating off the floor!" he'd insisted when Avarice had suggested an alterna-

128

tive to the seating arrangements. "You is not liking to eat off the floor, is you?"

When her mother had relented, Lilyth had despaired and abandoned her kidnapping plan. *He'd probably just get up and walk away. It's not like I could force him to stay in my room.* She thought back to the morning of the Harvest Festival when she had unsuccessfully tried to convince Tormy to be her cat.

The truth was, when she really thought long and hard about it, she doubted she'd have the heart to steal something from the odd little boy who had the habit of smiling with that insipid bony, skeleton grin of his as if they were all responsible for the rising and setting of the sun.

Kyr's just too helpless. Nope, I'll just have to figure out how to get a cat all on my own. Omen did it. How hard could it be?

During dessert, while trading barbs with Templar and Omen, Lilyth hatched a new plan. She excused herself from the table politely as soon as she could and walked out with as much dignity as possible, despite Templar's attempts to annoy her with his constant teasing.

Brat prince!

The moment she was out of sight, she bolted like a rabbit for her room. She raced to her dressing room, yanked off the beaded gown she'd been wearing, and changed into something she considered more suitable. As an afterthought, she picked up the ornate dress from the floor and placed it on the overstuffed Lydonian armchair.

She pulled on soft doe-skin trousers and a broken-in pair of traveling boots, sturdy and comfortable. The tunic she pulled over her head and belted around her waist was black and unadorned — not something she would usually wear, but tonight it suited her purposes.

I'm going on a top-secret stealth mission, and that means I have to wear black.

Her belt had a small sheath attached to it, and she slipped a razor-sharp dagger into it before pausing in front of her mirror to braid her long, black hair. *I probably ought to get myself a sword, but most of them are still too big and heavy for me.* She'd only practiced fighting with daggers.

All that was left to complete her supplies was some rope. According to the book she'd purchased in the market, *The Adventurer's Guide to Everything Adventurous,* she needed a weapon and a rope before setting out. She wasn't entirely certain what the rope was for, but she imagined she'd figure it out sooner or later. *If Omen can figure it out, so can I.*

There was a coil of strong but thin silk rope in the back of her large wardrobe, placed there months ago after she'd first read her book. *Just in case.* She collected it, and attached it to the back of her belt with a strong metal clip.

Lastly, she pulled on a pair of fine leather gauntlets and a heavy winter coat. *Prepared for anything.* She opened her bedroom door and peeked out into the hallway.

The hall was empty, the servants elsewhere. She took a chance, racing as silently as she could toward her father's office. She had to sneak down the back stairs and then wait in the tea room for ten minutes for one of the maids to leave, but eventually Lilyth managed to enter the room unseen. She hid herself behind one of the brocade curtains that adorned the enormous east-facing window behind the desk. She knew it was unlikely that her father would return to the office this evening — normally he spent his time after dinner in the music room, practicing the violin or one of

the many other instruments he enjoyed. It was equally unlikely he would find her before she could put her plan into
motion. *But nothing is certain.*

She hoped that Tormy would not poke his head into the
room. The curious cat had an uncanny knack for finding
her when she didn't want to be found. She'd learned early
on never to play hide-and-seek with Tormy — it was impossible to win. She was fairly certain that this evening,
however, she'd be safe — Tormy was busy with Tyrin and
Kyr. *Bet he forgets to check on me entirely.* She felt both relieved and annoyed. *He used to check on me hourly. No
matter.* All she had to do was wait.

Twenty minutes later, her patience paid off. She heard
her brother and Templar outside. Omen was bidding the
Terizkandian prince goodbye, and Templar was trying to
persuade Omen once more to come to the Night Games.
But for once, Omen sounded determined to take his respon-
sibilities seriously, and he refused the offer.

*What's happening to him anyway? He's not supposed to
be responsible. It'll never last!*

A moment later the door opened, and Templar stepped
into 7's office. He headed toward the Cypher Rune transfer
portal in the alcove. Omen followed, and took a moment to
touch the sigils carved into the wall in a certain order, acti-
vating the portal with the required code. Lilyth watched
carefully, noting each mark he touched.

Her father had made certain that the portal could not be
used randomly by just anyone. *Now I know the pattern!*

Omen waved goodbye to Templar.

Get on with it, you git!

The prince stepped onto the portal and touched the rune
that would take him to the corresponding portal in the dis-

tant city of Hex in the kingdom of Terizkand. A second later Templar was gone.

Omen took a small book from one of the shelves and left, never once glancing in her direction.

Wonder what he took.

She waited exactly one minute, counting the seconds silently. She figured that one minute would give Templar time enough to exit the portal on the other side.

. . . Fifty-eight manticores. Fifty-nine manticores. Sixty manticores. She ran forward, entered the code, and followed the prince to Hex.

She'd never actually been to Hex before, so she wasn't at all certain where she would end up. The Cypher Rune transfer portal in her father's office transported her across the world to the matching portal in Terizkand. She had expected to find herself in a similar room to her father's office with the portal etched into the stone floor.

Instead she found herself in a tree-filled courtyard in a park. This portal, while made of cut stone, was embedded into the floor of a marble gazebo.

Lilyth quickly ducked away from the gazebo and hid behind the nearest tree, worried that someone might spot her. But a quick look around revealed that, save for the retreating figure of Templar on the far side of the clearing, the entire area seemed empty. *Odd. Melian parks are never empty.*

But then she spotted the enormous walls surrounding the park and realized that this was an area walled off from the rest of the city. *A private courtyard, not a park. Why is it so huge?* There were several dozen full-sized trees in the yard. *More of a woodland glade than a simple courtyard.*

She hurried after Templar while quietly marveling at the

sights around her. She'd heard the stories about Hex of course, but until now she hadn't given them much thought. Her eyes widened in awe as she realized that the wild stories she'd heard about the city were true.

Hex was the capital city of Terizkand and the former stronghold of the last rulers of the land — the Giants of Ershakand. The giants had enslaved the human and elvin populations, until Templar's father, King Antares, had conquered the land. *Cities and castles built for giants — I hadn't imagined this.*

She'd spent her entire life in and out of various castles around the world, and she was very familiar with the basic layout of the structures. This was a castle, not dissimilar to many others she'd been inside, save that it was built for creatures nearly three times the height of a normal man. The arched doorway she followed Templar through was over twenty feet tall, and the hallway beyond was wide enough to drive wagons through. *It's the length of a city block! How does anyone move around in this place?* She supposed they had learned to adapt. She tried to picture what size her own bedroom might be if it had been built for a giant instead of a human. *Well, Tormy would fit right in. Could it be . . .*

Templar never looked back as he headed down the long hallway, and Lilyth followed at a distance, not wanting to risk getting too close lest he hear her. The enormity of the hall worked to her advantage.

Templar periodically called out to people in various rooms along the way — there were a few doors on either side. But as the enormous wooden doors were so massive, all of them stood open, and were likely to remain that way permanently. Templar's greetings gave Lilyth enough warning to pause before passing by them. She peered cautiously around the doorframes to make certain no one would see her.

The first stairway gave her some concern as she could see from a distance that the steps were made for a giant's gait, not a human's. But as she had suspected, the residents had adapted. Lining the far wall was a set of wooden steps lain over top the stone stairwell that allowed people to come and go without difficulty.

Following Templar down the stairs, however, wasn't entirely easy. She had to wait several minutes. Then she raced down the stairs and prayed she'd still be able to catch up to Templar, who had disappeared around a corner. *If I lose sight of him, I'll never find my way around.*

Luck was with her. Templar had paused to speak to someone. Ducking quickly behind a stone pillar that could have hidden several horses, Lilyth watched cautiously. Though she'd never seen her before, Lilyth suspected that the tall red-haired woman Templar was in deep conversation with was his sister, Corzika, High General of the Terizkandian army.

Corzika was extremely tall — nearly as tall as Templar who towered above average men. Strongly built and dressed in hardened black leather, Corzika was beautiful but fierce-looking. She kept her dark red hair cut short, and unlike her flashy younger brother, wore no jewelry, no adornment of any type despite being as much a princess of the realm as Templar was a prince.

She's also got the Night Dweller blood of the Terizkandian royal family, Lilyth reminded herself, despite the fact that unlike Templar, Corzika's eyes were turquoise blue.

"Keep an eye on the elves tonight," Corzika ordered

Templar, her stern voice as no-nonsense as Lilyth's mother's.

"The elves? Why?" Templar sounded startled.

Corzika's lips thinned, her eyes narrowed. "Something's going on with them. Particularly the Venedrine. I've been hearing stories all day that something has riled them up."

"That would be Omen." Templar waved his hand dismissively. "Or rather his brother who's apparently the last child of the Venedrine royal line."

"Another Deldano?" Corzika asked.

"No. The Dark Heart." Despite being Nightblooded, Templar spoke the name with a certain degree of reverence. Lilyth listened impatiently as he summarized Omen's story.

Corzika's frown had deepened by the time he was done. "Keep that to yourself tonight. There are many Venedrine who would not be happy to hear that a potential heir has resurfaced."

Eventually Templar and Corzika parted company, and Templar proceeded along his way. Lilyth silently followed after him.

Evening had settled in when Templar finally left the castle through the outer courtyard and approached the front gates. Lilyth, trailing behind, found herself staring in awe at the iron portcullis that stood open. Enormous chains as thick around as three men held the portcullis in place over the massive entrance. Lilyth could see the huge interlocking mechanism of wheels and gears that would raise and lower that gate — without magic to move it, it likely took twenty men to simply turn the wheel.

The torchlit courtyard was filled with people — servants coming and going, guards standing on duty or patrolling the area. The walls surrounding the castle, also built for giants and tall beyond anything she'd ever seen, were lined with guards. Various people called out greetings to Templar as he strode toward the gate. *He's extremely popular. Who would have guessed?*

Suspecting there would be no way she could remain unseen, Lilyth took a risk and simply followed after him, taking care to walk with purpose and determination, trying to appear as if she belonged there. It was dark enough that she doubted anyone would take notice of her unfamiliar features. Her gamble paid off, for while one or two guards glanced in her direction, no one said anything to her, and no one tried to stop her.

She emerged from the castle into the city of Hex and took a moment to gape once more at the sight before her. The castle was on a hill. *More like a small mountain, but to a giant it would just be a little hill.* The city lay below it at the bottom — and unlike most of the cities she'd seen in her life, it was built of stone. The only wooden structures she could see were scaffolding and stairwells allowing people to traverse the giant structures more easily. And all of it, city and castle, was surrounded by the most enormous walls she'd ever seen — giant-built as well, dwarfing anything a human society might construct. The houses — if they could be called that — were keeps unto themselves. The only way Lilyth could imagine them working as actual homes would be if the insides had been rebuilt with wooden walls to suit the smaller stature of the current residents.

Perhaps the most striking thing of all was the stone itself — every single stone in the city, every block that created the great walls, had magical runes carved into it — thousands, tens of thousands everywhere she looked. The runes glittered and glowed in the torchlight, all of them made of some sort of reflective material that caught the faintest light.

She knew that this was why the city was called Hex — the name given by the current inhabitants, and not the giants who'd lived there before. It was said that there was no city in the world with this many spells carved into the walls and stones. It was one of the reasons it had stood for so long — endured war after war over thousands of years without ever crumbling away to ruin. Lilyth couldn't even begin to conceive of the power and the force that must have been used to conquer such a place, and to do so against such formidable foes must have been epic beyond belief. She would have to get the story of it from someone soon.

Momentarily distracted by the sight of the city and its hex marks, Lilyth had to race after Templar to keep up. *If I lose him in this enormous stone citadel, I'll never find him again.*

Numerous people throughout the city recognized Templar, called out to him, waved in greeting, some stopping to talk to him, but Lilyth had little trouble keeping out of sight and out of notice. There were other girls her age running about the streets, finishing up evening chores. Though it was dark, the winter sun setting quickly, it was still early in the evening and there was plenty of activity on the roadways. No one took any notice of her.

She shivered as she followed Templar through the streets. While Hex was quite a bit warmer than Melia, the ground clear of snow, it was still cold, the air blowing in off the ocean chill and sharp. *I hope it isn't much farther!* She was beginning to grow more uneasy the longer the journey took — if she were gone for too long, her parents would notice, and then she would get in trouble.

Templar turned down another roadway, and Lilyth realized they were moving into a less populated area. The prince picked up his pace, walking more purposefully toward his destination.

He said he was going to the Glass Walk, whatever that is. While she didn't know where the Night Games were, she remembered Omen had spoken about the Glass Walk in his stories. *All I have to do is keep following Templar, enter the games and pick out a cat. I bet they have loads of them. I won't get an orange one though. I want my own color.*

She really didn't know what the Night Games were exactly. *Something like ringball only with fights.* She knew that Omen had won Tormy at a Night Game. *Which of course means, that's where the cats are from!* She just needed to find where the cats were kept and grab one. *I'll get a smaller kitten that I can carry. Easy enough. I'll be home before Mother knows I'm gone.* She figured she'd have another hour at least before her parents would check on her. As long as she could be back before then, she'd be fine.

Templar rounded another corner, disappearing from sight momentarily. A second later Lilyth heard a loud explosion, followed by a muffled yell. A shower of blue sparks flared from around the building, and Lilyth heard the sound of many booted feet racing toward the prince's last location.

She froze. *What was that?*

Three men barreled past her, one of them knocking her aside. They never even glanced in her direction, never giving her a second look as they disappeared around the corner.

Frightened, Lilyth crept forward, determined to find the

cause of the explosion. She peeked cautiously around the edge of the building.

The alleyway was glowing with the eerie city sigils — but these were somewhat different. Other sigils, glowing red with fire, were painted over top of the permanent hex marks covering the stone. While she'd only studied a little bit of magic, she knew enough to recognize a magical trap. Templar had been caught in it — likely never even noticing the extra marks over the original ones adorning every wall. *The trap must have exploded the moment Templar stepped on one of the marks!*

Guessing that the cry of pain and the heavy thud had been Templar being thrown through the air by the explosion, Lilyth spied him lying on the ground in the alleyway, unconscious. *He must have hit his head!* There were a dozen armed men surrounding him, several in the process of binding him in heavy, glowing metal shackles.

Lilyth ducked down behind the wall, crouching in the shadows. *They're kidnapping him! Taking him prisoner.*

Templar groaned, starting to awaken despite the force of the explosion. To Lilyth's shock, one of the men immediately bashed him over the back of the skull with the pommel of his sword, completely knocking him out again.

Lilyth bit back a gasp. *A blow to the head that hard could kill him!* While he claimed to be part Night Dweller, she didn't actually know if any of that was true — beyond the stories that said yellow eyes were the sign of such things. Regardless, she knew that he wasn't a demigod like her brother. *What if he can't heal the way Omen does? They might have just murdered him right in front of me. What do I do?* Anger closed her throat and formed a hard pit in her stomach. *There are too many. I can't do anything.*

139

She watched in grim silence as Templar was picked up by two men. The entire group began hurrying forward, moving swiftly and silently down the back alley toward some unknown destination.

Huddled in the darkness, she panicked, sweat dripping down her spine despite the cold. *If I can get back to the castle, I can get General Corzika!*

But it occurred to Lilyth that if she left now, she'd have no way of knowing where Templar was being taken. *How can they rescue him if I don't know where he's being held?*

She bit the inside of her cheek to keep from screaming.

What would Omen do? Determination washed over her.

Her brother would charge in and attack the men, fight his way through — which wasn't an option for her. *I'll just have to be clever then!*

She slipped out of the shadows and raced after the group of brutes, keeping her distance and staying as silent as possible. If she were caught she wouldn't just be facing a scolding from her mother.

Chapter 11: Transgression

After Omen had shown Templar to the transfer portal and collected a new book to read, he returned to take Kyr and the cats into the drawing room for the evening.

The boy was waiting anxiously beside Tormy, leaning against the large cat's furry body, little Tyrin perched upon his shoulder. Kyr's face lit up when he saw Omen. "Wait!" he said proudly in Merchant's Common, repeating back the word Omen had used moments earlier when he'd left.

"Good." Omen smiled in return and motioned the three to follow him across the hall to the expansive drawing room where his parents were also waiting. The moment he crossed the threshold, a tingle of magic washed over him. Kyr too gasped, feeling the sensation.

That's Mother's magic! Omen scanned the room for the source. Tyrin leaped from Kyr's shoulder to explore while Tormy padded carefully to where his favorite rug was spread out in front of the crackling fire.

Avarice stood at the hearth, arranging small crystals at either end of the mantle. The firelight flickered off the crystals, casting a warm glow throughout the room. Similar crystals hung from the chandeliers and from the various decorative protrusions of the ornately carved wooden cornices and dark cherry wood wall panels.

"Mother?" Omen frowned, confused. The room had long ago been decorated to Avarice's exacting tastes with plush furniture and fine paintings. It was unusual for her to further ornament the space, save for changing the rugs or cur-

141

tains as the season warranted.

Across the room, seated at one of the larger tables in a well-lit alcove, 7 sorted through stacks of books and old scrolls, seeming unconcerned by Avarice's impromptu additions to the room.

"Wards against the undead and wandering spirits," Avarice explained. "Can't be too careful."

"The air dances, filled with stars that sing," Kyr exclaimed in Kahdess. "Is my head floating?" The stiffening of Avarice's shoulders told Omen all he needed to understand his mother's actions.

"Those are the wards, Kyr," he explained softly. "Because of . . . your language."

Kyr tilted his head to the side, violet eyes perplexed. "Kyr's voice is wrong?"

"No," Omen said instantly, not wanting the boy to misunderstand or think he'd done something wrong. "It's just . . ." *How do I explain the undead to the boy? He has no idea what dangers exist in this world. To him it's all perfect.*

"Your world had no magic in it." Omen waved his hand through the air, indicating the entire room. "The dancing air and singing stars."

Kyr nodded his agreement. "The stars were silent, and there was only the endless wind that screamed with the voices of the burned and broken."

"Here . . . there's a lot of magic," Omen continued. "And sometimes it reacts to our words and deeds. Speaking Kahdess — your language — can awaken the dead, can summon spirits, and that can be very dangerous. That's why you need to learn Merchant's Common. Understand?"

A shriek of outrage interrupted Kyr's hesitant answer, and they spun to see Avarice plucking Tyrin from the long curtains that covered the bank of parlor windows. The little kitten had managed to make it halfway up the fabric.

"But they is climbing curtains!" Tyrin yowled, claws outstretched as he hung in midair, still reaching for the drapes. The little cat struggled in Avarice's grasp and murmured a volley of choice words.

Omen's eyebrows shot up. *Did I hear that right? Is he trying to curse in Sul'eldrine?* As far as Omen knew, there were no actual curse words in the holy tongue. But Tyrin was spitting out a mix of broken — or made-up — words that almost sounded like cursing.

Kyr rushed toward his kitten, hands outstretched, though he stopped himself from grabbing the cat from Avarice's grasp. Omen followed, moving in front of the floor-to-ceiling bay windows, blocking the tiny pull where Tyrin's claw snagged the fabric. *Mother doesn't need to see that right now.*

Avarice ignored Tyrin's outburst. "No!" She stepped toward Tormy and set the kitten down on the sheepskin rug next to the larger cat. "The curtains are Frelzairian brocade, and you are not to rip them. We don't rip curtains in this house."

Tyrin tilted his head to the side and narrowed his amber eyes. By way of agreement or naughtiness, the little cat forcefully kneaded at the rug, his tiny claws hooking long white hairs from the sheepskin.

Avarice's eyes flashed. "You little—"

But before the kitten could say anything else, Kyr dropped to his bony knees on the rug and grabbed the tiny creature, holding him protectively against his chest. The boy's large violet eyes swam with moisture. "Kyr is bad, Tyrin is good. Tyrin is the green. I am sorry. You can crush

Kyr's bones and grind him to dust. I don't mind."

Avarice took a small, involuntary step back, her lips tightening at the boy's words.

"What is he saying?" Tyrin demanded from Kyr's grip, obviously seeing the dismay in Omen's expression and the shock in Avarice's.

"He's trying to take the blame for your transgression!" Avarice's withering glare was filled with accusation, and Tyrin's ears flattened.

"I is not transgressingnate!" Tyrin insisted. "I is not naughtinessness on account of the fact that I is a kitten and kittens is not naughtinessness. And my Kyr is not naughtinessness neither!"

Omen knelt down on the rug beside Kyr. "It's all right, Kyr. No one is going to crush any bones."

"I is teaching Kyr *lunch*, and *dinner*, and *water* already." Tormy gave the floor a firm whack with his tail as he curled toward the boy. "I is not teaching him transgressionessness. That is being a biggestest word I is not knowing."

"Lunch," Kyr said with a quaking voice.

"Do you know the word discipline!"Avarice snapped at the two cats. Her gaze locked on the pathetic form of Kyr, skeletal and frail, holding the orange kitten in his painfully thin hands. She took in a deep breath, forcefully controlling her temper. She pointed a stiff finger at the costly drapes. "No curtains!" She pointed at the little cat. "Tyrin." Then she pointed at the curtains again. "No curtains."

"No curtains?" Kyr whispered, his accent thick and awkward.

Omen patted Kyr's bony shoulder and then snaked an arm around Tormy. "No curtains."

"Kyr is being so smartinessness," Tormy sang out.

144

Tyrin's whiskers flared, his amber eyes narrowing. "Why is you having climbing curtains if they is not for climbing?"

Avarice folded her hands, visibly stopping herself from reaching for the cat. "They are not—"

"Who wants to play Monsla?" 7 threw out as he casually unrolled the leather game board. He'd pushed aside the pile of books and scrolls he'd been sifting through. "I can't find anything about the curse." He tapped the long wooden table. "I think we can all use a little distraction."

The rising tension in the room viscerally deescalated as Omen's mother turned a smiling face to 7. "That sounds lovely, my dearest," she said and walked away from the feline standoff. She joined 7 at the table.

Omen was thankful to his father for bridging the tense moment. He hated to see his mother clashing with the cats and Kyr. He imagined there would be further domestic battles in their future. *Mother is very particular about how she likes things. Tormy's never been a problem, but that little Tyrin is going to be a handful.*

"Come on," Omen urged Kyr to join them at the table. "It's a game, you'll like it." He said the word *game* several times in Merchant's Common for the boy to repeat.

Avarice picked up a game piece and twisted it around in her hand. "It has been a while since we've played as a family." Omen knew his mother had always preferred Monsla to Battlefield, perhaps because the Lydonian game required deeper strategy, perhaps because it was faster moving, but mostly — he thought — because it could be played by four. His mother could be harsh and difficult, but he knew she loved her family above anything else. Playing a game was a good excuse to spend time together.

"I is the bestest at games!" Tyrin proclaimed, the curtains forgotten as he eyed the game board. Kyr placed him carefully on the table.

"Tyrin is the bestest," Tormy agreed. "On account of the fact that he is very smartinessness." The larger cat hopped toward them, planting himself beside Kyr, and placing his chin on the tabletop, eyes darkening with excitement as he stared at the shiny game pieces.

"I'll go get Lily," Omen offered.

"Water!" Kyr proclaimed in wide-eyed concern before Omen could go in search of his sister.

"Are you thirsty?" Omen looked around the room for a decanter of fresh water.

"I can send for tea." Avarice rose to summon a servant.

"The white sails fly free in the wind, and the ship turns away upon the water," Kyr explained, looking anxiously up at Omen.

Omen paused. "What?"

"The cage is cold and blistering," he continued. "It eats the singing stars and the night burns with anger."

Both Avarice and 7 were looking from Omen to Kyr in confusion. Omen shrugged helplessly. "This is new," he told his parents. "I have no idea what he's talking about."

"Lunch! Lunch!" Kyr exclaimed in Merchant's Common.

"It is not being lunchtime yet, Kyr." Tormy's nose twitched in the direction of the kitchens. "But I is feeling a mite peckish."

"Dinner!" Kyr pulled on Omen's hand.

Omen placed a hand on the boy's shoulder. "We just had dinner, Kyr."

Kyr looked genuinely upset now, dismayed as he seemed to realize they did not understand him. "The ropes are unbound — the ones who tend them, dead upon the deck. Lily opened the cage and freed the night. And the battle wages upon the waves."

7 put down the Monsla pieces he had been setting up. "What about Lily?"

Kyr shook his head. "Water!"

7 moved around the table and turned Kyr toward him. Tyrin leaped from the table to Kyr's shoulder, rubbing his head against the boy's neck. The kitten purred loudly as if trying to calm the boy down.

"His thoughts are all jumbled," 7 murmured.

"Lily!" the boy insisted. "Water!"

"Why does he keep saying Lilyth's name?" Avarice asked. Omen could hear the concern in her voice. He knew the phrases the boy had spoken in Kahdess had upset her.

She puts far more weight to his words because of the language.

"I don't know." 7's eyes narrowed. "He's upset about something. But there are so many images flashing through his mind it's a wonder he can form words at all. His thoughts are going in a thousand different directions. There's something about Lily and the ocean."

"Lilyth is upstairs in her room," Avarice insisted. "She's not outside at—" She broke off, her face filling with anxiety. "I'm going to check on her." Without another word, she rushed from the room.

"Can you help Kyr?" Omen asked his father. *I have no idea how sane he really is. What if his mind is too damaged to ever live a normal life?*

7 gave him a pointed stare. "I did tell you this wasn't going to be easy. After all the things that have happened to this child, we can't begin to predict what his future holds."

147

Omen swallowed heavily. "I know, but we can teach him things, right?"

"Kyr is not jumblinessness!" Tyrin insisted from his perch on Kyr's shoulder. "He is losteded and now he is foundeded. We is being brilliantnessness together. We is living with you and Tormy and we is being heroes."

"We is being heroes, Omy!" Tormy agreed happily. "Kyr is being happy. Member, member dinner, Omy? Kyr is liking dinner!"

Omen patted Tormy's head, scratching one of his fuzzy ears as he smiled gratefully at the cats. *If they think it will be all right, then it will be!*

"7!" They all heard the edge in Avarice's voice as she shouted from upstairs.

7 ran for the door immediately. Omen followed, Kyr and the two cats in tow.

They arrived in Lily's suite. Avarice was standing beside a chair, holding the dress Lily had worn to dinner. One of the maids was fretfully wringing her hands beside the hearth where a warm fire sputtered. The room was dimly lit by candles.

"Lilyth is gone!" Avarice spun as they entered. "Where is my girl?"

Omen hadn't seen a look of such agony on his mother's face since Lily had been lost in the forest several months ago. *She worries like that about all of us. It must be hard. Being a mom.*

"Begging your pardon, my lord." The maid curtsied quickly to 7. "As I was telling my lady, I came up to light the fire for Miss Lilyth, and she wasn't here. So I went searching for her. I even checked the yard and the stables. I can't find her." The young girl sounded terribly distressed.

148

7's eyes unfocused, and he turned quickly in a full circle. Omen knew he was using his mind to scan the entirety of the house, searching for some sign of the girl.

Tormy pushed his way past them both and plunged his head under Lilyth's bed as if seeking her there.

Omen's eyes fell on Lily's desk. There lay a book, *The Adventurer's Guide to Everything Adventurous,* and a half-finished letter. He snatched up the parchment, his stomach dropping as he looked at the words upon the page.

"Over here," Omen called out.

"Dear Father," he read the letter out loud. "I want a cat of my very own. I believe they give them out in Hex at the Night Games. Since it is very unfair that Omen has two cats, and I have none, I think it only right that you go to Hex to get a cat for me. I think I should have a cat of my very own because—"

He looked up from the page, meeting his mother's silver gaze. "She didn't finish her letter. But I think I know where she went."

Avarice looked at him, eyes narrowed. "You don't think . . ."

"Hex." He cleared his throat. "Lilyth went to Hex."

Chapter 12: Cages

The thugs moved swiftly through the streets, never once bothering to glance back to see if they were being followed. After a few blocks, Lilyth realized that they were heading directly toward the port, which confirmed in her mind that this was a kidnapping instead of an attempted murder. *If they want Templar on a boat, they mean to take him somewhere specific, not kill him.*

Upon reaching the docks, the band of kidnappers headed unerringly toward a large Kharakhian frigate. *Not surprised.* Though the vessel looked like a merchant ship, Lilyth knew enough about Kharakhians to guess it was crewed with seasoned fighters who would be well-armed and ready for combat.

She could see that the ship's lines were already unfastened, and the men waiting onboard were quick to usher the men carrying Templar up the gangplank and onto the main deck. They disappeared down into the hold of the ship immediately, and Lilyth saw the crew scrambling to pull away from the deep water slip. *If the ship gets out of the port with him, I'll never find him!*

Her feet pounded along the dock as she ran. She hoped that no one would notice her, and to her relief no one on deck looked back once the ship was unmoored and moving away from the stone pylon.

Heart in her throat, she reached the end of the dock and leaped toward one of the many large ropes hanging from the side of the ship. She caught hold of it with one hand and grasped a side-draped net with the other. For a moment she hung there, dangling over the dark waters of the inlet in silence as the vessel pulled away from the dock and headed out to sea. She stared back at the disappearing lights of the city as she clung to the side of the ship. *That may have been foolish.* She swallowed hard. *But it's done now.*

The ship glided through the black waters toward the tall, giant-built stone obelisks that lined the exit to the open sea. Enormous fires burned atop the pillars at the mouth of the deep water bay, and Lilyth focused on them as the ship rose and fell with each swell, her body paralyzed, her mind stunned. *Wished I'd actually learned that water-breathing spell I teased Omen about.*

Icy ocean spray hit her in the face, and a shiver of naked fear raced through her limbs. For an incredible second, she heard herself thinking, *Fingers, let go.* She'd heard that awful voice in her head before — sneaky, alluring, soul-crushing. "No!" She gripped the rope tighter, letting herself really experience the pain in her joints and wrists.

I can't just stay here. And I can't just cling to the side of this ship and do nothing! Her mother was always telling her that she acted without thinking. *So, think, Lilyth. Prove her wrong.*

As the ship sailed out to the open waters, the rising and falling of the hull became rougher. The fires of the watchtowers disappeared, and only the crescent moon overhead offered any light at all. The water beneath Lilyth's precarious hold on the side of the ship was utterly black, and her fingers and toes were growing numb with cold.

All right. . . think . . . I can't hang here the entire journey. This isn't like mountain climbing. My fingers are freezing. My toes are numb. And if the ship is going all the way to Kharakhan, we'll be at sea for weeks, maybe months!

Panic welled up inside her again, but she fiercely tamped it down. *I can't do anything by myself — but maybe Templar can. I have to free him . . . that's it! If I free Templar, he can help me. He'll know what to do!*

Focused on her goal and free of the oppressive whispers, Lilyth began climbing upward using the ropes and the nets that lined the side of the ship to navigate the outer hull. Above her she could see the tall stern of the ship and imagined the main cabins situated there. As she continued climbing, she noticed portholes further up. *If I could get inside through one of those, I might be able to find Templar.*

She reached the row of portholes after several minutes. Her muscles ached, but she put the pain out of her mind and cautiously pulled herself up to peer inside.

Several rough-looking men sat around a table just below her. She ducked to the side swiftly, biting back a frightened gasp and hoping they hadn't seen her. Golden lantern light shone through the thick glass. *They're eating dinner — no way I'm getting in there!*

Concentrating to secure her grasp, she moved down a bit further, hand-over-hand, continuing to make her way along the back of the ship toward the starboard side. There was a wooden runner just below her that she could rest her toes on, helping support her weight. But as she shimmied around the side, her hands and arms ached more than she'd ever remembered, even when they'd scaled Mount Elden in Lydon. *I'm starting to think Dad psionically helped me.* She knew enough psionic manipulation to levitate a little, but had neither the focus nor the time to experiment. *Should have thought this through.* As she rounded the back end of the ship, she spied a wooden hatch lower down on the hull.

She had been making her way around the hull by grabbing onto the ropes and nets running along the upper frame of the ship, easily accessible to the outer railing. But the hatch was too far below her. The rope she was currently holding did not dangle down far enough to get to the lower deck. *Wait! I have a rope!* She almost laughed out loud. *That book was right!*

Repositioning her feet on the wooden rim supporting her weight, she looped her left arm through the ship's rope. Lilyth reached toward her belt clip with her right hand and grabbed the length of silk rope. She pulled it free and tied it off to a metal fastening holding a fishing net. *I should have paid more attention when Liethan Corsair tried to teach me about ropes and knots!*

The Corsair family, one of her mother's closest allies, were all sailors and knew everything there was to know about ships and water. But as Lilyth had never aspired to being a sailor, she had mostly ignored their various attempts to engage her interest in all things nautical.

She was, however, quite clever and well-practiced in a number of crafts. She sewed and knitted extremely well, and knot-tying was applicable in both endeavors. While she doubted her knot was anything typically found on a ship, she was fairly certain it would not come loose.

Once her rope was firmly attached, she tied several larger knots along the length of the rope, knowing that she'd need something to grip when she lowered herself down. She felt strong still, but knew she would grow tired if she had to use her arms alone to climb downward. So far her journey around the back end of the ship had been easy enough with the wooden rim beneath her feet. But there were no rims further down. *I can grip the knots with my feet.*

153

Satisfied she'd be safe enough, Lilyth grabbed hold of her rope with both hands and carefully began lowering herself down. Gripping tightly with her boots, she moved from knot to knot downward trying to ignore the violent shivers starting to wrack her frame. *Glad I put on the gauntlets.* Without them, she knew her hands would have been raw.

Reaching the hatch opening, she picked at it with her fingers. It was a fairly tight seal, but she suspected it was only held in place by a simple wooden toggle that could be twisted from the inside. She drew her dagger after realizing it was not going to come open easily, and she carefully slid the blade between the bottom seam, moving it along the middle of the hatch until she found the toggle. Some careful force caused the toggle to move, twisting to the side until the hatch swung open. She sheathed her dagger and cautiously peered through the opening.

The room was dark and — judging by the smells — had to be the ship's galley. Lily was starting to feel hungry, but by the look of this kitchen, she would be hard-pressed to eat anything stored on its filthy counters or prepared in its crusty pots.

The hatch itself seemed to be a garbage hatch on the side of the galley, or a means to get some fresh air into the lower deck. Since the evening meal was done, the room stood empty.

An adult likely could not have squeezed through the hatch, but Lilyth, at only ten years old, was small and slender, and able to slip through the opening easily. She scrambled across the wooden counter, but paused before climbing down.

Orienting herself, she tried to recall the basic layout of seagoing vessels. She had spent many a summer afternoon playing hide-and-seek on one or another visiting Corsair ship with her friends Aurora and Aurelius Corsair.

This area had two doorways — one that was sealed with a heavy wooden door and another dark opening that led to the main storage compartments lower down. *That's probably the safest place to hide.*

Lily moved silently into the cargo hold, finding it filled with wooden crates and barrels. The only illumination was the faint gleam of moonlight through the open hatch of the galley behind her — barely enough to save her from missteps in the gloomy darkness. But as her eyes adjusted, she was surprised to note the many distinctive shades of grey coming into sharp focus. She gave it no further thought but hurried quietly toward the tower of crates. *If I climb on top of the crates, I should be able to crawl to the other side of the hold.*

She cautiously scaled several crates until she was able to wedge herself into the small space between the wooden lids and the overhead. She began crawling the length silently, realizing with some revulsion that she wasn't the only one using the crawl-way. Rats scurried among the crates in the darkness. Lilyth shuddered, worried that she was going to set her hand down on one. More than once, she thought she saw beady eyes gleaming in the shadows. *This is why I need a cat!*

The main hold was broken up into sections, the frame of the ship acting as partial walls between each area. She was able to move from one to another simply by crawling along the top of the crates through the various openings. *This ship certainly has a lot of supplies. I suppose it makes sense that they would load up with material before leaving the port. No point in making a trip with an empty ship. No profit in it. But why do they want Templar?*

As she crawled toward the deepest area of the ship, she realized that there was a section up ahead that was walled off from the rest of the hold. This area was divided into smaller storage rooms. But like the rest of the hold, it had a small opening near the top of the dividing wall. Light shone through this opening, and after the pitch blackness of the hold, it seemed bright and welcoming.

She crept silently toward the opening and peered down into the room below her. The small cabin was filled with more crates and packages. In the center of the room were two unusual metal cages.

Templar was inside one of them.

The cages themselves were made of a glowing red metal. It wasn't copper — far too red for that, but not dissimilar. The metal itself gave off an inner light so that even without the lantern hanging near the door Lilyth suspected the room would have been illuminated. *Wonder if the metal is hot.*

Templar hunched in the center of the cage, crouched to keep his head from brushing the top of the metal frame. Both cages were narrow, leaving very little room to move around — certainly not enough for a man to lay down, though she supposed he could sit. The prince, however, was holding himself quite still.

His sword belt was gone, as were his gauntlets and the leather frock coat he'd been wearing over his outer tunic. Even the daggers from his boots were missing. His bare hands were stripped of all his rings, and the gemstones were gone from his ears. There was blood on his hands and a smear of blood across one of his cheeks. *I can't tell if he's badly injured.*

156

He stood completely still, his body tense, and for the first time since she'd known him, those unearthly yellow eyes of his were burning with glowing light.

I've never seen them do that before. She found herself shuddering. She'd half convinced herself that the strange color was just an anomaly. She couldn't ignore the glow, however. *Mother says Night Dwellers have the fire of chaos inside them — that's what you see in their eyes.*

Templar looked angry. She'd never actually seen him angry before, and she found the image disturbing. Templar was always quick with a smile or laugh. But now there was something truly frightening in his eyes, a hardness in his expression that made her wonder if she'd been blind to his true nature. She had heard all the stories about his dark heritage, but he'd always seemed like a good guy to her. *A lout to be sure! All of Omen's friends are annoying goons. But he's always been fun.* Now, however, she could see something more. *He's dangerous. Maybe he should be in a cage.* She dismissed the fleeting thought, feeling a moment of shame for having allowed it. *He's Omen's friend.*

Three of the men who had captured Templar were standing next to the cage, watching him. While the two on the side looked somewhat wary, the one in the center — the captain Lilyth suspected — was smiling smugly.

"I wouldn't try that again," the captain told Templar, and Lilyth wondered what it was he'd tried. "These cages are made from Night steel. I knew it would stop your magic from working, but I hadn't believed the rest of the stories. It's true — the stuff burns Night Dwellers. Guess the stories about you are true as well. Night Dweller!" The captain laughed hard — and the two men with him joined in, though they looked more nervous than amused.

157

Night steel! Templar won't be able to get out of there. Lilyth had heard of Night steel. It was a metal that prevented or suppressed all magic — which in a world teeming with magic made it an extraordinary weapon. *It's rare. Really rare. How would a bunch of scummy kidnappers get any?* The stories also said that while it suppressed everyone's magic, it was even worse for Night Dwellers. Even touching it would burn anyone with Nightblood, no matter how small the trace. She could see now that Templar's hands were not just bloody — they were burnt. That he wasn't crying out in agony impressed her.

"You won't be going anywhere for the duration of this trip," the captain said to Templar. He was speaking Kharakhian, his accent marking him as native born.

Lilyth tried to calculate how long it would take to get to Kharakhan — weeks she supposed. *Do they truly mean to keep Templar in that small cage for the entire trip? He can't even lean against the bars without getting burned. How do they expect him to sleep?*

"What do you want with me?" Templar demanded, his voice like ice. Like the captain, he spoke in Kharakhian — though his polished accent made the words sound strange to Lilyth. Despite understanding the dire situation he was in, Lilyth could see that he was neither frightened nor worried — just incredibly angry.

The captain waved his question away with one hand. "That's none of your business," he said dismissively.

Templar's gaze shifted briefly toward the second empty cage. "You didn't expect me to be alone."

The captain scowled at him, his brow furrowing. "I said it was none of your business, Nightspawn!"

"The other cage was for Omen Daenoth, wasn't it?"

Templar pressed.

Lilyth suppressed a gasp.

"You expected *both* of us to be in that alley," Templar continued. "I always take that shortcut to the Glass Walk. Which means this has something to do with the Night Games."

The two men standing next to the captain looked alarmed, both taking a step back and shaking their heads in denial. "You said he wouldn't be able to use his powers inside that cage!" one of them exclaimed, his voice tinged with hysteria. His hands moved to the sword at his side. "How does he know?"

The captain struck the man hard in the shoulder and hissed, "He can't use his powers! He's just making guesses, idiot. Now shut your hole!"

Templar's eyes narrowed. "Two cages of Night steel." His words curled around his tongue like a scorpion curling around a stone. "They don't come cheap — and you can't simply purchase them in a market. They had to come from someone very powerful — either someone who wants to keep us from playing the games or someone who wants us to play for them."

The captain slammed his hands against the bars of Templar's cage. "I told you! It's none of your business!"

"A human or an elf would have simply dealt with us directly." Templar ignored the captain's warning. His eyes flashed again with yellow fire, and Lilyth realized that despite the dire situation, he was enjoying the captain's distress. "And it's unlikely a human or an elvin lord would have access to Night steel. Which means you most likely got it from a Night Dweller. Do your men know you're making deals with Night Dwellers?"

The two frightened men beside the captain made the warding sign against evil while the captain leaned forward, sneering at Templar. "I didn't make a deal with anyone!" he snapped. "This is a simple transaction — *you* for a great deal of *money.* That's all anyone needs to know."

Templar let out the laughter he'd been holding in, seeming unable to help himself.

The captain's face twisted with anger.

"Let me clarify something for you." Templar chuckled. "Night Dwellers don't make simple transactions. If they gave you a cage to keep me in, it means they want me alive. Which means sooner or later, they will let me out of this cage — at which point I'll come after you. And that will be a really bad day for you."

"I'll be long gone by the time they let you out!" the captain insisted, though to Lilyth it looked as if he were somewhat less certain of himself.

"With this ship?" Templar scoffed. "Where will you go? I'm the crown prince of Terizkand — my father has alliances with kingdoms all over the world. What port will you ever be able to enter freely? Let me go now, and I might be inclined to forget all of this."

To Lilyth it looked as if the two men with the captain were hoping he would take Templar's offer — certainly, the prince sounded reasonable. But the captain shook his head vehemently. "We won't need the ship after this — we'll have enough money to retire anywhere we want."

"And will all your men be getting an even split of the profits?" Templar asked, his tone smooth.

Lilyth saw the furtive looks the two men were throwing each other. *They don't like this — but they're afraid to go against their captain. It's Templar they should be afraid of.*

160

The captain seemed to come to a similar conclusion, and he motioned the men away. "We're done talking! Enjoy your cage!" He spun on his heels and headed for the door. His two men followed swiftly after him, both throwing nervous looks back at the cage.

Templar chuckled softly, his eyes flashing.

Once they're were gone, Templar winced, showing he was not as immune to the pain as he'd pretended. He stared down at his burnt palms. Lilyth could see that they were blistered and bleeding. She winced in sympathy.

Templar's brow wrinkled in concentration, and Lilyth suspected he was attempting to heal himself. But whatever he was doing had no effect. He cursed under his breath.

Lilyth wiggled forward through the small crawlspace above the rafters.

Templar's sharp gaze moved upward directly toward her hiding place.

"It's me. Lilyth," she whispered, swinging down from the exposed beams and dropping silently into the room.

Templar blinked at her in dumbfounded disbelief. "Lily!" he hissed, taking care to keep his voice down. "What are you doing here? Get out of here!"

She glared at him. *Lily* was what her family called her, and ever since Templar had first heard it he'd taken great delight in using it just to annoy her. But she supposed getting in a fight over that right now wouldn't be particularly helpful. "I followed you, obviously."

He blinked. "Why?"

"I wanted a cat." *If he was able to figure out the captain's plan so easily, surely he could have figured that much out as well.*

"And you think I carry them around in my pockets?" he

demanded.

"You know where they come from," she told him. "I just wanted to get one of my own."

He tilted his head up as if intently studying the ceiling. "Look, I don't know where the cats come from — according to Tormy, they come from the Cat Lands. I have no idea where that is."

"They come from the Night Games," Lilyth insisted. "That's where you picked out Tormy."

Templar reached for the cage bars, only to stop himself before he actually made contact. "Tormy wandered into the Night Games by accident and got shoved into a box because apparently the Night Dwellers that run the game don't like creatures who speak Sul'eldrine. There aren't any other cats there. Your parents are going to kill me!"

"Likely story." Not at all certain she believed him about Tormy and the Night Games, Lilyth frowned. "I'd rather think the people who kidnapped you are the bigger concern right now. Though you're right — I should have been back home hours ago." Her stomach churned with anxiety.

She took a step closer to the glowing cage, eyeing the door. There was a large lock holding it firmly shut. "Is this really Night steel?" She reached out and touched the metal with the tip of one finger, jerking her hand back instantly. It didn't burn her — it just felt cold and strangely dead. She licked her dry lips.

"Yes," he admitted. "If these idiots were smart they would have just sold the cages — they're worth a fortune. I don't suppose you have any supplies on you?"

"A dagger and a rope — though I already used the rope. It's outside, but I can go get it."

Templar's eyes narrowed. "I don't think a rope is going

to help. I don't suppose you have any lock picks?"

"Should I?" she asked. The book, *The Adventurer's Guide to Everything Adventurous,* had talked about ropes and campfires and the importance of having good boots. But it had never mentioned anything about lock picks.

"Right, then," he said, more energetic than before. "We'll need to figure out how to get my belongings."

"Where are they?" she asked, looking around the room for his sword belt.

"Probably out there with the guards." He motioned toward the door.

"I'll go get them." She turned to leave.

"Lilyth!" he hissed, stopping her instantly. "Don't you dare go out there! I just told you, there are guards out there."

"I'll knock them out first," she reassured him.

"And just how do you think you're going to do that?" he demanded. "You're ten years old."

"Psionically," she replied. "Obviously."

He briefly squeezed his eyes shut, his fist closing over his wounded palms. "Lily, the guards out there were tasked with guarding a Night Dweller. Along with being excellent fighters, they most likely have magical and psionic defenses. If you try to psionically attack them, they'll fry your mind."

"Don't be silly," she insisted. "They can't do anything to me." She turned toward the door again.

"Lily!" he called again, a whispered hiss but more insistent than before. He sounded panicked. "You're not your brother! You're not a demigod. You're human. You won't heal the way he does. Get back here!"

Lilyth took in a measured breath and smiled. "You

163

know, for his supposed best friend, you really don't know much about Omen, do you? It isn't his *god blood* that makes him extraordinary." And with that she pried open the door, making a shushing motion with her hands as he started to protest again. She didn't want to be overheard sneaking from the room.

Chapter 13: Nightblood

Templar's panicked warning notwithstanding, Lilyth peeked down the passageway.

The narrow corridor was dark. It ran along the bulkhead, and Lilyth could hear the sound of waves crashing against the wood. The faint reddish glow of firelight at the far end was the only sign of the guards Templar had mentioned.

Templar fell silent as Lilyth took a few slow, cautious steps. Her eyes had grown so accustomed to the dim light that she could traverse the passageway without any trouble. She crept forward nervously, grateful for the darkness.

The red light proved to be a small lantern. It was set on a wooden crate situated in front of small stairs. Seated on stools on either side of the wooden crate were the two men she'd seen earlier in the captain's company. The men spoke in low tones as they slapped cards down on the crate.

Lilyth paused just out of range of the small sphere of lantern light. *If I move any farther forward, they will catch my movement. If I make the slightest noise, they will hear.* She eyed the other crates in the passageway — she guessed Templar's belongings were in one of them. *So close.* But if she tried to open them, the two men would see her.

She bit her lip. Her father had taught her a variety of psionic skills and certainly her mother had taught her several magical spells over the years, though she was less confident in her spell casting. The problem was, Lily realized with a start, that much of what she'd learned was designed to teach her discipline and basic skills to make her stronger, but nothing for combat. *They haven't taught me anything*

165

practical.

She knew she was very good at lifting things, and while she could not yet manage to move great weights like her father or brother could, she could manipulate multiple objects simultaneously.

Lifting is just like applying pressure to something from beneath, she reasoned. Which meant that in theory she could use the same principle to apply pressure to the veins in the necks of the two men, cutting off the blood flow to their brains and rendering them unconscious.

She wasn't certain she could hit such a small area without being able to see both targets clearly, but moving closer was not an option.

Something else . . . A suggestion then. But Templar had been right when he'd pointed out that the two men guarding him were likely to have psionics of their own and would be able to sense her intrusion. She'd have to be stronger than they were — stronger than both of them combined even. Her suggestion would be met with resistance, and she would have to overcome it through sheer will alone.

Nothing for it, she decided with grim determination. *Just start subtly, don't let them sense it until it is too late.*

She focused on the required pattern. While magic could be learned from a book, the psionic patterns could only be taught by another psionicist, transferred directly from mind to mind. Everything she knew had come from her father, and the patterns he'd shown her were clear and vibrant. But it had been up to her to internalize them, find a personal mnemonic device that would recall them with perfect clarity.

She knew that for her brother, all patterns, whether magical or psionic, translated into music. Most patterns were like that — translating into music or drumbeats or colors or even words.

Lilyth's patterns were all bound to a sense of movement — an abstraction she'd learned from her mother. Her mother internalized magical patterns into kinesthetic movement. For Lilyth it was nearly the same; she only had to imagine the motions, and the sense of movement would vibrate through her limbs like the rush of wind through the trees or blood through her veins.

The Loiritic Patterns for suggestion, she reminded herself. She'd learned all five of them, and decided on the strongest in the series. This pattern took the form of swirling wind and fluttering clothing, and she pictured the motions in her head, recalling the movements within her muscles. Instantly the pattern formed in her mind, clear and bright and pulsing with power.

If you get caught . . . She pushed away the wicked voice.

As the power rose within her, she reached out slowly, cautiously, keeping tight control of the energy, containing the movement in small swirls within her mind. She pushed forward. Neither man was actively shielding from attack, but she sensed the outer edges of their defenses. Like all psionicists, they had learned to maintain passive shields. The moment they felt her touch, the shields would flare to life. She had to be quick — before they could raise an alarm.

You're just a little girl. You're all alone. She clamped her teeth together and shut out the bad thoughts.

Sleep! she commanded, pushing forward with a surge of strength, the pattern in her mind growing with rising swirls of motion.

The man on the left hardly even noticed her presence,

his shield falling around him as the pressure of her mind pushed into his. But the man on the right fought back, his shield expanding like a smothering wall of darkness, holding back the force of her mind. Lilyth knew she could not hesitate even a second. She let loose the full force of her power.

Her pattern exploded into a rush of motion, torrential winds swirling and howling through the whorls and corridors in her mind. She felt the force all the way down to her bones.

Both men dropped like stones, the cards falling from their hands, their limbs growing boneless as they toppled over and slumped to the ground fast asleep. One of them bumped against the crate as he fell, nearly knocking the lantern over.

Lilyth altered her pattern and caught the lantern with her power, setting it back in place.

Then it was over — the two men deeply asleep, no sound from above beyond the creak of wood and the crash of water against the hull as the ship moved further out to sea.

Letting out a sigh of relief, Lilyth crept forward and turned her attention to the crates along the wall. There were bottles of wine in the first crate, and several hard wheels of cheese in the second. But the third crate, nearest the two sleeping men, held Templar's belongings — his coat, the metal studded leather bracers and the gauntlets he typically wore, a small cloth bag containing various pieces of jewelry, and his sword belt.

Clipped to the belt were his sheaths containing the strange white blades made of giant bone, one a full-length sword, the other more of a long dagger. She lifted the belt from the crate, finding that his weapons were far lighter than she'd expected.

She gathered all and, after throwing a wary look back at the two sleeping men, hurried down the dark passageway toward Templar's cage.

The look of relief on Templar's face made her smirk. *He was worried.*

"What happened?" he demanded.

"I knocked them out." She held up his belongings. "Here are your things. Now what?"

He paused as if uncertain whether or not to believe her, but his gaze quickly locked on the items she held in her hands. He reached toward the bars of his cage, but flinched back before accidentally touching the metal. "Give me the gauntlets, and there should also be a small leather bag in the pocket of my coat."

Lilyth set Templar's things down, then grabbed his gauntlets and pushed them through the bars of the cage. He pulled both on quickly. She winced at the thought of Templar dragging the leather over the blisters covering his hands. Averting her eyes, she dug inside the inner lining of his coat and found the small leather bag. She pushed that through to him as well.

He pried open the small bag and pinched two thin pieces of metal between his fingers.

Lock picks, she guessed.

Templar cautiously reached between the bars of his cage and fitted the two pieces of metal into the lock on the small door. Despite the gauntlets, he flinched with pain.

"Is it burning you?" she asked, concerned.

His lips thinned, a muscle in his jaw twitching as he ground his teeth. "No — not through the leather — but I can still feel it — like some hungry void eating my magic. It's nasty stuff even if you're not Nightblooded."

She watched in fascination as he twisted the pieces of metal around — going pretty much off feel alone since he couldn't get his face close enough to the bars to see what he was doing. It took several moments, but she heard the distinctive click when the lock sprang open.

Templar immediately shoved open the door. He had to crouch low to exit the cage — the opening designed more for a large dog than for a man. He breathed a deep sigh once free and shook his entire body as if shaking off water. Then he bent down to retrieve his property — pulling on his coat and bracers before strapping his sword belt around his waist.

"You are very useful," she thought she heard him say, but he wasn't looking at her.

"What's that?" she dared to ask.

He didn't repeat the compliment.

Templar retrieved the small pouch containing all his jewelry last. He poured out a number of rings and small studded earrings.

She frowned, wondering why he was so concerned with primping under the circumstances.

"Here, you should wear both of these," he told her and handed over two small rings with chips of amethyst embedded into the precious metal.

She recognized both as the white-gold rings he normally wore on both his pinky fingers.

The adrenaline was slowly leaving her body, and she felt herself starting to shake. She took the rings and watched as Templar peeled off his gauntlets and began slipping the rest of the rings onto his various fingers. When he'd finished, he started fitting the gems into his ears. To her surprise, she noticed he actually had to pierce the flesh of his earlobes to put in the metal studs as the holes had already closed up.

"Why do you want me to wear your rings?" she asked, voice shaking.

"One will keep you warm," he said. "Have you even noticed . . . It's the middle of winter, and we're pretty far out to sea by now. It's bad enough down here, but it will be freezing above deck."

Lilyth touched her face. Her skin was chilled. She looked down at her blue and trembling fingers. "I hadn't—"

"The other ring will make you less noticeable," Templar went on. "Not invisible mind you — just less likely to be noticed in a fight."

Lilyth looked at the rings. "You mean, they're all magical?" she asked, breathless.

He fastened a ruby stud in his left ear. "Of course they're all magical — why else would I wear them?"

"Fashion." She raised one shoulder in a halfhearted shrug, working hard to appear unimpressed both by the magic and the gesture.

He gave her a sardonic smile. "Well, I did have some of them redesigned to look good," he admitted. "But no, they're all magical. Even my signet ring." He held up his right hand to show her the ring he wore on his first finger — it bore his father's crest — the silver lightning bolt of The Redeemer embedded into a black onyx stone.

Why do Nightbloods have a divine symbol for their house? She kept herself from asking. "What does it do?" she asked instead.

"Heats up in the presence of the undead." Templar pulled his gauntlets back on.

"Why would you need something like that?"

"I've had some odd problems lately in certain parts of Terizkand," he replied. "Now, let's get out of here."

"How exactly are we going to do that? We're at sea. We can't swim all the way back." She was a decent swimmer but didn't think she could manage to swim to shore through the winter waves of the Terizkandian ocean.

Templar gave her a pointed stare. "I'm going to have to take over the ship. And it's not going to be pretty."

She understood the logic in what he was saying, but couldn't imagine what he had in mind. "How?"

He drew his swords. In the red light of the glowing Night steel cage the two white blades of bone pulsed with cold fire. "The old-fashioned way," he replied. "The ship is fairly small — and they wouldn't have been able to get a full crew to agree to kidnap a crown prince — especially not me. My family isn't known for their forgiving nature. I'm guessing at best there are maybe twenty people on board the ship. I can't afford to . . ." He broke off.

"I get it." Lilyth's mother had educated her on the realities of the world despite the peaceful life she lived in Melia. "You can't afford to show mercy. What do you want me to do?"

"Stay out of my way," he told her honestly. "The magic I'll be using won't distinguish friend from foe. You stay out of sight, and keep back, understand?"

A part of her wanted to protest — wanted to insist that she could help — but she also understood the seriousness of the situation. She nodded silently and pushed the two rings he'd given her onto her thumbs. While she noticed nothing specific about the one ring, she did feel a wave of warmth wash over her when she slipped on the other. *Not too loose. The fit is probably magical too.*

Templar opened the door heedfully and peered out into the passageway. Then the two of them slipped from the room and down the corridor toward the small lantern and the sleeping guards.

When they reached the two guards, Templar paused to check them both, shooting Lilyth an impressed look.

She felt the swell of magic around her as he waved his hand over them — casting some spell she guessed would ensure they remained asleep no matter what sounds they heard from above. Then Templar and Lilyth headed up the wooden stairs toward the main hold.

There was a door at the top of the staircase, and beyond the doorway Lilyth heard men's voices.

Templar touched her wrist firmly. "You stay here," he whispered. "No matter what. If something goes wrong — you climb back up into that crawl space in the other room. They don't know you're here. You stay hidden all the way to the next port. Then you get off this ship, find a Machelli Guild house and get home."

She was unable to speak around the lump of fear in her throat. He winked at her, a familiar cocky grin taking over his features. "I don't exactly expect anything to go wrong," he promised her. "I'm really good at this sort of thing." She blinked once, biting her lip to stay silent.

"Good kid." Templar stepped out into the passageway and closed the door firmly behind him.

A moment later Lilyth heard shouts coming from the pirates, followed by the clash of swords. The hissing and burning sounds of magical lightning cracked, and blue-white light flared around the edges of the door. Teeth clamped shut, she waited in the darkness, listening to the sounds. *I have my psionics. I have my psionics.*

The fighting continued for some time, but moved swiftly away from her as Templar apparently made his way through the main hold and headed toward the upper deck. He was no longer making any effort to be quiet.

He's drawing them away — getting all of them focused on him, she realized. Several explosions shook the ship, and shouts mixed with screams. She could hear Templar's voice rising above the others, speaking words in the Night Tongue that she didn't understand. While she knew that magic could technically be cast in any language — her mother preferred her native Scaalian — the darker, more violent spells were always cast in the Night Tongue.

Eventually, the sounds drew far enough away from her that Lilyth risked opening the door. She peered into the corridor. The room ahead was silent, but in the dim light of swinging lanterns she saw dark shapes on the floor. They were not moving. She cautiously crept past them, keeping her eyes focused forward.

What if Templar doesn't come back for you? What if he dies? The vile voice of doubt returned, tearing at her resolve.

She moved ahead. The outer passageway was also still. She heard the sounds of battle moving toward the top deck. Anyone below in the hold was either dead or had fled upward to continue fighting. She passed several more shapes — all still. In the dim light, she could see the gleaming stains on the wood. She swallowed hard.

You're alone.

The ship shook and shuddered as another explosion rocked it — the motion sent her slamming into the wall. She caught herself, but her boot struck something soft. Her hands flew to her mouth to stifle a gasp as she realized that she'd just stepped on the outstretched hand of a dead man.

You're lost.

Scrambling up, she forced her eyes away from the man. *I've never seen . . .* She stepped over him gingerly and headed toward the clash of swords, which was growing louder.

I want my mom and dad, she thought and braced herself.

The door to the deck had been blown open — large scorch marks covering the wooden beams of the frame as if Templar had just blasted them open with the force of magic. Ducking her head around the frame, she risked a peek outside.

A growing bank of fog hid the moonlight, leaving only swinging lanterns to illuminate the deck in the darkness. The ship rose and fell upon the waves. *The ocean doesn't care about us. Why would it?*

Cold air struck her face, but the warmth coming from the ring Templar had given her seemed to push the bite of frost away, surrounding her in a cocoon of heated air. Tendrils of hair escaped her braid in the wind, and she pushed them back from her face as she studied the scene before her.

Templar was in the center of the deck, bone blades in either hand as he spun and turned in a swift dance of sharp edges against the group of men attacking him. Around him swirled burning ropes of bluish lightning that lashed out like whips or striking snakes, scorching everything they touched. The magical lightning wrapped around the limbs and throats of the men attacking, searing their flesh as they tried to deflect the swift strikes of bone blades.

Through it all, Templar fought like a creature possessed,

black hair whipping about his pale face, lips pulled back in a snarl. His eyes burned with yellow fire.

From her hidden vantage point, Lilyth saw more than one man back away and leap over the side of the ship — preferring to risk the danger of the winter waves rather than face the Night Dweller their captain had unleashed upon them.

Lilyth flinched with every swipe of Templar's sword. Her heart pounded in her chest as she understood perhaps for the first time what it meant that Templar, like her brother, was not truly human. *I'm going to be that strong, someday,* she swore to herself. One day she would be able to stand alongside Templar and hold her own.

The fight was over far quicker than she expected. The captain fell to Templar's blades and with his demise, the remaining men all leaped overboard, disappearing into the darkness of the water.

Dead littered the deck at Templar's feet. No one remained. *The rest all jumped instead of surrendering! Why take that risk?* While she guessed that sailors would likely be strong swimmers, she knew the chances they'd make it to shore in the winter seas were slim.

She paused, waiting for the fire to fade from Templar's eyes as he whipped his head from side to side looking for more opponents. Slowly he lowered his blades, the bluish lightning flickering around him fading as well. She could see blood soaking his clothing and hoped none of it was his. She thought about the blisters on his hands. *Wielding those swords must have hurt.*

He turned his gaze toward her. The fire faded to the familiar yellow gleam. "Thought I told you to stay put," he croaked, his voice hoarse from shouting. But at least his words were spoken in Merchant's Common.

"I was hidden," she insisted, cautiously stepping up onto the deck. She glanced warily at the bodies strewn about. "Now what?"

"You know how to sail a ship?" he asked.

She shook her head emphatically. *Not safe. It's all your fault. You're going to die.* She pushed down the swell of fear. *I will not cry. So stop it.* The troublesome thoughts retreated, and she tried to breathe evenly.

Templar flicked the blood off his blades and reached down to grab a discarded cloak from the deck to clean them. "Me neither," he admitted. "We're going to have to get those two men you knocked out to do it for us."

"Why didn't anyone surrender?" she asked. "Why did they all jump?"

"Better chance of survival." Templar's cadence was matter-of-fact, but the rasp in his voice gave him away.

He tries to be cold-hearted, but I think he's just like Omen.

"Terizkand has been in a state of perpetual war for years," he went on quickly. "We're still fighting the giants in the north. Prisons are a luxury of a stable, civilized society — and regardless, treason against the royal family is punishable by death. They're better off taking their chances in the sea."

He sheathed his two blades, before checking the bodies of the men on the deck — as if to assure himself they were all dead.

"This is how it is, Lilyth," he said hoarsely. "I am sorry you had to see this. Your parents—"

"Are you wounded?" she cut him off, eyeing the blood on his clothing.

"No," he assured her. "Not my blood — and they didn't have any magical weapons and only one spellcaster in the group. The captain wasn't very bright I'm afraid — didn't think it through."

"And they were fools for following him," Lilyth said in a tone she'd heard from her mother.

He finished his search and then motioned Lilyth to follow him back down into the hold — taking his time to check the rest of the ship, ensuring that there was no one else on board.

When they reached the two men still asleep below deck, he paused before waking them. He removed his left gauntlet and pulled off one of the rings on his hand.

He whispered soft words into the ring. Lilyth felt the rise of power as the ring began to burn brightly between his fingers. Templar pressed the emblem on the ring into the forehead of the first man, and then the second — a burning sigil of red fire remained upon their skin, glowing brightly in the dim light. Both men woke at the same time and stared at Templar with blank expressions, their eyes empty.

Lilyth shuddered, not sure what she was witnessing.

"Up," Templar commanded them both.

Silently they both rose to their feet — or tried to. One of them slumped toward the left as he stood and fell against the wall. The other teetered back and forth as if drunk. The look of consternation on Templar's face worried Lilyth.

"Stand up," Templar commanded again, more firmly.

Again the two men tried to obey. The one slumped against the wall staggered upward, only to fall over sideways as if unable to make his legs work correctly. The other listed forward, hunched as if incapable of holding his body upright. The blank expressions on their faces never

178

changed.

Lilyth felt anxiety rising inside her as she witnessed the strange behavior. She wanted to turn away, but she forced herself to keep looking at the sailors. *Is this supposed to happen? Did his spell do something bad to them?*

"What was that spell?" she asked, fearful.

"Just a basic compulsion spell," Templar said, his brows furrowed as he studied the two men. He reached out and pushed at the one man still standing — he toppled over easily. Templar crouched down again, lifting the chin of the other man. He peered intently into his eyes as if trying to read what had gone wrong with his spell. A look of comprehension crossed his face for an instant, followed by a grimace. Then all emotion vanished from his expression.

Templar waved his hand over the two men once more. The swelling crackle of magic filled the narrow passageway, and the men closed their eyes, falling swiftly back to sleep. Templar stood.

"Well, looks like we're sailing the ship ourselves. Come on." He headed decisively up toward the deck.

Ask . . . No . . . Ask.

Lilyth trailed behind him, looking over her shoulder. "Why didn't your spell work?" she asked, afraid to hear the answer.

Templar waved his hand dismissively. "Oh, it's nothing to worry about," he assured her. "Sometimes spells just don't work for a variety of reasons. Most likely the Night steel is still affecting my magic." He sounded remarkably unconcerned.

His sleeping spells worked. Lilyth gnawed her lip uncertainly. *His lightning worked just fine.* And she was fairly certain that Night steel didn't affect magic without physical

179

contact or at the very least close proximity. She looked back at the men again.

"Are you sure . . ." The terrible thought manifested fully. She nearly sank to her knees. She thought back to the strange manner in which the men had moved — as if drunk, or as if their limbs no longer worked properly. *Or as if their minds no longer functioned!*

A shiver cut through her. Her knees began trembling. "I did that!" she gasped.

Templar stopped upon the stairs. He muttered a curse under his breath, caught her arm, and tugged her up the stairs toward the open air of the deck.

"I did something to their minds, didn't I?" Lilyth demanded. *Dad warned me! He told me not to attack another psionicist's mind — that it was dangerous. That it could lead to. . .* "I damaged their brains, didn't I?" She could hear the hysteria in her own voice, but couldn't seem to stop her words. "My father said it was dangerous; he said not to do it! He said it could cause brain damage. But I thought he meant me! I didn't mean to destroy—"

"Lily!" Templar cut off her words with a hard shake to her arm. He'd reached the door leading back to the deck and pulled her into the fresh air. "It's not your fault!"

Her stomach churned. "But I broke their brains! Are they going to die?"

"Calm down!" Templar insisted firmly. "Listen to me. You didn't break their brains — they're just damaged, and —"

"Can a healer fix them?" She thought about the healers she knew — many were extraordinarily powerful. *Maybe my dad could . . .*

"Maybe." Templar sighed. "I don't know. But it doesn't

matter. They would have killed you if they found you. And in any event, they kidnapped me. If you hadn't knocked them out, I would have killed them myself. And when we get back to Hex, they're going to be executed. Nothing you did caused that — they were responsible for their own actions."

Executed. Tremors wracked through her, but she latched onto a glimmer of hope his words had sparked. "But if they're not in their right minds, you can't execute them — right? Not if they can't even remember what they did!" *Maybe I saved them — that by hurting them I really saved them!* She gazed hopefully up at Templar.

His eyes narrowed briefly, his lips tightened.

He's Omen's friend, he protected me. He'll help them, right?

"Maybe," Templar said after a long, tense moment, "I can give them to my grandfather. Maybe he'll take them to the Temple of The Redeemer and put them into service there. Maybe they don't need to be executed."

Lilyth blinked back the tears that welled in her eyes, and she nodded her head fiercely. *He said maybe.*

"But Lily, regardless what happens to them, you are not to blame. This isn't your fault. Ultimately, my sister will decide their fate. You put them out of your thoughts." Templar's expression was grim but determined.

Don't think about them. Lilyth swallowed the heavy lump in her throat. "But you'll tell your sister about your grandfather, right? And the temple. You'll tell her to take them to the temple?"

He nodded his agreement. "I'll tell her." He looked up, his gaze sweeping over the deserted deck. The sails were flapping in the wind, the crash of waves and the creak of the wooden hull droning on. The bank of fog had grown thicker. It surrounded them, leaving them trapped in an eerie bubble of darkness.

There were a few burning oil lamps hanging from chains nearby, but several of them had gone out, and without the light of the moon overhead, Lilyth could see little beyond the ship's railing.

Templar motioned Lilyth toward a short staircase that led to the upper deck where the ship's wheel was located. "Sit here," he told her, pointing to one of the steps. "I'm going to see if I can figure out how to steer this thing."

Lilyth sat, her shaking legs practically giving out beneath her. She huddled into her coat, squeezing her eyes shut as she tried to block out the thoughts beating at her mind. *I'm in so much trouble!*

Chapter 14: Lost

Lilyth tried to block out all thoughts of the two men below as she watched Templar move around the ship. *Stop thinking about it. It'll be fine!*

Templar lit several of the lamps on deck before circling the masts to study the ropes and sails and the complex jumble of pulleys that made up the rigging. He then headed toward the pilot station where he studied the wheel.

Lilyth kept her attention locked on him, driving back nagging thoughts: *Bad. What you did was bad. You are bad. Lost girl.* She studied Templar's face as if examining a painting — the set to his jaw, the deep line between his brows. He wore the same expression her brother wore when trying to learn something new. *Pure frustration.*

Eventually, Templar returned to the main deck. He raised his hand, and a ball of bright flame appeared between his fingers. He tossed it high into the air. Lilyth watched as the flare rose into the night sky and then exploded in a flash of brilliant red and orange sparks that spread out like a flowering tree. *Mother said she would teach me that spell, but she never did. Maybe Templar . . .* As the sparkling light from his spell slowly faded, he returned to her side.

"I have good news, and bad news," he announced. He unclipped his sword belt and sat down on the stairs beside her, laying the two blades across his lap. "The bad news is, sailing a ship is a lot more complicated than it looks. And I'm pretty certain it requires more than one person to manage everything."

183

"I can help," Lilyth offered immediately, desperate to be useful.

A grin crossed Templar's lips. "I'm pretty sure it requires more than two people as well. Besides, even if we did manage to figure out how the rigging works, I'm not certain what direction to go."

"Don't we just turn around and go back the way we came?" She'd never given sailing any serious thought, had no idea how the complex systems of ropes and pulleys worked. She knew the sails had to be positioned against the wind a certain way to provide basic thrust, but how that was accomplished was a mystery.

"You can't just flip a ship around," Templar explained. "And I don't think something like this can sail backward. Assuming I could figure out how to turn the ship — and that's a big if — the turning radius is pretty wide. The moment we started to turn, we'd lose our sense of direction in this fog."

"You said there was good news?" Lilyth blinked nervously.

He looked momentarily startled. *He doesn't have any good news.* Her heart sank.

"Oh. . ." He looked across the deck again. "Well . . . the good news . . . we can't be that far from shore, and there isn't much wind. The fog seems to have slowed our momentum and the sails are fairly slack at the moment. Come morning, when the fog lifts, I suspect we'll be able to see the shoreline."

"And the light you created just now?" She pointed upward to the sky where he'd thrown the ball of sparks. *I think it's fire magic. Mother's flares are illusions.*

"A signal to the shore," Templar explained. "As I said,

184

we're not that far out. And Hex is a busy port — there will be other ships coming and going. Someone will spot us on approach or departure. I'll shoot a few more flares into the sky every few minutes."

Lilyth's gaze skirted the bodies still littering the deck — the red stains beneath them were starting to spread. *Glad it's dark.*

Templar cast a cleaning cantrip over himself, and then another for good measure, removing the blood splatters completely. He examined his hands. They were both badly blistered, blood and seeping fluids smeared across his skin.

"Can't you heal your hands?" Lily knew some basic psionic healing but had never practiced on anyone else.

Templar flexed his fingers, wincing at the pain. "Burns from Night steel have to heal naturally. They'll be fine in a few days."

She shivered. "I always thought the stories about you being a Nightblood were . . ." She waved her hands vaguely in the air. "You know . . ."

"Made up?" he asked, bitter amusement in his rough voice. "It's not really something you admit to unless you absolutely have to. Most people don't react well."

"My parents are going to kill me," Lilyth said softly after a few moments had passed. They would know she was gone. *All I want is to talk through all of this with them. But they're going to be furious. What am I going to do?*

"Probably." Templar pulled a small pouch from another pocket of his coat and opened it. He removed several soft cloths, a bottle of sword oil and an odd golden-colored whetstone.

"I'll never get a cat." She felt miserable. *I sound like a spoiled brat. I don't deserve a cat. Father won't . . .* She cut

185

off the thought. *If I hadn't snuck away, those men wouldn't be hurt. But if I hadn't done that, Templar would still be in that cage. And he couldn't send up flares to get us rescued.* "What about your parents?" *Maybe his parents will be understanding. And then they can talk to my parents.*

Templar drew the longer sword from its sheath, holding the white bone blade out in front of him to inspect the edge. As far as Lilyth could see it was undamaged. "My father will be annoyed," he explained. "I should have been paying better attention — shouldn't have stepped into that trap in the first place."

"What about your mother?" she asked. In the time she'd known him, she'd never heard anything about Templar's mother or a Queen of Terizkand. "Is she kind?"

He wiped the sword down with one of the cloths, feeling the blade periodically with his fingers. "She's dead."

"I'm sorry," Lilyth said quickly.

"Don't be." He grinned, no mirth reaching his eyes. "She tried to burn me at the stake when I was five, so I'm not really unhappy she's gone."

"What?" *That can't be right.* "Burn a five-year-old? Her own son? What kind of a monster—"

Templar laughed bitterly. "My mother was the daughter of the king of Windheim. That's a kingdom on the east coast of Terizkand. It was very wealthy, very powerful — and it had magical defenses strong enough to withstand the giants when they took the rest of the land. When my father was first fighting the giants, he needed allies. He made a deal with the king of Windheim — married the king's daughter to seal the alliance. They agreed that any child born would be the heir to both kingdoms — that would be me."

"You're the crown prince of two kingdoms?" Lily narrowed her eyes to study him more closely.

"Just the one," he replied. He took the sword oil and poured it onto the cloth and carefully began applying a thin coating to the blade. "When I was about five years old I got angry over something — my eyes flashed yellow. They used to be blue like my father's and my sister's. Unfortunately my mother saw the flash of yellow and knew what it meant. Consorting with Night Dwellers was forbidden in Windheim. I guess my father hadn't shared that little detail with his bride. My mother turned on me — and I mean that literally. She and her father and the rest of their court tied me to a stake and lit me on fire. Luckily my father arrived in time to save me. None of the Windheim royals survived my father's wrath. Windheim is now a province of Terizkand, not a kingdom unto itself."

Lilyth gulped down the knot in her throat. "You said your eyes flashed yellow," she said in an attempt to move the conversation away from his murderous dead mother and his being nearly burned at the stake. "Why are they yellow all the time now?"

"Something to do with the fire — or at least that's what the healers told us. I was burnt pretty bad — guess I got angry enough that my eyes just never changed back." Templar shrugged.

That didn't exactly change the subject. She couldn't think of what else to say and pushed her lips into a pout. *My mother loves me. She's all sorts of scary, but she loves me.*

"Now, what about you?" Templar asked, seemingly offhand. "Are you going to tell me how a ten-year-old was able to knock out two men? And while you are at it, tell me what you meant about Omen's god blood not being what makes him extraordinary."

It wasn't a story the Daenoths shared with people, and in light of what had happened to the two men, Lilyth wasn't really certain she wanted to talk about it. But she supposed Templar deserved an explanation. "It has to do with my great-grandfather — Marric Daenoth. He wasn't from here — wasn't from this world."

"He was from another realm?" Templar tried to clarify. Finished with his sword, he set it aside and removed the smaller blade from the second scabbard.

Lilyth shook her head. "No, another planet." She pointed upward toward the sky. "From out there — the stars." Seeing the blank look on Templar's face, she waved her fingers dismissively. *Too much, Lilyth. That's crazy talk to him. Shut your mouth!* "That part isn't really important. Marric Daenoth was from a different place far away. He was a scientist — that's like an alchemist. Specifically, he studied . . . well, let's say he studied people's blood and what makes people unique."

"All right." Templar nodded as if clear on the concept, though Lilyth suspected he didn't truly know what she meant.

Faker. She forgave him.

"Marric already was a powerful psionicist, but he wanted to be stronger — so he experimented with other types of blood, trying to create hybrids, and new types of creatures with different psionics."

"He bred psionic animals?" Templar asked. As he had with the first blade, he began inspecting the edge of his second blade, fastidiously checking it for nicks or scratches.

"No." Lilyth pulled her coat tighter around her shoul-

188

ders. "Humans — he wasn't a nice man. In any event, eventually his research led him to an ancient creature — something long dead, but preserved well enough that he could extract viable blood from it."

"What kind of creature?"

"That's hard to explain — it was something old and massive — a creature the size of an entire world, something from the dawn of time — which is much older than you might imagine—"

"One of the Old Ones from the abyss?" Templar asked, pausing momentarily in cleaning the blade. He looked at her with the same wariness she had felt when she'd watched him fight.

Great. Now he thinks I'm a monster . . . Maybe I am.

"That's a good way to describe it." Lilyth unfastened her braid and combed her fingers through her stubborn curls. "I am surprised that you've heard of such things. I'd been taught their very name is secret."

"Those things were said to come from the nightmares of the Elder Gods — creatures of pure chaos and death," Templar supplied.

"I don't know about any of that," Lilyth admitted. "But it was probably something that should have been left alone — which was the opposite of what Marric did. He used the blood from that creature in his experiments — and it worked beyond his wildest imagination. He created twin boys — Cerric and Torric — who possessed psionic powers stronger than anything Marric had ever seen. Problem was, he wanted the power for himself — so, he kept the boys locked up, experimented on them, tried to figure out how to splice their . . . blood . . . into his own. But eventually, they fought back. Marric was no match for them. They killed

189

him."

Templar snorted in amusement as he began oiling the second sword. "That's what happens when you cage something stronger than you."

I don't understand him. He thinks it's funny.

Her gaze flicked toward the dark forms of the dead captain and the remaining crewmen who had failed to jump from the ship in time to avoid Templar's wrath. She supposed there were parallels to their family histories. "Torric wanted nothing more to do with Marric," she continued. "But Cerric was fascinated by Marric's experiments — wanted to figure out what more he could do with them, if he could make himself even more powerful than he already was."

"From what you describe — how much more powerful can you get than a god of the abyss?"

"Well — that was just it — while they were extremely powerful, it turns out that Marric had managed to isolate two strains of blood from the creature. The only one he could activate was the recessive strain. Cerric and Torric had the recessive powers. Marric had never been able to activate the dominant strain. Cerric wanted to figure out how to turn it on."

Templar frowned at her, and she realized she was using words that she'd been taught by her father. *He wouldn't know any of the science.* "Recessive, in this case, weaker. Dominant is the— "

"Yeah, I understand dominant." He laughed.

Lilyth looked up at the glittering night sky. While she remembered all the stories her father had told her, there was much about that tale that she couldn't quite picture — traveling among the stars for one. "Cerric continued the experi-

190

ments," she explained. "And his search eventually brought him here — to this world where he discovered other powers. He continued the experiments on our world, and eventually he discovered that my grandmother, Queen Wraiteea, had a unique blood type, which he could use to succeed where his father had failed. My father was born with the dominant trait — fully active."

Templar looked utterly flummoxed. "You're telling me that your psionics are the equivalent to the mind powers of the Old Ones of the abyss?"

"My father's are," Lilyth confirmed. "Omen and I have the recessive trait like Cerric and Torric — which is just a fraction of the Old Ones — but still unmatched by anything else you'll ever come across."

"I don't know if I should be impressed or terrified," Templar joked. "I mean, I had heard stories about how strong the Daenoths' mind powers are — but I didn't expect this. What happened to your grandfather?" He finished cleaning the sword and sheathed it, then started putting his supplies away.

"Like Marric, he wanted the power for himself. He tried to figure out how to take my father's abilities. When he finally realized that he was no match for my dad, he sought other powers to get what he wanted. He'd heard stories about the imprisoned Elder God Cerioth — imprisoned by the other Elder Gods in a musical instrument. Cerric spent years searching for the Elder Temple that held The Dark Heart — the lute. He thought he could use Cerioth to control my dad. He learned the hard way you don't control an Elder God — the moment he touched the lute, Cerioth turned him to ash, right in front of my father."

Templar stoppered the small bottle of oil and slipped it

back into the leather pouch. "But the lute didn't burn your father? He kept it — at least that's what all the stories say. Your father alone held The Dark Heart, played music with it, and eventually freed Cerioth in exchange for saving the life of your mother and their unborn son, Omen."

"It's a crazy story," Lilyth conceded. "It isn't something my father talks about — but yes, for whatever reason Cerioth didn't kill my father when he picked up the lute. I don't know why."

"You do realize that your parents are going to blame me for you being here, right?" Templar told her. "And from what you're saying, I should be afraid of your father?"

"Oh, no." Lilyth shook her head. "It's my mother you should be afraid of. Even with all my father's powers, Mother is far scarier." She sighed heavily, realizing that despite her teasing, she was the one who was going to be in trouble. Her mother was going to be furious. "I just wanted a cat."

"I get that." Templar slipped the sword kit back into his inner pocket. "They are rather amusing. I thought Omen was out of his mind when he insisted on keeping Tormy. All the trouble that caused . . . still the fuzzy critter has grown on me. But I don't think you can just go and get one — they have to find you. I think you'll agree that Omen doesn't actually own Tormy. It's more the other way around."

"I know," she moped, finding the thought depressing.

The wind picked up as they sat on the deck, both lost in thought — luckily the ring Templar had given her kept the cold from her bones. Templar tossed another glowing ball of light into the air a few minutes later. They both watched as it exploded in a showering fall of colored light that hung in the air for a long moment before flowing downward and winking out.

Lilyth's thoughts went once more to the two men below deck. "Do you think your grandfather—" she began only to be cut off by the sound of a bell ringing through the fog. They jumped to their feet and peered into the murky darkness.

"Thought it would take longer." Templar sounded surprised, but wary.

Fear stole over Lilyth again. It did seem unlikely that a ship could find them that fast. "Do you think it's more pirates?"

"No, whoever it is saw my signal." Templar sounded certain. "Pirates don't typically approach ships when they know there's a mage on board. It's too easy to light a ship on fire. Most likely, it's a passing merchant ship." He hesitated a moment before tossing another ball of light into the air.

The bell grew louder, and a moment later Lilyth spotted lights gleaming in the fog. "There!" She pointed.

Templar quickly retrieved his sword belt, strapped it around his hips, and pulled on his gauntlets. He moved to the railing and leaned forward, eyes narrowing. The approaching light banked in a graceful curve away from them as the vessel turned to pull alongside them. Through the fog, Lilyth could make out shadows forming as the ship neared. A flag flew from a tall mast, illuminated by a bright, magical lamp.

A look of relief washed over Templar's face, and he threw Lilyth a confident smile. "It's flying the flag of the Sul Havens."

"The Sul Havens." Lilyth approached the railing. "That's

the Venedrine, right? Elves." *Mother said Kyr is Venedrine.*

"Not just the Venedrine — there are a lot of elvin clans who live in the Sul Havens," Templar explained. "But there were several Venedrine ships in Hex's port."

The vessel emerged from the fog, glittering lamps illumining the deck. A large, silver bell hung from the prow; it rang slowly as the ship pulled up alongside them. A dozen tall, slender men stood along the railing of the deck. They called out to Templar as they neared, the elvin ship gliding smoothly through the water.

Templar grabbed the coiled mooring line and tossed it toward one of the waiting deckhands. Lilyth backed nervously away as several of the strangers leaped across the expanse between the two ships, heedless of the plunging gap and the cold dark water below. They immediately rushed to various parts of the ship, swiftly tending to the sails and the wheel, bringing the ship under their control. A few glanced warily at the bodies still littering the deck, but said nothing to Templar as they went about their business.

Lilyth moved to one side, staying out of their way. She'd had little dealing with elves in her life. These men were all ageless and beautiful, their sharp features cold and haughty. They threw a few glances in her direction, but none made an attempt to approach her.

They seem to know Templar, she noted, taking comfort in that. They had called to him by name. And certainly the Terizkandian prince no longer looked worried.

Another elvin man boarded the ship a moment later. Unlike the sailors, this man was dressed in velvets and silks, his ears adorned with numerous jewels, as were his hands. *Like Templar.* As the elvin man turned to survey the deck, taking in the bodies and the blood, the light caught upon his face, revealing a faint dusting of glitter upon his cheeks. His eyes were lined with dark kohl, and there were strands of tiny golden beads woven through his hair. *All right, maybe not entirely like Templar.* In all the time she'd known Templar, she'd never seen him with paint upon his face.

"Reegorn!" Templar called out to the man, approaching him with a smile.

The elvin man inclined his head, his movements graceful and deliberate. "Prince Templar, I am pleased we were able to find you. Had it not been for your lights, we would have passed right by you in this foggy shroud."

His words indicated that he knew Templar had been in trouble — that this wasn't a random encounter. *How could they know already?*

Templar too looked surprised. "Not that I'm not pleased to see you, but how did you find me?"

"When you were late for the party, we became concerned. So unlike you," Reegorn explained. "And then our seers all grew agitated."

Seers? Mother said something about the Venedrine being powerful mystics. While Lilyth didn't pay much heed to prophecies or mystical warnings, the Machelli clan was a superstitious lot, and she understood the complexity of fortune-telling.

"Your seers?" Templar's expression curled into one of extreme skepticism.

Reegorn inclined his head again. "Our seers have been agitated for a few days now." The elf's stern face took on a grave expression. "They have been speaking of the rise of an ancient curse. All of them. In unison sometimes. It's very disturbing. They speak of a vast host of the dead shouting warnings across time and space and the rise of an ancient blood curse. When you did not show up earlier this evening, they indicated that you were somehow connected to this curse, and that we are all in grave peril."

"Wait a minute!" Templar exclaimed, looking as startled as Lilyth felt. "Are you talking about The Dark Heart's curse?"

Lilyth's heart nearly stopped.

Reegorn's eyes flashed. "What do you know of that?"

Templar threw a look toward Lilyth.

Don't . . . This is about Kyr. She wished she could send her thoughts to Templar's mind.

"Very little," Templar replied slowly. "The Soul's Flame warned Omen Daenoth that the curse had returned."

Reegorn gasped and took a step back. He braced his hand against the railing of the ship, his jeweled rings flashing in the lamplight. The sailors around him, though busy with the ship's rigging, were all listening in. Lilyth spotted more than one of them making a warding sign against evil.

"You . . . spoke . . . with The Soul's Flame?" Reegorn's voice was breathy and unsteady.

"Me?" Templar gave a hard, decisive shake of his head. A gust of wind blew past them, snapping the sails loudly and causing the fog to swirl. "The gods don't speak to me. But Omen—" He broke off, as if not certain how to explain. Lilyth could hardly blame him. Her brother's connection to the gods, and the casual way he spoke of The Soul's Flame, always confused her.

"We've all heard the stories, of course." Reegorn looked warily at the fog churning around them. The night had grown noticeably cooler, and Lilyth was grateful for the magic ring Templar had given her.

Reegorn pressed his hand to his chest, covering his heart

in a reverent manner. "We owe our very existence to The Soul's Flame. Long ago The Soul's Flame interceded on our behalf, he and his brethren. There are many of our number who are devoted to him." He took a deep breath, as if preparing for something difficult. "May I know the exact words he spoke?"

Templar looked deeply uncomfortable. "Like I said, I wasn't there. You'll have to ask Omen if you want to know more."

"The seers spoke of a lost child," Reegorn pressed, his gaze intent. "Do you know what they might have meant?"

Impulsively Lilyth stepped forward, panic pounding inside her. *We shouldn't tell them about Kyr. Omen wouldn't want that!* "I'm lost!" she exclaimed quickly. "I shouldn't be here."

Reegorn's gaze swept over her, and Templar swiftly moved to her side. "Reegorn, this is Lilyth Daenoth — Omen's sister," he said. "And she's right, she shouldn't be here. We should get her home. Her parents and her brother are no doubt extremely worried about her."

Reegorn inclined his head. Lilyth could see the tightening of his lips and a flash of annoyance in his eyes. *He knows we're not telling him something.*

"Of course, Prince Templar," the elf agreed. "My men will have us back to Hex in no time."

"And there are two men below deck who should be taken into custody," Templar added.

Reegorn called out to the elvin sailors. The ship turned, banking to the side as they steered a course back to Hex. The Venedrine vessel beside them pulled away, remaining parallel as they cut through the darkness and black water. Lilyth could hear the toning of the elvin bell fading as the ships drew farther apart.

Templar motioned Lilyth toward the prow, away from Reegorn and the others.

"Do you think—" she started to ask, only to have him silence her with a quick shake of his head. He tapped his left ear lightly.

Elves have exceptionally good hearing! I knew that! Lilyth nodded once. *He doesn't think we should mention Kyr either. General Corzika said the same thing.* She pictured the strange little boy licking butter from his fingers along with his kitten. *Kyr's no threat to anyone. Is there really some horrible curse hunting him?* She swallowed hard. *We have to protect him.*

She shivered, a sharp stab of fear piercing her heart. *If there is a curse, it will come for Kyr, and Omen and the cats, and maybe the rest of us.* She squeezed her eyes tightly shut, feeling ill and wishing now that she'd never left the house. Around them, the fog billowed. The crash of waves and the harsh taste of salt in the air filled her with growing anxiety. She closed her eyes and willed the ship to sail faster. *Home. Please, home.*

Chapter 15: Homebound

The elves steered the ship steadily onward. Eventually the light from the large Hexian watchtowers appeared on the horizon. But it took nearly another hour before they reached the port. The ship slid silently into position along the deep water slip, and the elvin sailors tossed several ropes to the waiting dockhands.

Long rows of armed soldiers lined one of the docks. A gangplank was lowered, and the ship was immediately boarded by soldiers. An older, stern-faced guardsman bowed to Templar and spoke quietly in Terizkandian.

Reegorn followed as Templar led Lilyth down the gangplank to the dock where General Corzika waited. Corzika's short-cropped hair gleamed like blood in the torchlight. A spike of fear slid through Lilyth's chest, and she straightened to her full height. *Am I going to be in trouble with her too?*

Corzika and Templar exchanged a long look but said nothing to each other. Lilyth wondered at the woman's lack of concern for a kidnapped brother. Then it occurred to her that perhaps the siblings were communicating telepathically — like Lilyth did with her family. *She should still at least try to look happy that Templar is safe!*

Corzika turned to Lilyth, inclining her head politely. "Lilyth," the general greeted, and for a moment Lilyth was taken aback at the familiar use of her simple name by someone she had never formally met. She had to remind herself that this was Terizkand — not Melia, not Lydon. The customs were different — and they didn't use the same

199

set of honorifics common between strangers in Melia. Omen was forever scolding Templar for greeting Melians with too much familiarity, and for whatever reason Templar blithely dismissed the proprieties demanded by polite society.

"We had best get you home before your parents return and tear down the walls of our city looking for you."

Lilyth blanched. Her father was more than capable of doing just that — despite the walls being giant-made. "They came to Hex? They know I'm here?"

"They do," Corzika stated gravely as they began walking toward the roadway. A carriage waited for them — a team of four horses hitched to it. "Your parents know you came through the portal. I promised them that I would find you. I doubt they expected you to be out at sea on a ship, however. I imagine they will have words with you when you return home." Her cold blue gaze slid briefly toward her brother as she added, "Both of you."

"You're going to throw me to the wolves, just like that?" Templar protested — though to Lilyth his tone sounded somewhat mocking as if this was a familiar exchange between the two of them. "And after all the trouble I've gone through to get you a new ship and two lovely cages of Night steel that you can melt down for weapons."

The lack of surprise on Corzika's face confirmed to Lilyth that some form of telepathic communication had gone on between them. *Which means they have to be closer than they seem.*

"Your kingdom thanks you for your generous donation," Corzika stated mildly. Something bright gleamed in her eyes. "But, yes, the wolves are yours to deal with. Consider it your reward for being dumb enough to walk into a trap in the first place."

To Lilyth's surprise, Templar's shoulders slumped, though he looked more embarrassed than upset.

"What about those two men?" Lilyth asked worriedly. "Did you tell her to—"

"It's fine," Templar cut in. "She'll take them to our grandfather." He looked pointedly toward his sister who seemed more annoyed than concerned.

"I will have them taken to our grandfather and the Temple of The Redeemer," she assured Lilyth. "Now, come. Your mother's wrath is quite fearsome to behold. I'd rather not deal with it again tonight."

She motioned them toward the carriage.

"Prince Templar!" a voice called out. They all turned. Reegorn stood nearby on the roadway. "Are we in danger?" The proud, arrogant expression did not waver, but Lilyth could hear genuine fear in his tone.

Templar's jaw tightened. "I don't know," he answered honestly. "I think any danger centers around Omen Daenoth. The warning would indicate that The Soul's Flame is still looking out for you. You should trust in him."

Reegorn looked as if he were about to question him again, and Templar shot a quick glance toward his sister before stepping forward and inclining his head formally to the elvin man. "Reegorn, you have done me a service tonight, and I am in your debt. If I can learn more about this curse and the threat you face, I will come speak with you and your people. And if there is a threat, I will defend the elves with my life."

What about Kyr? Will he defend Kyr?

"As will I." Corzika inclined her head to the elvin man.

Reegorn can't say anything further without offending

both of them, Lilyth realized.

Reegorn bowed in turn. "Your most humble servant thanks you. I will return to the Glass Walk and convey your words to my people."

At that Corzika ushered both Lilyth and Templar into the waiting carriage, and they left Reegorn and the docks behind.

Corzika escorted Templar and Lilyth to the castle and to the inner garden that housed the transfer portal to Melia. Lilyth stepped onto the familiar, sigil-covered circles of the portal with some trepidation and waited as Corzika activated the rune that would take her instantly home.

7 and Avarice were waiting for her as she stepped off the portal into her father's office. Omen too was standing nearby, a worried look on his face. There was no sign of Kyr or the cats.

Lilyth sighed heavily as she realized that they were most likely absent so that they could not comment on any punishment her mother might level upon her.

Her parents hugged her as she stepped forward, and she felt the swift sure touch of her father's mind as he lifted all the events of the last few hours directly and painlessly from her thoughts. She knew from experience that her mother was likely telepathically informed of all that had transpired a few seconds later. She took comfort in the warm hugs, knowing that her mother's wrath was soon to follow.

"What were you thinking?" Avarice hissed at her, her silver eyes flashing with fury.

Lilyth gulped nervously. *She's really mad.*

Templar, who had followed her through the portal, stepped to one side and nodded to Omen.

Omen just shook his head and moved in to ruffle Lilyth's

tangled hair. "I'm glad you're all right, Lily."

"Do you have any idea what could have happened to you?" Avarice continued, ignoring Omen's words.

"I wasn't in any danger," Lilyth protested and knew instantly by the darkening of her mother's eyes that she'd chosen the wrong tactic. "And if I hadn't been there, Templar would have been locked in that cage for weeks, maybe months! I saved him!"

"She is right about—" Templar started to say only to be interrupted by a dark glower from Avarice. He fell silent instantly.

"Templar is not your responsibility!" Avarice shouted. "Templar can take care of himself."

"I just wanted my own cat," Lilyth murmured glumly.

"Lily, if you wanted a cat so badly you should have just said something." Her father sounded reasonable and calm.

Lily's face twisted with incredulity. "I did—"

7 smiled. "I'm sure I can—"

"No!" Avarice barked.

Lilyth flinched as even her father fell silent. She hadn't been joking when she told Templar that, despite the differences in their power, Avarice was the one to be afraid of. And she knew her father well enough to know that if Avarice insisted on something, he would not go against her.

"No cat!" Avarice pointed a finger at her. "You're grounded, Lilyth Machelli Daenoth! No cat, no presents, no new clothes or toys or horses or shoes. No new anything for you *for a year!* You will stay home, you will focus on your studies, and you will not set one toe out of line. Does everyone understand?"

Lilyth gulped again, shock washing over her. *She's more than just mad. She's furious.* The fact that both her father and her brother silently nodded their heads in agreement made Lilyth hold any words of protest that might have escaped her mouth. She thought about the two men she'd knocked out, guilt washing over her.

"You could have died. Do you understand that?" Avarice pressed.

Lilyth nodded her head reluctantly. "Yes, ma'am," she murmured, knowing better than to talk back.

"Templar, thank you for keeping my idiot daughter alive, but I suggest you go home now before I ground you as well," Avarice bit out angrily.

"Yes, ma'am." Templar nodded in quick agreement. He paused before stepping onto the portal, placing a heavy hand on Lilyth's shoulder. "Sorry about the grounding," he told her politely. "But thank you for getting me out of the cage."

She felt him slip something into her coat pocket. She kept silent, forcing her expression to give nothing away.

"Before I go," Templar spoke to Avarice and 7. "The Venedrine know something is going on. I'm not much for mystics and seers, but they said their seers are all talking about the return of an ancient blood curse, and a lost boy. I'll do my best to keep any word about Kyr from being spread around, but you should all watch yourselves."

With that Templar stepped onto the portal, shot a cocky grin toward Omen, and then vanished from sight.

"Get to bed!" Avarice ordered, and Lilyth scampered from the room.

She raced through the hallways and headed upstairs to her bedroom, defiantly slamming the door shut. Anything more and she was afraid her mother might extend her grounding for another whole year.

"A year!" Lilyth stomped her feet and whipped her curls back and forth violently. Then she sank down on the floor in front of the fireplace, exhausted. One of the maids had already lit the fire, and the room was toasty warm — not that she was cold. She pulled off her gloves and stared down at the two rings on her fingers. Templar hadn't asked for either of them back, and considering she wasn't going to be receiving any new presents for a whole year, she wasn't inclined to return them.

"Those men will be fine," she told herself, hoping it was true. "They'll go to the Temple of The Redeemer, and the healers will help them." She didn't want to think about what might happen after that, not entirely certain she wished to know if they would be executed. Templar had said his grandfather would take care of them, and that he was a good man.

A knock at her door startled her. "Come in," she called.

The door opened and her father and brother peeked inside. "You all right?" Omen asked her, his eyes worried.

Before she could answer, a large, fuzzy orange form pushed his way past the two of them and barreled inside. Tormy flounced forward, all white and orange and shimmering. He flopped down onto his belly in front of her. "Lily!" he exclaimed. "We is all worriednessness, on account of the fact that we is not knowing you is missing, and Kyr is saying the stars is singing and lunch even though he is not being hungry. Exceptedness for cookies. We is always hungrinessness for cookies."

Lily leaned forward and wrapped her arms around the large orange cat, burying her face in his soft fur. "I don't know what that means," she mumbled.

"For some reason, Kyr seemed to know you were missing," Omen explained as he and 7 approached, kneeling down beside her on the floor. "He was very agitated."

"Maybe he's a mystic like all the rest of the Venedrine," Lilyth mused. Tormy's rumbling purr relaxed her. "Mother's really mad, isn't she?"

"It will be fine," her father assured her. "She was frightened. You could have been hurt, or killed."

"I'm the dangerous one." Lilyth blinked heavily as she tried to fight back tears.

"Lily, we are very strong," 7 agreed. "I told you and your brother that. That's why you have to stay in control of your powers, so you don't hurt someone truly helpless. But those men weren't helpless, and they would have killed you if they'd seen you. And you did save Templar. That's what your powers are for. To protect yourselves and those around you."

She nodded and gave a deep heartfelt sigh. "Am I still grounded for a year?"

7 and Omen both laughed at that. "You know we can't change your mother's mind." 7 smiled and gave her a tight hug before rising to his feet. "Now get some sleep. You've had a long day."

Omen and Tormy rose as well, all three of them heading toward the door. "You shouldn't have snuck out of the house," Omen told her, then he grinned. "But it was pretty brave what you did. Reminded me of me." Lilyth stuck her tongue out at him as they left.

She turned to stare into the flames of her fireplace, her mind churning with the events of the night. She remembered then that Templar had slipped something into her pocket. Reaching for it, she pulled out a small leather bundle. She recognized it immediately — it was the leather pouch that contained Templar's set of lock picks. Opening it up, she stared at the neat row of small metal devices of various sizes that lined the pouch — several dozen of them for every type of lock imaginable.

Lilyth bit her lip to keep a smile from growing. If she learned how to pick locks, she could get herself into and out of all sorts of things. And if she opened enough doors — sooner or later she was bound to find a cat on the other side.

Chapter 16: Sundragons

Heavy winter coat bundled around his shoulders, Omen stood on the western cliffs of Melia, over-looking the ocean. A stone staircase led down from the upper gardens and patios of Daenoth Manor to a grassy plateau. From there, another longer staircase wound to the beach.

White sand spread out in a crescent before tipping around another peaked outcropping on the northern point. Beyond it lay the busy city port. On that far outcropping, the enormous glittering form of one of the Melian Sundragons perched beneath the winter sky. Heedless of the cold, the dragon watched over the port and any ship that might brave the winter seas.

Omen raised one hand to shade his eyes against the glare of the icy sky. The distant dragon's golden scales gleamed through the mist blowing in off the water. Omen could even see the sparkle of the dragon's underlying gemstone color. *Sky blue — that's Sundragon Amar.*

Anyone raised in Melia, as Omen had been, knew the twelve Hold Dragons on sight in both their human and dra-conic forms. Melian children had all the dragons' secondary under-scale color memorized by the time they were four.

High-pitched giggling recaptured Omen's attention, and he turned his gaze back to the three forms of Kyr, Tormy, and Tyrin, who all sat upon the top step of the long stone-cut staircase.

"Watch them carefully," his father had said.

Airy huffs of laughter came from Tormy, who lay belly

down on the ground, front paws dangling over the side of the top step. Kyr, wearing one of Omen's childhood coats, hunkered beside the large cat and marveled at the sea. Little Tyrin leaned into the boy's other side, trying to buffer himself from the cold.

Tormy's and Tyrin's fur looked alive in the wind — shimmering waves of orange and white rippled beneath the winter sunlight. The stocking cap upon Kyr's bony head hid his current lack of hair, but his painfully thin, bare neck poked out from the gape in the too-large coat.

Omen shivered in sympathy. He doubted the cats were truly cold, their thick fur protection enough. *But Kyr has to be freezing. He needs a scarf.*

The boy made no indication of discomfort, or any sign that he wanted to go inside. *He loves the sight of the sea.* Two days ago, when Kyr had first seen the vast ocean from their lower balcony, the boy had stared in unmoving awe. He'd been beside himself with delight, viewing the crashing waves. While neither Tormy nor Tyrin shared his enthusiasm for water, they were more than happy to sit outside with him and enjoy the panorama.

"There you are," a familiar voice greeted.

Templar was making his way down the upper staircase from the house. It had been three days since his kidnapping, and he'd made himself scarce, no doubt afraid of incurring Avarice's wrath.

Omen had known that Templar wouldn't stay away for long; the prince grew bored easily and seemed to enjoy the Daenoths' company.

Omen was glad for it.

"I'm still not taking Kyr to the Night Games," Omen stated without preamble.

209

"I know!" Templar grumbled as he came to stand next to him, taking a moment to fasten the buttons on his long leather overcoat as a strong gust of icy wind hit him from just over the rise of the cliff. He stared at the cats and Kyr on the lower steps. While they were obviously deep in conversation, from this distance it was difficult to hear their words. Not that Kyr was likely saying anything.

"What are they doing?" Templar asked curiously.

"Kyr wants to go down to the beach," Omen explained. "The cats are insistent that they wait until the tide goes farther out. Don't want to get their paws wet. They're currently negotiating. I think they're trying to explain the concept of tides to Kyr."

"He understands the fuzz-faces?"

While Kyr had picked up a few words of both Sul'eldrine and Merchant's Common from the two cats, he'd spoken very little himself. The lack of a shared language, however, didn't seem to bother the cats in the slightest. The cats chatted blithely while Kyr pretended to understand.

"He's learning," Omen told Templar. "And Tyrin's picking up Merchant's Common remarkably quick. He's extremely clever."

"Smarter than Tormy?" Templar asked in amusement.

Omen said nothing, refusing to make such a comparison.

"Did you ask them about the whole twin thing?" Templar pressed.

Omen stifled a chuckle, not wanting to draw the attention of the cats. "They insist they are identical and continue to be utterly astonished at my ability to tell them apart."

Templar and Omen shared a grin. There were times when there was nothing more to do but to accept the absurd.

210

"So how's Lily holding up?" Templar asked after a few moments of silence.

"Constant temper fits," Omen replied. "Not in front of my mother of course. But a year-long grounding — that's bad, even for her."

"How long is that year likely to last — a few weeks? A few months?"

"A year." Omen didn't have to think about it. "My mother doesn't joke around about stuff like that. If she said a year, it will be a year. End of story. What about you? Did you get in trouble?"

"You know, contrary to whatever assumptions you made, I didn't actually do anything wrong," Templar pointed out. "I was the victim in all this. I was attacked, injured."

"By someone who wanted you to play in the Night Games?" Omen shook his head, bewildered.

"I assume that was the reason." Templar gave an indifferent shrug. "There were two cages — one for you as well. The pirate captain never said exactly what they were doing, so it could have just as easily been someone who wanted to extort money from our fathers."

A low rumble thundered in the distance, and both of them paused to look around. While the sky was grey with winter mist and fog, there were no signs of a brewing storm. The cats too had stopped their chatter and were looking northward along the shoreline toward the distant outcropping where Sundragon Amar had lifted his great head.

"The dragon is moving!" Templar hissed, still wary of the massive creature.

"I'm sure it's—" Omen started in on his typical reassurance that no, the dragon wasn't dangerous, but before he

211

could finish, the dragon opened his jaws, enormous teeth gleaming in the light, and let out a trumpeting bellow that echoed across the land in all directions.

Sundragon Amar rose, enormous wings unfurling and catching in the wind. From eastward across the city Omen heard an answering roar like the blaring of distant battle horns.

"That came from one of the Holds!" Omen felt alarm wash over him at the sound. He'd never heard the dragons roar before. The sound was a mixture of bone-shaking low frequency and the high musical tones of flutes and pipes that reminded him of summer concerts in the park and the warm firelight of the winter hearth. Though he could not make out the meaning of the roar, he was certain there were words embedded deep in the trumpeting notes.

Another roar came a moment later, from farther away, southeast across the city. *That came from the direction of Lord Darshawn's Hold and the other sound had to have come from one of the Deldano Holds.*

A moment later he heard the pealing of the temple bells sounding through the city — not the delicate musical tones of the winter blessing, but the repetitive warning clangs of alarm. While it was not something Omen had heard in his lifetime, he knew the sound was a warning to all Melians.

The glittering shapes of dragons appeared in the sky.

Sundragon Amar launched himself into the air, the great wings unfolding as he rose to meet the other forms circling high over the city.

Omen gaped in shock.

"That's Varanth and Geryon!" Omen yelled over the noise. While it was not unusual to see one dragon fly over-head from time to time, it was rare to see multiple dragons

212

in the sky. Omen also knew that Lord Geryon was one of the few Hold Dragons who actually preferred to remain in human form — for him to have transformed into his draconic shape and take to the sky meant that something was wrong.

The three Sundragons circled like hunting hawks.

"What's happening?" Templar asked, hand moving to his side where his two bone swords hung. Templar wasn't Melian and like all foreigners was leery of the dragons, seeing them as more predator than protector.

"Kyr! Tormy!" Omen hurried toward his brother. The boy was staring at the flying dragons, his face fixed in wonder at the sky. The enormous beasts circled overhead in tight spirals.

Another bellow rang out from a Hold all the way across the city.

"We is not doing anything, Omy!" Tormy proclaimed. "We is not waking the dragons up, honest, honest!"

"We have to get inside!" Omen barked out, wishing that he had thought to bring his sword. Standing in his own gardens, he hadn't felt the need to arm himself.

He heard a sharp shout and turned to see his mother standing at the top of the stairs near the patio garden, Lilyth beside her. Both of them were clad in riding breeches and boots, with matching velvet coats of emerald green, each wearing their long dark hair in braids. They had been out riding earlier — Avarice's attempt at keeping Lilyth occupied and out of further mischief.

"Inside!" Avarice shouted down to them, a razor's edge to her voice.

Omen grabbed hold of Tormy's ruff, tugging him up. "Get up the stairs! You too, Tyrin! Run!" he ordered the

213

cats. He grabbed Kyr's thin arm. "Come on Kyr!"

Kyr might not have understood the words shouted out in Common, but he certainly understood the urgency of tone. The boy scrambled to his feet.

But no sooner had they spun around toward the house than a sharp force ripped Kyr from Omen's grasp.

Absolute terror scorching through him, Omen pivoted to see a black shadowy mass forming around Kyr and lifting the boy away. It tossed him several feet across the rocky cliff to land near the edge of the plateau.

The dark shadow loomed over Kyr. The seemingly incorporeal creature was made of living black mist, thousands of ropey tendrils and swirling limbs flailing through the air. One of the long black coils wrapped around Kyr's throat, holding him pinned to the ground as he clawed at the overpowering horror with desperate hands.

"Kyr!" Without hesitation, Omen rushed to his brother's defense. Pounding music pulsed through Omen's mind as he summoned the first psionic pattern he could think of — a force of sheer crushing power, which he aimed at the shadowy mass harrowing Kyr.

Omen's force of energy struck the creature, and for a moment it seemed as if the shadows swirled and moved around the pulse in a chaotic dance of wind and fog. But the blow passed harmlessly through it, and the black misty rope around Kyr's throat tightened.

"Omen!" Templar shouted.

Omen looked, hand raised. Templar had drawn both of his bone blades from their scabbards and tossed the larger of the two swords toward Omen. A crackle of lightning raced around Templar's body as he summoned his magic.

Omen caught the bone blade out of the air and swung it

with all his might at the shadowy creature even as Templar's blazing flash of blue lightning struck the shade.

The creature shimmered and flared backward. It momentarily released Kyr, who rolled to his side and clawed at the dead winter grass as he coughed desperately and gulped for air.

Omen and Templar pressed forward, striking the shadow again and again, swords bashing through its flimsy form with every hit. Omen put the full force of his psionics behind each blow, hitting the creature with enough force to crush bone to dust.

For a moment he thought their attack successful. The creature reared back like a billowing curtain and swirled away in a gust. But then it solidified and hardened, blacking out the sky as it swelled with an ear-splitting hiss. It lashed forward and struck both of them, pounding each square in the chest.

Omen felt the force of the blow lift him up and throw him through the air. Briefly airborne, shadows swirling over his skin, he switched the song in his mind to one that raised a physical shield around him. A glimmer of light had already begun to form around his body even as he fell to the ground with bruising force. He brought up his shield not an instant too soon as his body impacted against a sharp boulder with terrible violence. Had he been unshielded, he would have broken his spine. The breath fled his lungs, and he gasped for air. Painfully, he twisted to his side and tried to roll to his feet. The shadows withdrew to attack elsewhere.

Omen spared a moment to see Templar lying dazed on the ground. Blood covered the side of his face. Templar's eyes flashed yellow with fire, and he too rose to his feet, lightning flaring around him again.

The sound of hissing and shrieking drew Omen's eyes back to the creature. Tormy, ears flat against his head, teeth bared, stood over the still gasping form of Kyr. The cat hissed with fury, striking out at the shadow with both front paws, claws extended. Little Tyrin had hold of the sleeve of Kyr's coat and was trying to pull him up the hill, but the tiny kitten was far too small to make any difference.

Beside Tormy stood Avarice, both hands blazing with blood-red light like a poisoned fire. She threw sphere after sphere of crimson flame at the creature. Her fire swirled into a vortex of burning rope and wrapped around the shadow, enclosing it in an inferno of light.

The shadow beast twisted and writhed within its fiery prison, spinning upward into the sky as it sought to escape. But despite the burning mass, with each twist of flame the creature grew darker, more solid — larger with each passing second.

"It hasn't fully manifested yet!" Templar shouted.

Naked fear swept through Omen. The thing had already swatted him and Templar aside like flies, and it was growing stronger. Instinct screamed at him that one blow would kill his mother, despite her remarkable force of magic.

Omen clawed for the battle song again, re-forming the pattern that fueled his psionic blows. He rushed to stand at his mother's side and pushed with all his might, trying to contain the creature within a bubble. He desperately hoped his mother's magic could burn the shadow if he kept it in place.

As if understanding what Omen was trying to accomplish, Templar bolted to Avarice's side. The blue lightning of his magic crackled outward to surround the creature, electrifying it at the same time as Avarice burned it. Out of the corner of his eye, Omen spotted Tormy aiding Tyrin. The large cat caught Kyr by the back of the coat and tried to drag the boy toward the stairs and the relative safety of the manor.

In an instant, the creature lashed out again, exploding outward with such force that the backlash threw Omen, Avarice and Templar to the ground, their combined magics and psionics ripped apart in one terrible blow. The creature swelled in size and reared up above them like a column of darkness, rising high into the cloud-covered sky.

Inky tatters ripped through the air around the shadow — black spears aimed toward them. Omen desperately raised his psionic shield, straining to extend it over his mother and Templar before the piercing blades struck them.

A crashing blow hit his shield with devastating force. He tried to hold onto the only thing keeping the shadow from crushing them utterly.

It's breaking!

He felt his shield crumble.

My mother. Templar. No!

Omen screamed like an animal.

But just before their only protection failed totally, a blinding flash of light shot past them.

The creature was ripped away.

Sundragon Amar had swooped down from the sky and caught the writhing mass of blackness within his two back claws. He lifted it up and away, into the winter sky. The rush of wind from the enormous dragon wings whooshed over them as the dragon banked out to sea.

Omen howled and pumped his fist in the air.

But immediately a terrified cry caught his ears. While

being dragged away, the creature had reached out with one long trailing shadow-strand and had torn Kyr away from Tormy, lifting the helpless boy into the air.

Amar, the shadow creature, and Kyr ascended high into the sky.

"Kyr!" Omen screamed, his voice breaking. He reached out with his mind, trying to latch on to his little brother with his psionics. He felt it momentarily, felt his mind catch hold of Kyr. *I can't just pull. I'll snap him in half.* He tried to pry the black shadow's fingers from around Kyr's leg. *Have to catch him if he falls.* But as the three of them flew farther away, Omen's grip on Kyr slipped, the pattern in his mind disintegrating with the distance.

Another brilliant streak of sunlight swooped toward them. This shape was much smaller than Amar, and Omen recognized him immediately as Sundragon Andrade, the youngest of all the Hold Dragons, and the smallest. But Andrade had the added benefit of also being one of the fastest, his smaller form giving him the ability to maneuver in the air with speed and agility. The small dragon swept past Amar and twisted in midair to dive beneath the great dragon. He snatched hold of Kyr's thin form with one claw, ripping him away from the shadowy tendril.

Andrade banked to the north while Amar pivoted in the air and headed southward.

But dragon or no dragon, the shadow creature was not done with its tricks. It swirled suddenly and grew again, spreading outward in a dark mass that lashed out in all directions.

In a mere moment, Amar was encased in the black mist, swallowed up. Then the swirling coils expanded and caught the fleeing form of Andrade, wrapping around the smaller dragon and pinning his wings tightly against his body.

Omen's heart raced as he beheld the powerful force that the creature exerted like a whip snapping out and lashing backward. It flung Andrade down. Unable to unfurl his wings, the mighty Sundragon crashed on the beach.

Omen scrambled toward the stairs, taking them three at a time as he ran, eyes on the downed dragon. Blood rushed in his ears like a torrent of water. "Kyr!"

The dragon had pulled the boy inward toward his body, clutching him tightly to his chest as he hit the sand and tumbled head over tail across the beach. The dragon and boy lay dazed and unmoving upon the sand.

Overhead, Amar still struggled against the shadow. Two more sun-gold dragons had joined in. Sundragon Geryon, older and larger than even Amar, had caught the struggling dragon with one claw and was beating his wings hard against the air to keep him aloft while Sundragon Varanth dove in, jaws opened.

Flames burst from the dragon's mouth, swirling around both the shadow and Amar in a blinding white-hot blast of molten light. The shadow swirled away, releasing Amar who stretched his wings once more.

The three dragons banked in their flight and turned tightly to surround the creature as Omen ran across the wet sand toward his fallen brother.

Please . . . He couldn't finish the thought.

Chapter 17: The Dark Heart

Andrade was just beginning to stir, his wings sliding back across his body as he tried to right himself. He got his back claws beneath him and pushed himself upward sluggishly. Then he released Kyr from his grasp. The boy curled on his side and dug his hands into the wet sand, trying to crawl away.

Omen slid in beside them and touched Kyr's shoulder. "I'm here." His hand came away wet, and he realized that during the fall one of Andrade's claws had pierced Kyr's delicate skin. Blood seeped through the boy's coat, and his left arm hung limply at his side — the bone angled unnaturally, broken clean through.

"They can't hold the shadow," the musical voice of Andrade rumbled, and Omen turned to look up at the dragon. While Andrade was one of the smallest of the Sundragons, he was still over fifteen feet long and towered over both of them even while hunched.

Despite having grown up in Melia, Omen had never been this close to a Sundragon. Tremendous heat radiated off the creature's scales.

Andrade's gaze was on the sky, and Omen followed his line of sight to behold the three large dragons battling the shadow. The fray was so high in the air that their roars and screams were muted.

In unison, the three enormous Sundragons scorched the creature with white-hot draconic fire, but rather than retreating, the shadow only grew in size, uninjured, darkening and spreading. One massive coil reached down to the ground as if rooting the creature in place. It rose up like an ancient redwood tree — hundreds of feet in height. Swirling whips of darkness slashed out — cutting the dragons like blades. Dark crimson blood splashed across their thick dragonhide.

The trio of dragons flew at the shadow, cutting with claws and teeth and then raining a column of dragon fire down upon it — but nothing seemed to touch the ever-expanding darkness.

A moment later one of the dark coils wrapped around Sundragon Varanth and flung him down. While Omen knew that the dragons' ability to fly was enhanced by magic — reducing their weight so it would be possible — the magic did nothing to change their great mass. The dragon struck the ground with terrific force and carved a deep furrow along the beach as he tumbled to a halt.

A second tendril of darkness caught Sundragon Amar and flung him down as well. He twisted in the air, barely managing to fold his wings against his body before he plunged like a boulder into the ocean.

Only Sundragon Geryon remained in the sky, his claws buried in the shadow, expansive wings beating madly as he tried to uproot the creature from its writhing grapnel in the ground.

They're trying to get it away from Melia, Omen realized.

"I can take the boy," Sundragon Andrade called out. "I can take him and run. It will follow, but I will stay ahead of it. I will not stop."

In a flash of insight Omen understood what Andrade was offering — taking Kyr would eliminate the threat to Melia. The creature was here for Kyr and nothing else. But he also understood that Andrade would not be able to stop his race — not ever. And even a Sundragon could not fly indefinitely. Sooner or later the shadow would catch him, perhaps kill him to get to Kyr, and Kyr would be at the creature's mercy.

"It won't stop either!" Omen shook his head. *This can't happen! There has to be a way to stop it. There has to be something we can do!*

"Omen!"

He spotted his mother and Templar racing toward him across the sand. *We need Dad — he took the portal to Lydon earlier this morning. When was he coming back?* Omen couldn't remember.

"Get up!" Avarice shouted at him, reaching his side and dropping down to her knees beside Kyr. The boy was trying to rise — trying to get to his feet despite his injuries. Omen wrapped his arms around Kyr, steadying him as his mother hauled them both up. "We have to get Kyr back to the house."

"Will the wards on the house keep that thing out?" Templar shouted. Blood streaked across his face and dripped down his chin from the wound in his scalp.

"Don't know," Avarice shot back. "If we can get him to the portal, we can take him to Lydon or Terizkand. We can keep moving him around — confuse it."

Brilliant! That would work!

Beyond them, Sundragon Geryon had been knocked back. Varanth had steadied himself upon the beach and had relaunched into the air. Rising from the surf, Amar clawed his way out of the water with an angry screech. But the momentary reprieve from attack was all the shadow creature needed to refocus its attention on Kyr.

The dark entity turned in the sky — masses of swirling

tendrils flailing about as they re-formed and shot toward the group standing unprotected in the crashing surf and wet sand.

Andrade roared, a billowing stream of flame bursting from his jaws. He seared through a cluster of shadowy spears, but the shadow itself just swerved and avoided the fire.

Omen released Kyr and jumped forward, putting himself between his brother and the oncoming darkness. Grinding his teeth, Omen raised his shield — trying to extend it out far enough to encompass them all.

He reeled the instant the shadow hit his shield full force. For one brief moment he held back the harrowing blow with the sheer power of his will. He howled, enraged as he pushed against the entity. His sight went white, and the battle song in his mind thundered. He held the pattern clear and sharp. But beneath the unrelenting force of the blows crashing down upon him, his shield began to crack and shatter — falling away as the pattern exploded in flares of iridescent pain.

Omen dropped to his knees.

A flash of blue surrounded him as his shield collapsed. He recognized Templar's magic covering them, driving the shadows back. But Templar's spell flickered and sputtered at the gross force weighing down upon them.

As Templar's magic shattered in an explosion of blue sparks, a screen of silver light took its place — his mother's spellwork holding them safe.

Omen gasped, working to rekindle his battle song and forcing the psionic pattern back into place. His barrier flared just as his mother's screen of light crumpled in on itself and failed.

223

We can't hold it back! Both Templar and Avarice staggered beneath the power of their collapsed shields. Omen feared they wouldn't be able to take a second round, and his psionic barrier was already cracking.

But even as his pattern unraveled, a flash of warm red light surrounded them all. The red light flared outward in a searing wall and then struck the core of the shadow. The warm light thrust the creature back so forcefully that the entire swell of darkness swayed back out over the ocean where Sundragon Amar was launching himself into the air once more.

The dragon roared and breathed fire at the swaying shadow, grabbing its attention for a moment.

The red light vanished. Etar, The Soul's Flame, stood before them.

"Etar!" Relief washed over Omen at the sight of his older brother. "You said you couldn't get involved! Have you changed your mind?"

Etar's face was grave. "I am forbidden from coming between the curse and its prey."

"But you just did!" Omen saw no point in sticking to the letter of the promise now that it had been broken.

Etar shook his head. "I protected you. The dragon protected Kyr."

Andrade had placed his glittering body over the crumpled form of Kyr lying in the sand. Etar's shield may have driven the creature back, but the shadow force would have struck Omen and the others before reaching the boy.

"How do we stop it?" Avarice bellowed. She'd drawn a long dagger from a hidden sheath at her back and was clutching it with knuckle-white fury.

"You cannot," Etar said simply.

A string of Scaalian curses escaped Avarice's throat, and for a moment Omen thought she would bury her dagger in Etar's chest. Instead she waved the blade in the air, blood from her own hand spattering the sand. *She's summoning blood magic!* Omen knew how dangerous such spells were — just as he knew that his mother would stop at nothing to protect her family.

Above them, shadowy tendrils had wrapped around the throats of both Geryon and Amar. The strength of the hold ripped the dragons from flight and cast them down. They both fell like stones, and only Geryon was able to get his wings folded against his body before he struck the ground. Amar roared in pain as his left wing caught beneath his body. He rolled across the sand.

He's coming straight toward us! Omen realized, stunned. The enormous dragon was about to crash into everyone standing on the beach. *Mother! She won't survive the impact!*

Sundragon Varanth, farther south on the beach, took a great leap and vaulted over top of all of them — coming down on Amar's form, claws extended as he sought to catch his dragon brother and stop his momentum.

But with the dragons distracted, the shadow returned its attention to the group on the sand. Again it reared upward and back, then shot downward with all its tendrils — aiming them like a thousand javelins falling from the sky.

Etar raised his hand again — red light flaring out in a shield that encompassed Omen, Avarice, and Templar. Andrade, still standing over Kyr, roared again — jets of his fire streaming upward toward the approaching darkness.

But this time, as the full force of impact rained down on Etar's unbreakable shield — one long, lashing tendril of darkness snapped out and around it. It flung Andrade backward as if he weighed nothing at all, and then wrapped like a serpent around Kyr's right leg.

Avarice's slashing magic cut at the coil, creating gaps and gashes, but not affecting its strength or momentum.

"No!" Omen shouted and leaped for his brother. He caught hold of Kyr's coat. He knew that if the shadow was able to move the great weight of the dragons, his own strength would be nothing against it. The coil would just lift him off the ground along with Kyr. So instead, he fastened his mind onto the tendril of darkness, forming a telekinetic pattern which he had often employed to move objects. He hauled back with all his strength.

Kyr screamed.

For one horrible instant Omen feared he'd grabbed Kyr instead of the tendril, and that between the creature and him, they were pulling the boy apart.

Cold terror broke the song in his head, and his grasp slipped when it should have fastened. But Avarice and Templar dove toward them, dropping their weapons, hands outstretched — Templar's hands glowed with blue electricity, Avarice's with red hot flames. They both locked onto the black coil, trying to force it to stay in place.

Omen pushed his psionics, blaring the song in his head. Kyr wrapped his right hand around Omen's wrist, fingers like vises. The child's broken left arm flopped uselessly as he tried to pull himself away from the ropey mist wrapping tighter and tighter around his leg. Omen knew there was no strength in him. Kyr's stocking cap had come off, and his pale, bone-bare skull looked fragile and pitiful as his too-thin face twisted with tears.

His heart breaking, a new song flared in Omen's mind,

the psionic pattern forming cleanly and sharply. He latched onto the tendril again, mad with rage, trying to hold back the instant when his little brother would be ripped away and torn apart by the hate-filled darkness swelling above them.

No, I can't let go! He couldn't accept it — would the shadow take Kyr's broken remains and drop him once again in the dead world, or take him somewhere else, worse perhaps, to let him suffer an immortal death beyond imagining? *I have to stop it!*

Filled with the savage need to bite and tear at the coil, Omen screamed. Outrage and desperation swallowed him as he felt his mind breaking — felt the force of his pattern flying apart. His power failed him. He could not stand against the curse of an Elder God.

And then — he already saw himself and his family shattered and lifted away into nothingness — the world around them went utterly and deathly silent.

Omen thought he'd gone deaf. No sound, no wind, no surf, no dragon roar — just utter silence.

The force on his mind vanished — the tendril he'd been pulling against was gone. Kyr was free.

Omen looked up, thinking that perhaps somehow Etar had interfered after all. But Etar stood still, hands at his sides, unmoving.

Above them, the enormous shadow still swirled madly, still flaring with masses of deadly darkness, but it seemed unable to reach past a ring of light that surrounded it. It lashed outward, upward, striking soundlessly against the cone of light protecting them.

The light was not coming from Etar or any of the dragons. Instead, it was emanating from the pale, golden-haired man standing a few feet away from them in the wet sand,

227

one hand outstretched, gaze focused intently on the shadow creature, face grim.

"Dad!" Omen rasped. Deep relief coursed through him.

"Get them out of here, Avarice," 7 ordered, his voice the only thing to penetrate the strange blanket of silence surrounding them.

7 stepped forward, one hand stretched toward the shadow creature, eyes fixed on the blackness. Despite the utter calm and deep focus etched into 7's face, Omen could see the tightening of his father's jaw, the way the muscles in his neck stood out in strain, the way his entire body looked rooted to the ground. "Get them out of here," he said through gritted teeth.

Avarice took hold of Kyr and Omen, pulling at both of them, yanking them to their feet. There was a wild, desperate look in her silver eyes. "I won't leave you here alone!" she shouted to 7.

Somehow his father was holding the creature at bay — somehow 7 had surrounded it with a shield of light, holding it immobile with his psionics when nothing else had stood against it.

The light from his father's shield flared up like the noonday sun, hundreds of feet in the air. It muffled the shadow, swallowing it whole. And then the ball of light contracted, hurtling downward, shrinking, and pulling the shadow with it.

The misty form of the creature grew darker and darker, solidifying within the ball of light as it folded in on itself. When the ball of light was no more than a few feet across, held aloft in the air, the bright sphere and its dark center stopped shrinking. Omen realized that his father couldn't force the mass to shrink any further.

"We'll open a portal to another realm! You can throw it through," Sundragon Amar's deep voice growled. The dragon rose sluggishly, his wing torn and bloody.

"It can travel through any realm, through any time," Etar said, deep sadness marking his voice. "There is no realm you can send it to that it cannot escape from."

Omen glared at his brother. "You told me to bring Kyr here. You had a plan! What's your blasted plan, Etar?"

"Only one can stop this." Sorrow darkened Etar's eyes, and he looked down. "Only one who can—"

"Why have you involved others in your oath breaking, Eldest Child?"

The question came from the air itself, breaching the unnatural stillness of 7's shield and echoing across water and sand. A haze of soft red light surrounded them all, blocking out the light of the sun so that only the blazing illumination of 7's shield broke through.

A presence manifested, something old and ancient and at the same time familiar. Omen felt it all around him.

The Dark Heart.

And though Cerioth's words had been spoken in Sul'eldrine, to Omen they sounded like music, the same song that pounded in the lower registers of all his psionic patterns, the same song he heard vibrating in the frequency of 7's music when he played his violin at twilight, the same haunting music he heard echoing through every chamber of Etar's realm.

"I have not broken my oath, Father," Etar answered back in Sul'eldrine, head bowed. But beneath the fall of his hair, Etar's eyes gleamed with satisfaction, a touch of a smile upon his lips.

Etar knew this would happen!

"I have not broken my oath — not one word," Etar repeated firmly. Omen could hear the crackling hiss of power as 7's shield tightened and re-formed, the dark shadow creature fighting back as if fueled by the presence of the Elder God who had created it. 7's gaze never wavered, his focus held steady, but Omen could see the strain in his father's eyes, sweat forming on his skin.

He can't hold that thing indefinitely!

"You play with words," the voice of Cerioth rose in accusation. "Do you think my curse a game? A product of temper perhaps with no meaning or reason?"

"I don't know why you created this curse!" Etar held steady. "It has gone on too long, destroyed too many. This is not in your nature!"

"You are too young to understand my nature, and you cannot see the path this curse holds clear."

The words sank into Omen's heart, and he shuddered, unable to fathom what good such a dark curse could conceivably be doing.

"And now you have involved these children in your act of defiance," Cerioth's voice rumbled like thunder around them.

"It is because of a child I am here!" Etar exclaimed. "Would you condemn your own son for a sin he did not commit? And what of the others here — they have taken no oath. They will not stand aside. Will you condemn them as well?"

"They will stand aside, or they will die." Cerioth's voice was deep and final, no sign of yielding in it.

Omen tightened his grip around Kyr — the boy was shaking uncontrollably.

The red light swirled and coalesced around 7. "Lower

the shield and release the curse, 7," Cerioth commanded. "Lower the shield or you will die."

"Then I die!" 7's voice was tight and strained, but Omen recognized the finality in the tone.

"Lower your shield or your mind will burn," Cerioth commanded again. It seemed to Omen that something shifted and changed in the tone — the music of the words taking on a soothing sound as if attempting to cajole 7.

"No!" 7 said again, his gaze never wavering from the shadow in front of him, his shield holding steady.

"You cannot hold it!" Cerioth bit out. Omen could hear The Dark Heart's anger, but concern ran deep beneath the heated words. "Your mind is breaking. If you do not release it, you will burn. You will die, and the curse will be free, and your death will serve no purpose. You must release it!"

"No!" 7 said again.

The light flashed and flared, and Omen could feel the deep terrible anger welling through the presence surrounding them, ancient and unspeakable. "I have repaid the debt I owe you! Your son and wife live! Will you throw away your life for the sake of a child you do not know? Release the curse before it is too late!" Cerioth's voice was wild now, burning with rage and, inexplicably, also vibrating with sorrow and fear. Omen could hear the desperate notes as clearly as any counterpoint.

"No!" 7 shouted again, and Omen felt his mother wrap her arms around both him and Kyr. He grabbed hold of her as they watched, limbs trembling, faces ashen — both staring at 7 as he defied an Elder God.

7's entire body glowed, the sheer amount of energy heating the winter air around them.

For a moment time stood still. Omen saw his father

alone before the Elder God, saw his mother and Templar alongside him, defiant. Far up on the hillside he could sense his sister watching in horror, the little girl holding back two struggling cats who were fighting to reach their side. And beside him was Kyr, broken, bleeding, terrified. *I'm going to lose them all.*

He tightened his hold around Kyr, his mind raw and open, shields gone as he connected with those beside him. *I'm sorry. I wanted to save you.* He sent the words to Kyr past the raw fraying of his mind, and found to his utter bewilderment that the child was not alone.

Connected mind to mind, he saw the world through the boy's eyes — he and Kyr were surrounded, not just by his family but by a growing horde of thousands of ghostly shapes. The spectral people stood upon the sand and the water and lined the cliffs of Melia — thousands, tens of thousands, mouths open and screaming, shouting in Kahdess, a cacophony so deafening that Omen could not hear the individual words.

Terror swarmed through Omen's heart. He tried to find his brother in the chaos, tried to find something that felt familiar and gentle like the little boy who'd protected the tiny weed with his own flesh and blood. *Kyr!* He reached — no pattern, no finesse, just raw emotion grasping for something familiar. A bright light flashed before his eyes — he grabbed it, latching onto it within the maelstrom of madness.

The voices grew silent. The dead stopped shouting. Kyr blinked up at him. *There is only the one, the thing that crawls, the thing that bleeds. There is only Kyr, and you found me.* The voice was soft and fleeting in his mind.

Slowly, Kyr turned toward 7. Through the smothering

silence of 7's shield, and the musical presence of The Dark Heart's energy, the boy shouted in Kahdess, his voice gone hoarse from screaming: "The wheel has turned for the last time!"

The Language of the Dead sounded fearsome and wrong in the presence of two gods and the golden Sundragons.

Kyr's words continued. "The one who died will not return again. This is the last step!"

Omen had no idea what his words meant. Neither, it seemed, did anyone else. Even Etar stared at the child blankly. But the presence of power dissipated instantly — the music of the Elder God growing soft and then silent.

"What did you say?" Cerioth's voice was little more than a whisper, and Omen could feel all of The Dark Heart's attention now focused on the bone-thin, bloodied shape of the half-elvin child.

"The lesson has been learned," Kyr continued, eyes feral and frightened. "And the promise stands at the point of breaking. The dark heart shall be lost."

There was a gasp like a gust of wind blowing through all of them, and the beating pulse of a single distant drum sounded in the distance. The light of Cerioth flared for a moment, and they all heard the words he whispered: "The sin is forgiven."

Cerioth was gone — and with him the dark shadow blown apart by a blast of wind coming in off the cold sea.

7 staggered, his face bloodless, and his shield of light shattered utterly as he fell to his knees, fingers sinking into the sand.

Avarice was at his side a moment later, leaving Omen to hold Kyr.

There was a moment of complete, stunned silence as

they all stood there, uncertain.

Omen felt his entire body shaking, his teeth chattering. Beyond his parents, the Sundragons watched them. Geryon raised his head, turned toward the city, and let out a loud musical bellow that moments later was echoed back far in the distance. *He's calling to the other Hold Dragons, letting them know the danger has passed.*

The wind shifted, and the temple bells rang once again, pealing out the song that played at the morning watch hour.

Omen knew that was a signal to the citizens that all was well. *They probably didn't even see the shadow from the city.* He couldn't believe how quickly it had all happened. *How quickly it could all have ended for us.* His stomach clenched, and he squeezed the beginnings of angry tears from his eyes.

Disoriented, he tried to see the strange vision of spectral people surrounding him again. But whatever connection he'd briefly made to his brother's chaotic mind had ended. The dead were gone.

Across the beach, his sister and several other people rushed toward them — Tormy leading them all in a mad dash across the sand. Tyrin perched like a tiny puff of fluff on Lilyth's shoulder. *I have to thank her. She had to have used her psionics to hold Tormy back. If they had followed us into battle, they might have been killed.* The large cat outweighed the little girl by several hundred pounds and the force required to hold him impressed Omen. *Have to sneak her a present for that.*

"Still think the Night Games would be more dangerous than staying home?" Templar's voice broke the silence.

Templar had streaks of blood running down his face, his clothing covered in wet sand, his hair plastered around his

234

head. Yet he grinned broadly.

Omen let out a harsh laugh and clapped his friend on the shoulder.

Chapter 18: Music

Hours later, back within the relative safety of Daenoth Manor, Omen sat quietly in the library beside his mother and sister. A roaring fire blazed in the stone fireplace, and Tormy was stretched out on the woolly sheepskin rug in front of the hearth. Kyr reclined against him, and Tyrin was sleeping on the boy's stomach. Across the book-lined room near the heavily curtained window stood 7, violin in hand, golden head bowed as he played a haunting melody — eyes closed, lost in the music.

Lilyth was reading, absorbed in some tome about distant lands. His mother sorted through family correspondence.

They'd all seen the healers earlier — several Untouchables from the Temple of the Sundragons had arrived to help them in the aftermath of the battle.

All four of the Sundragons had been injured, as had Templar and Omen. Kyr's injuries had been the most serious, however, and Sundragon Andrade had insisted he be treated first. The dragon had been guilt-stricken that he'd inadvertently pierced Kyr with his claw when he'd snatched him from the shadow. The boy had broken his arm in the subsequent fall, despite Andrade using his own body to shield him.

Now half asleep, Kyr watched the flames contentedly. Omen had to smile, sadly remembering how the healers had marveled over Kyr's silence, given the severity of his injuries. The boy hadn't even cried out when they'd manipulated his broken bone back into place before healing it. Throughout the entire procedure, Kyr had simply clutched

Tyrin tightly to his chest and gazed at Omen with wide, worried eyes, following his every move as if afraid he was going to vanish.

"It's all right Kyr," he had told him. "You're staying here."

"I like green!" the boy had told him earnestly in Kahdess as if trying to convey a world of meaning along with his words.

Surprisingly it was Templar who had set Kyr's mind at rest. "Then you are going to love springtime," he'd told him in fluent Kahdess, laughter in his voice. "Omen and I will have to take you fishing in Revival once the weather warms up." The promise of things-to-come eased the worry on Kyr's face.

"Fishing?" Omen had repeated the word back in Merchant's Common, wondering if he'd mistranslated the Kahdessian word Templar had used. In all the time he'd known the Terizkandian prince, he hadn't made mention of enjoying such a peaceful pastime as fishing. Tormy and Tyrin perked up their ears at the mention of fish.

"We have thirty-foot-long freshwater sharks in the swamps of Revival." Templar had nodded with enthusiasm. "They go dormant in winter, but come springtime, things get really lively!"

I really have to go visit Revival! Omen thought, as he stretched his legs out in front of him. He'd only been to Hex, but the more he heard about the rest of Templar's country, the more eager he was to explore it. *Though I doubt Kyr will be up to shark hunting by spring.*

The sound of his father's music changed then — dropping down into a lower minor key as he worked on some new composition. He was still lost in the sounds, eyes closed, body swaying as he played effortlessly. He'd been quiet most of the evening, and Omen was beginning to worry. He wanted to reach out psionically and touch his father's mind — make certain that he was uninjured from the attack, but he didn't dare.

"Is Dad all right?" Omen asked his mother softly. Lilyth looked up at that, head tilted to hear their mother's equally quiet response.

"He's fine," Avarice assured her children. "Your father is just tired."

"Are the dragons angry with us?" Omen asked carefully, glad that Kyr couldn't understand their words. "Will we have to leave?" It had occurred to him earlier that day that the Sundragons might blame him for the attack — his family wasn't Melian; Kyr wasn't Melian. *This is not a Melian problem.* The Sundragons had no reason to allow any of them to remain within their borders. *Hold Lord Sive is forever complaining about how dangerous we outsiders all are — maybe he's right?*

"No," Avarice stated firmly. She set her letters down, turning her shrewd gaze on both her son and daughter. "The Sundragons understand that we bring certain danger to Melia — all of us, not just you through your connection to Cerioth. When 7 and I first came here, Cerioth was still imprisoned — your father literally brought an imprisoned Elder God into this land in the form of a musical instrument. And I and my companions brought other dangers with us as well. And yet the Sundragons allowed us all to remain. They understood that those dangers exist whether we are here or not. They let us remain because we consistently prove we are valuable allies who will protect this land. Do not forget that. It's the same reason King Antares allows his son to spend so much time here instead of fulfilling other duties in Terizkand, or why I allow you to go off to play your ridiculous Night Game."

"You don't allow me to play," Lilyth pointed out, only barely masking her annoyance.

Avarice shot her a stern look. "That is because I'm very much aware of what it entails and what you are not yet capable of surviving. One day you will bring your own set of troubles to our lives — I do not need you borrowing your brother's."

"Is that why you let Kyr stay?" Omen asked.

Avarice gave him a wry smile. "I let him stay because you asked me to, and because in the short time he's been here I've grown fond of him. But like all members of my family I expect he will one day prove his worth."

Omen glanced down at where his little brother was dozing. He wondered if he should tell his mother what he'd seen when he'd connected with the boy's mind. *I don't actually know what I saw — it was too chaotic, too overwhelming. How can Kyr even function if that's what he experiences every day?*

"He's already done something extraordinary," he said instead. "I don't know what his words meant, but whatever they were, they made Cerioth stop the curse."

"I think that was the plan right from the start," Avarice mused.

"You mean Etar's plan?" Omen asked, having replayed the events of the day over and over in his mind. He'd been convinced Etar had tricked him into saving Kyr — though Etar had been right in pointing out that it had all been entirely Omen's idea in the first place. But certainly getting 7 involved had been Etar's idea, which still baffled Omen.

239

But Etar couldn't have predicted what Kyr would say. *How did he know Cerioth would stop the curse?*

"I don't think it played out quite the way Etar expected," Avarice reasoned.

"What do you mean? It seems to me he had it all planned out."

"I think he expected Cerioth to exempt Kyr from the curse, not forgive the sin and destroy it utterly," Avarice replied. "I think there was a great deal more to that curse and the reason behind it than Etar realized. He was simply acting on a hunch that Cerioth would not let 7 die."

"If he'd been wrong . . ." The very thought gave Omen a queasy feeling.

"7 is not going to let some trick of the gods destroy him," Avarice stated definitively. "Regardless, you need to pay better attention to what you're committing yourself to. You're too easily manipulated."

"But he didn't really manipulate me. I mean . . ." Omen rubbed at his eyes. He agreed with his mother, but he just couldn't really see the moment it had happened. "Tormy and I wanted to do something, and I asked him to send me on a quest." He felt it best he not mention the glowing mice.

Torment flashed across his mother's face. "Then you had best find a way to keep your boredom in check." Her voice was like silk. "Or you will become your own worst enemy."

Omen leaned back in his chair and looked down at the two cats and Kyr. Most of the time, Tormy kept him busy with one crazy game after another — and if not Tormy, then Templar or some of his other friends. Everyone had more than enough things for him to do. And now with the addition of Tyrin and Kyr, he didn't suppose there would be a whole lot of time for boredom in his future.

"It all worked out in the end," he decided. "I rescued Kyr and we stopped the curse. And now we have Tyrin too."

"I still don't have a cat," Lilyth grumbled under her breath. Omen reached over and ruffled her curls in sympathy.

"Come on, Lily, let's go join Dad." He rose swiftly to his feet and crossed to where his lute was leaning in a rack against the wall. Despite her grumbling, Lily set aside her book and followed him, picking up the violin resting beside the lute.

A dozen other instruments were on display, well-tended and oiled — lutes, mandolins, flutes, drums — of all shapes and sizes. Omen could play all of them, but he preferred the lute.

7 opened his eyes as Omen approached. He smiled peacefully and changed the song to something familiar to all three of them.

Omen sat down on the nearby bench, lute in hand, and joined in. Lilyth followed suit a moment later, playing the harmonies to their melody, all three practiced at playing together.

Near the fire, the cats had both woken up, and Kyr turned to watch. He folded his arms over Tormy's back and rested his chin on his hands as he gazed at the trio.

Tormy's and Tyrin's amber eyes gleamed in the firelight. Their ears swiveled forward, and the glow caught in the soft white ruff at their necks, making them practically shimmer.

Avarice turned her chair, folding her hands in her lap, a tranquil smile on her face as she listened to the music with her eyes closed.

Yes, Omen thought, his heart lighter. *It all worked out in the end.*

Want More?

If you've enjoyed RADIATION, please consider telling a friend, or leaving a review. Help us spread the world Of Cats and Dragons. And, as Tormy would say, that is being greatlynessness!

More OF CATS AND DRAGONS tidbits and artwork are waiting for you on our website:

OfCatsAndDragons.com.

Join the adventurers by signing up for our Newsletter.

Audiobook Lovers!

Find OF CATS AND DRAGONS on Audible.

Thank you!

Camilla

As ever, I want to thank my husband, P.J., for his continuous support of my writing and this project in particular. He is an eagle-eyed editor, a story doctor, and the brilliantly protean narrator of our audiobooks. I could not have done any of this without him.

My partner in Werewolf Whisperer crimes, Bonita, has had our backs throughout this long process. She's lent an ear, an eye, and her tireless enthusiasm.

Carol

I want to thank my family and friends for all their support and well-wishes. I'll keep fighting.

We also want to thank all of our friends who listened to the tale of the tale unfolding, and threw nothing but positive energy and love our way.

And a big thanks to our very first fan, Noreen. We knew we had something special when she kept asking, "What's next?"

About the Authors

Carol E. Leever:

Carol E. Leever, a college professor, has been teaching Computer Science for many years. She programs computers for fun, but turns to writing and painting when she wants to give her brain a good work out.

An avid reader of science fiction and fantasy, she's also been published in the Sword and Sorceress anthologies, and has recently gotten into painting illustrations and book covers. A great lover of cats, she also manages to work her feline overlords into her writing, painting and programming classes often to the dismay of her students.

Camilla Ochlan:

Owner of a precariously untamed imagination and a scuffed set of polyhedral dice (which have gotten her in trouble more than once), Camilla writes fantasy and science fiction. Separate OF CATS AND DRAGONS, Camilla has written the urban fantasy WEREWOLF WHISPERER series (with Bonita Gutierrez), the mythpunk noir THE SEVENTH LANE and, in collaboration with her husband, written and produced a number of short films, including the suburban ghost story DOG BREATH and the recent 20/ 20 HINDSIGHT. An unapologetic dog lover and cat servant, Camilla lives in Los Angeles with her husband actor, audiobook narrator and dialect coach P.J. Ochlan, three sweet rescue dogs and a bright orange Abyssinian cat.

Get in Touch

Visit our website at OfCatsAndDragons.com

Like us on Facebook @OfCatsAndDragons and join the Friends Of Cats And Dragons Facebook group.

Find Carol:

caroleleever.deviantart.com

Find Camilla:

Twitter: @CamillaOchlan
Instagram: instagram.com/camillaochlan/
Blog: The Seething Brain

Or write to us at:

meow@ofcatsanddragons.com

Made in the USA
Las Vegas, NV
16 December 2021

38232620R00152